Chiapas Maya Awakening

I0564579

Chiapas Maya Awakening
Contemporary Poems and Short Stories

Edited by Sean S. Sell and Nicolás Huet Bautista

English translation by Sean S. Sell

Foreword by Marceal Méndez

Introduction by Inés Hernández-Ávila

UNIVERSITY OF OKLAHOMA PRESS : NORMAN

*Published through the Recovering Languages and Literacies of the
Americas initiative, supported by the Andrew W. Mellon Foundation*

Slightly different versions of the Spanish and Tsotsil and Tseltal Mayan portions of this book were previously published in *Ma'yuk sti'ilal xch'inch'unel k'inal: Silencio sin frontera* (Chiapas, Mexico: Centro Estatal de Lenguas, Arte y Literatura Indígenas [CELALI], 2011). The poems by Ruperta Bautista Vázquez in this book did not appear in the previous volume.

Chiapas Maya Awakening: Contemporary Poems and Short Stories is published as part of the Recovering Languages and Literacies of the Americas initiative. Recovering Languages and Literacies is generously supported by the Andrew W. Mellon Foundation.

Library of Congress Cataloging-in-Publication Data

Names: Sell, Sean S., editor. | Huet Bautista, Nicolás, editor.
Title: Chiapas Maya awakening : contemporary poems and short stories / edited by Sean S. Sell and Nicolás Huet Bautista ; English translations by Sean S. Sell ; foreword by Marceal Méndez ; introduction by Inés Hernández-Ávila.
Description: Norman : University of Oklahoma Press, 2017.
Identifiers: LCCN 2016019935 | ISBN 978-0-8061-5561-6 (pbk. : alk. paper)
Subjects: LCSH: Mayan literature—Mexico—Chiapas—Translations into English. | Mayan literature—Mexico—Chiapas. | Mayan literature—Mexico—Chiapas— Translations into Spanish.
Classification: LCC PM3968.55.E5 C53 2017 | DDC 897/.427—dc23
LC record available at https://lccn.loc.gov/2016019935

Contents

Contents

Illustrations

The artists created the illustrations that appear in this volume to accompany specific poems or stories and did not provide titles for their pieces. The titles given below indicate the poem or story the image is meant to illustrate.

Figures

Map

Foreword
to the English Multilingual Edition

Chiapas Maya Awakening is a significant showing of contemporary literary accomplishment in the indigenous languages of Chiapas; in particular by young Tseltal and Tsotsil writers who, in the act of creating and simultaneously shaping literature, eagerly seek and forge the pathways of their poetic and narrative voices, the same ones that little by little are laying the foundations of a literature arising from "minority" cultures and presenting their different social contexts.

The themes addressed are based on the silence that underlies the apparent calm and submission of the indigenous people, which at the same time break cultural and linguistic barriers forced on them by the impoverished circumstances that keep them oppressed, in search of ways to conduct a dignified, more human life; still not as fulfilling as it should be, and representing a reduced number of people. But the causes of misfortune come not only from outside, from the "other" who has been contradictorily both enemy and leader; they emerge also from among the fellow victims of the overwhelming reality: envy, hate, indifference, neglect, and the bad luck that becomes tragedy, which are inherent in the daily lives of the individuals, the communities, the cultures. The texts collected here give account of this.

The present collection of stories and poems is a sampling of the results of the Seminario de Análisis y Composición Literaria (Literary Analysis and Composition Seminar) conducted in 2007, one of various projects of artistic formation offered to young Maya and Zoques of Chiapas by the Centro Estatal de Lenguas, Arte y Literatura Indígenas (CELALI) and now under the auspices of the Ministry of Indigenous Peoples and Cultures. Among the objectives of the seminar was to professionalize the incipient activities in writing and promote publication in the original languages of Chiapas. With this action, they sought to help poets and storytellers know and apply to their

Editors' note: A version of this foreword appeared, in Spanish only, in the indigenous- and Spanish-language edition of this book, *Ma'yuk sti'ilal xch'inch'unel k'inal: Silencio sin frontera*, published in Mexico by the Centro Estatal de Lenguas, Arte y Literatura Indígenas (CELALI; State Center for Indigenous Languages, Art, and Literature) in 2011.

creations the universal tools of literary composition, as well as to explore other possibilities based on the stylistic resources from their mother languages and their "oral literature," in particular from oral narratives and ceremonial prayers and speeches, and this project is ongoing. In sum, they seek to produce and disperse a literature that defines and reclaims the existence and the creativity of the indigenous peoples in a setting of cultural diversity.

After a decade of hard work on this material, the bilingual literary works have conquered spaces beyond the borders of Chiapas and Mexico; they are achievements that without a doubt represent the commitments and responsibilities of their authors, as well as of the new generations of writers who now, after much effort and dedication, share the fruits of their work to have dialogue with other people, the readers.

MARCEAL MÉNDEZ
Department of Literature and Art, CELALI

Presentación

[Foreword to the Spanish/Indigenous-Language Edition]

Cuentos y poemas: Ma'yuk sti'ilal xch'inch'unel k'inal, Silencio sin frontera, es una muestra significativa del actual quehacer literario en las lenguas indígenas de Chiapas; en particular de jóvenes escritores tseltales y tsotsiles que, a través del ejercicio de la creación y simultáneamente con la formación literaria, buscan y construyen afanosamente el cauce de sus voces poéticas y narrativas, mismas que poco a poco irán cimentando las bases de una literatura que surge de las culturas "minoritarias" y proyecta sus diferentes contextos sociales.

Los temas abordados giran en torno al silencio que subyace en la aparente calma y sumisión de los pueblos indígenas que al mismo tiempo rompen sus fronteras culturales y lingüísticas, obligados por la situación paupérrima a la que fueron y siguen sometidos, en busca de caminos que conduzcan a una vida digna, más humana; no ya placentera como debiera ser y como la vive un número reducido de personas. Pero las causas del infortunio no vienen sólo de afuera, del "otro" que ha sido contradictoriamente enemigo y dirigente; sino que emergen también de entre las mismas víctimas de la realidad agobiante: la envidia, el odio, la indiferencia, el descuido y el azar que se convierte en tragedia, son inherentes a la cotidianidad de los individuos, de los pueblos, de las culturas. Los textos aquí reunidos dan cuenta de ello.

La presente colección de cuentos y poemas es una muestra del resultado obtenido de un Seminario de Análisis y Composición Literaria realizado en el año 2007, uno de los varios proyectos de formación artística que ofrece a jóvenes mayas y zoques de Chiapas el Centro Estatal de Lenguas, Arte y Literatura Indígenas, antes del Consejo Estatal para las Culturas y las Artes de Chiapas, y ahora dependiente de la Secretaría de Pueblos y Culturas Indígenas. Entre los objetivos del seminario se encontraba el de profesionalizar el incipiente oficio de la escritura e incrementar las publicaciones en las lenguas originarias de Chiapas. Con esta acción se buscaba que los poetas y narradores conocieran y aplicaran en sus creaciones herramientas universales de la composición literaria, así como ensayar otras posiblidades a partir de los

Nota editorial: Esta presentación apareció en la versión bilingüe de este libro publicado en México por CELALI en 2011.

recursos estilísticos propios del idioma materno y de la "literatura oral", en particular de la narrativa oral y los rezos o discursos ceremoniales, y la tarea sigue en pie.

En suma, se buscaba producir y difundir una literatura que defina y reivindique la existencia y la creatividad de los pueblos indígenas en el marco de la diversidad cultural. Después de una década de trabajo arduo en esta materia, las obras literarias bilingües han conquistado espacios más allá de las fronteras chiapanecas y mexicanas; son logros que sin duda representan compromisos y responsabilidades para sus autores, así como para las generaciones nuevas de escritores quienes ahora, después de mucho esfuerzo y dedicación, comparten el fruto de su oficio para dialogar con las personas, los lectores.

MARCEAL MÉNDEZ
Departamento de Literatura y Arte del CELALI

Chiapas Maya Awakening

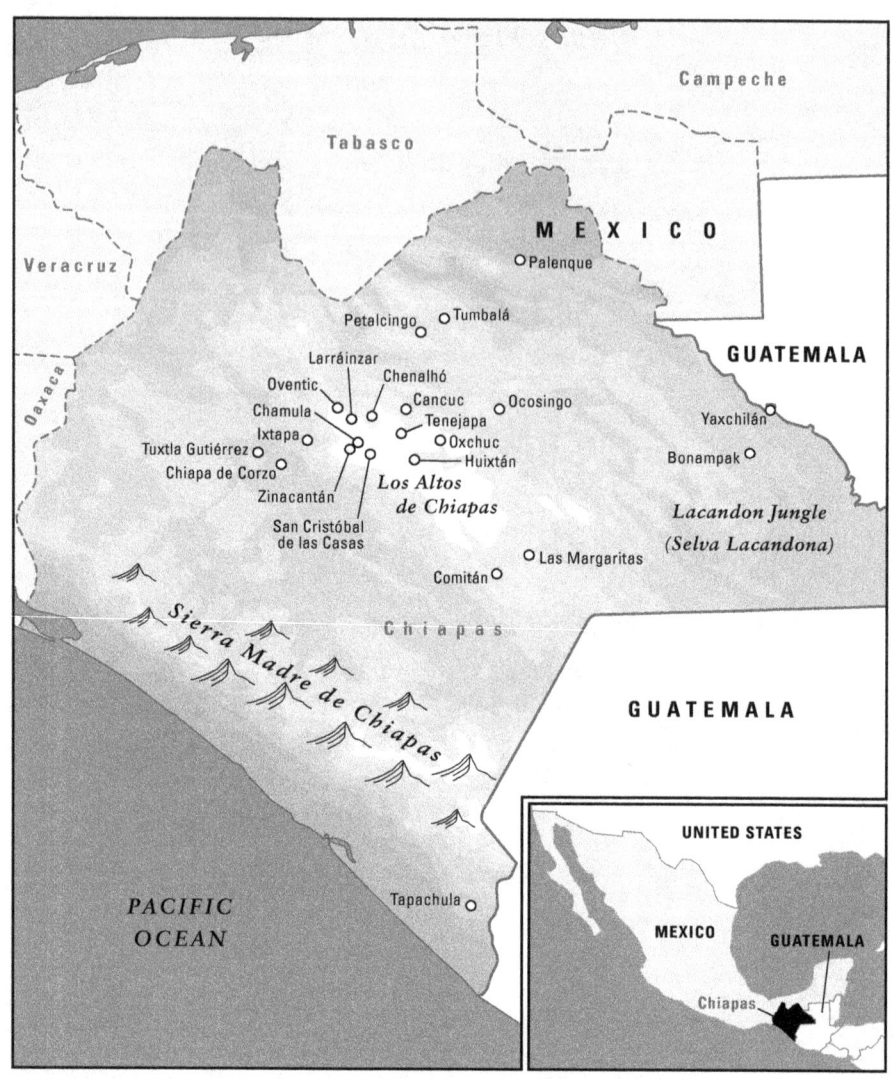

Chiapas, Mexico

The writers in this book generally come from the central highlands—Los Altos de Chiapas—at elevations of more than 7,000 feet (2,100 meters). Although the western part of the state of Chiapas reaches the Pacific Ocean, the Sierra Madre de Chiapas range creates a substantial barrier between Los Altos and the ocean.

Overall, Chiapas is rugged, tropical, mountainous, and beautiful.

Map by Erin Greb. Copyright © 2017, University of Oklahoma Press.

Introduction

Inés Hernández-Ávila

The original title to the multilingual (indigenous languages and Spanish) collection on which this book is based is *Ma'yuk sti'ilal xch'inch'unel k'inal: Silencio sin frontera*, and it was produced as a result of a seminar on Literary Analysis and Composition that took place in 2007, one of several projects offered to young Maya and Zoque writers of Chiapas at CELALI, the Centro Estatal de Lenguas, Arte y Literatura Indígenas (State Center for Indigenous Languages, Art, and Literature). The back cover of the original text explains the "silence without border" concept:

> Los temas abordados giran en torno al silencio que subyace en la aparente calma y sumisión de los pueblos indígenas, al mismo tiempo que rompen sus fronteras culturales y lingüisticas. El silencio que asesora un pensamiento, un sentimiento . . . es más poderoso que un grito. Sumérjase en la lectura, intente platicar con su ch'ulel y entonces el silencio hablará por si solo.

> [The themes addressed revolve around the silence that underlies the apparent calm and submission of indigenous peoples, at the same time that they break their cultural and linguistic borders. The silence that guides a thought, a feeling . . . is more powerful than a shout. Submerge yourself in the reading, try to speak with your *ch'ulel* (spirit), and then the silence will speak for itself.][1]

This collection is but one of approximately 150 titles produced by CELALI over the course of its history. The new title for this multilingual edition, with the works translated into English and the addition of poems by Ruperta Bautista Vázquez, is *Chiapas Maya Awakening: Contemporary Poems and Short Stories*, edited by Sean S. Sell and Nicolás Huet Bautista. The new title calls attention to the awakening, or *florecimiento*, the flourishing of contemporary Maya literature in the state of Chiapas, Mexico. While this flourishing of indigenous literature (and other arts) in Chiapas can be called a renaissance, the term is perhaps too limited to apply to what is actually happening throughout the Maya world and, for that matter, throughout the

---

1. *Ma'yuk sti'ilal xch'inch'unel k'inal: Silencio sin frontera*, back cover.

worlds of indigenous peoples in the Americas in the twenty-first century. This is a phenomenon that has been building and steadily gaining ground over a long time, some might say centuries.

In the essay "La voz indígena ante el nuevo milenio" (The indigenous voice before the new millennium), Natalio Hernández writes,

> No hay que olvidar que América descansa, en gran medida, sobre una matriz cultural indígena. A pesar de los cinco siglos de predominio cultural europeo, prevalece la raíz indígena, la espiritualidad indígena, la esencia indígena que matiza y permea la forma de ser y de pensar de cada sociedad y país de América. Por lo mismo, no es cierto que la cultura occidental logró aniquilar a las culturas nativas de América. Ignorar esta realidad, sería como intentar construir un nuevo edificio sobre arenas ovedizas.
>
> [We must not forget that America rests, in large part, on an indigenous cultural matrix. In spite of the five centuries of European cultural dominance, the indigenous root, the indigenous spirituality, the indigenous essence that qualifies and permeates the way of being and thinking of every society and country in America prevails. In other words, it is not true that Western culture managed to annihilate the Native cultures of America. To ignore this reality would be like constructing a new building on top of shifting sands."][2]

Natalio Hernández, Nahua, is one of the leading indigenous intellectuals in Mexico writing about this renaissance, or *despertar*. A poet, essayist, and one of the founders of Escritores en Lenguas Indígenas, A.C. (ELIAC; Writers in Indigenous Languages, A.C.), he is the author of *El despertar de nuestras lenguas: Queman tlachixque totlahtolhuan* (Mexico City: Editorial Diana, Fondo Editorial de las Culturas Indígenas, 2002). In this collection, the focus of one of his chapters is the indigenous literature of Chiapas. He writes of the "alumbramiento cultural de los últimos 25 años del siglo XX" (cultural birthing of the last twenty-five years of the twentieth century [93]). He cites the First Indigenous

---

2. Natalio Hernández, "La voz indígena ante el nuevo milenio," in *In tlahtoli, in ohtli/La palabra, el camino: Memoria y destino de los pueblos indígenas* (In tlahtoli, in ohtli/ The word, the path: Memory and fate of indigenous peoples; Mexico City: Plaza y Valdés, 1998), 51.

Congress of Chiapas that took place in 1974, organized by the diocese of San Cristóbal de las Casas and the state government of Chiapas (93).

In an essay that appeared on the site *El Mayoral* in July 2015,[3] José Daniel Ochoa Nájera (head of CELALI's languages and translation department), wrote that Enrique Pérez López, director of CELALI, also recognizes the 1974 First Indigenous Congress as a significant moment in the struggle of indigenous peoples; Pérez López notes that the congress was organized at the initiative of Bishop Samuel Ruiz García. His remarks were made on the occasion of the eighteenth anniversary of the founding of CELALI, celebrated on July 20, 2015, although the actual date of the opening of CELALI was July 19, 1997. Ochoa notes that in this time period diverse forms of dialogue between indigenous peoples and the nation-state were emerging (including, of course, the Zapatista Army of National Liberation movement); spaces for dialogue were created, albeit sustained asymmetrically, as he notes, given the undeniably unequal power relations, but the spaces were created by indigenous peoples themselves. The challenge he posits is "¿Cómo cada uno de los agentes se atreven a reconfigurar y cambiar el modo en que se suceden las relaciones?" (How will each of the agents take on the reconfiguring and changing of the way in which these relations take place? [*El Mayoral*]). The indigenous writers, artists, and intellectuals of Chiapas (and Mexico and beyond) are clear about their role as protagonists, clear about exercising their agency to bring about social, cultural, political transformation, thus the term "agents."

In relation to defining moments in the trajectory of Mexican indigenous literature and the validation of *la palabra de los pueblos,* "the word(s) of the peoples," Andrés Aubry, in his article "El Congreso Indígena de 1974, 30 años después" (The Indigenous Congress of 1974, thirty years later), published in *La Jornada,* October 15, 2004, credits Bishop Ruiz with transforming an event that was originally scheduled to be a commemoration of the birthday of Bartolomé de Las Casas[4] into an event that integrated the presence and voice of indigenous peoples of Chiapas through this congress. Indigenous

---

3. This essay was posted to José Daniel Ochoa Nájera's Facebook page on July 27, 2015.

4. Aubry cites other reasons for the celebration besides the birthday of de Las Casas—the date coincides with both the six-year term (1970–76) of President Luis Echeverría and that of the then governor of Chiapas, and with the date of the 150th anniversary of the first ratification of the incorporation of Chiapas as a state in the Mexican nation ("El Congreso Indígena"). Bartolomé de Las Casas is the well-known first resident bishop of Chiapas and held the official title protector of the Indians. He was a historian, an advocate for indigenous rights, and a Dominican friar.

peoples manifested "massively and eloquently their sociohistorical identity and their place in the country" (Aubry). Bishop Ruiz argued to the authorities that indigenous peoples had to be involved at the celebration of these two events, and thus was born the Bartolomé de Las Casas First Congress of Indigenous Peoples.

Another defining moment, according to Pérez López, was the 1981 MONTIACUL: Congreso Mundial de Cultura en México (MONTIACUL: World Congress of Culture in Mexico); this congress heard demands from indigenous peoples for creating the conditions by which indigenous cultures could be strengthened—this is when the indigenous cultural movement in Mexico emerged onto a world stage, and from then on there was a constant march forward (*El Mayoral*). The Zapatistas declared their revolution on January 1, 1994. CELALI began its path on July 19, 1997, but both of these projects emerged from the earlier-mentioned pivotal events (among others) that gave clarity to their visions. Ochoa Nájera affirms that the history of CELALI cannot be reduced to their eighteen years of existence; they are part of the collection of social movements in Chiapas that have always had the goal of being considered an important component of the cultural complex named Chiapas (*El Mayoral*). However, during its first eighteen years, CELALI has engaged in the following projects that have earned it respect and admiration (and at the same time some detractors): indigenous language revitalization through the teaching of Mayan languages; the production of dictionaries; the development of pedagogy to teach the languages; the promotion of literary creativity in all genres as a way to strengthen the Mayan and Zoque languages; the publication of texts (pedagogical, literary, linguistic); the organization of community festivals, in particular those of the Maya-Zoques; the promotion and training of visual artists. This collection is one example of their work.

Literary Renaissance in Chiapas

The literary renaissance, or *florecimiento*, in Chiapas takes place in a context that is national and hemispheric. In the essay "El renacimiento de las lenguas indígenas: La experiencia de Mexico,"[5] Natalio Hernández notes that indigenous people are at the end of an old way and at the start of something new and at the same time very ancient. He writes that since 1992,

---

5. Natalio Hernández, "El renacimiento de las lenguas indígenas: La experiencia de México," in *Literatura indígena de América: Primer Congreso* (Guatemala City: Asociación Cultural B'eyb'al, 1999), 48.

the Mexican Constitution recognizes the linguistic and cultural diversity of Mexico, that is, the pluricultural composition of the nation, sustained by indigenous peoples, and a commitment by the Mexican state to promote the development of their languages and cultures (48). As a founder of the national organization Escritores en Lenguas Indígenas, A.C. (ELIAC; Writers in Indigenous Languages), he cites the work of that association to promote indigenous languages and literatures. He also notes the international gatherings that have been held, one of which was in Quintana Roo, Yucatán, in 2000, the Encuentro Continental de Escritores en Lenguas Indígenas (50). However, there were at least two other *encuentros* before the one in Yucatán. On September 15–20, 1997, the Encuentro Continental de Escritores en Lenguas Indígenas de América (Continental Gathering of Writers in Indigenous Languages of America) took place in Puerto Ayacucho, Venezuela. Representatives from Chiapas included Enrique Pérez López and María Roselia Jiménez Pérez. In 1998, the Primer Congreso de Literatura Indígena de las Américas took place in Antigua, Guatemala, hosted by the Asociación Cultural B'eyb'al and coordinated by the Canjobal Maya novelist Gaspar Pedro González.[6] Representatives from Chiapas included Enrique Pérez López and members of Fortaleza de la Mujer Maya (FOMMA; Empowerment of Maya Women), a theater company that includes the FOMMA founders Isabel Juárez Espinosa and Petrona de la Cruz Cruz. Representatives from Canada, the United States, Mexico, and Central and South America attended both of these meetings and engaged fully in the formal sessions and the literary recitals. Maya writers in Chiapas are aware of the international developments in contemporary indigenous literature.

In the publication that emerged from the 1998 Congreso in Guatemala, Gaspar Pedro González, a Canjobal Maya, in "La literatura maya contemporánea: Como base la oralidad" (Contemporary Maya literature: Orality as the base),[7] writes of the new current of literature that is being produced. He notes that after the first wave of missionaries that came to America used Mayan languages as an important tool for the "conquista cultural" (cultural conquest), they eventually abandoned this tactic in favor of more violent

6. July 14–16, 2015, marked the 25th Medellín International Poetry Festival and the 2nd World Poetry Summit for Peace and Reconciliation. Indigenous writers have had a strong participation in these festivals.

7. Gaspar Pedro González, "La literatura maya contemporánea: Como base la oralidad," in *Literatura Indígena de América: Primer Congreso* (Guatemala City: Asociación Cultural B'eyb'al, 1999), 89.

legal and religious ones that denied indigenous peoples the right to cultural practices, languages, religious practices, dress, their calendric system, and writing (89). Culture had to be practiced clandestinely during this time of darkness (something that the poet Feliciano Sánchez Chan, a Yucatec Maya, also says), and Maya writers, like the author of the *Popol Wuj*, were not acknowledged. This clandestinity could appear to be silence, when in fact it is anything but that.

One of the keys to the significance of indigenous languages is the way in which the languages have embedded in them complex belief systems, or what the Pawnee scholar Walter Echo-Hawk would call "indigenous wisdom traditions."[8] In his essay, González critiques the term "folklore" because it restricts ancient indigenous knowledge to "lesser than" categories, such as "curious," "exotic," the "good savage" (90). For a long time, he writes, popular wisdom has received an inferior categorization: artisanry versus art, the oral tradition versus erudite literature, ethnography versus history, paganism or polytheism versus religion, witchcraft versus the popular medicinal traditions. But in the present, "se comienza a escuchar la voz de los pueblos que siempre han tenido literatura en la palabra hablada y se comienza a ubicar estos materiales en su lugar correspondiente" (the voice of the peoples who have always had literature in the spoken word is beginning to be heard, and there begins to be a way to situate these materials in their corresponding place [90]). González says that there has been a shift from focusing on the idea of folklore to a consideration of orality and "oral literature" (90). The oral tradition is clearly apparent in the works in this collection, reflecting traditional *enseñanzas* (teachings) on the one hand, and the articulation of history and the lived experiences of the peoples on the other. As Marceal Méndez says in the foreword to this volume, the writers fuse the professionalization they learned from the CELALI writing seminar with their own "stylistic resources from their mother languages and their 'oral literature,' in particular from oral narratives and ceremonial prayers and speeches." The *palabra hablada* (spoken word) of indigenous peoples, as González says, gives strength and inspiration to contemporary writers.

8. Walter R. Echo-Hawk, *In the Light of Justice: The Rise of Human Rights in Native America and the U.N. Declaration on the Rights of Indigenous Peoples* (Golden, Col.: Fulcrum, 2013), 258–60, 270–78.

The Writers of Chiapas

Writers in Chiapas form a large community of Maya intellectuals and pro-moters of indigenous languages, cultures, and creative expression working in the state. From a Mexican national perspective, they contribute to an important movement of indigenous writers and they are increasingly becoming known internationally for their work. Four of the volumes published by CELALI and the Consejo Nacional para la Cultura y las Artes (CONACULTA) document the writers, visual artists, weavers, and potters currently working in Chiapas. *Semblanzas de escritores mayas-zoques de Chiapas*, edited by Pedro Antonio Martínez Gómez (2002), includes biographies and publication lists of twenty-eight writers, one of whom is Ruperta Bautista Vázquez, whose poems appear in this collection.

The writers included in this collection are certainly promoters of language revitalization through the art of creating literature in their indigenous languages. Manuel Bolom Pale, Andrés López Díaz, María Concepción Bautista Vázquez, Ruperta Bautista Vázquez, Angelina Díaz Ruiz, and Miguel Ruiz Gómez are Tsotsil; Adriana López, Juan Julián Cruz Cruz, and Alberto Gómez Pérez are Tseltal. They consciously engage in a revindication of cultural knowledge in terms of oral narratives, literary orality, prayers, ceremonial speeches, and other expressions of their maternal languages to promote language revitalization through the creation of literary pieces in indigenous languages. This cultural knowledge is communicated in the literature often through the indigenous languages first; then the writers translate their works into Spanish to reach audiences beyond their communities. Sometimes the writers write first in Spanish and then translate into their indigenous languages.

Each of these writers has surpassed an exceedingly formidable challenge to participate in the world's literary and academic discourse. Most indigenous Maya children do not advance in their schooling beyond the sixth grade. The dreams of many young Maya to find a way to express their personal perspectives and aspirations are crushed by the continuing racism, poverty, and structural violence that impact their lives. Even for the writers herein, who have achieved some success and recognition, themes of anger and desperation run through much of their work; their ability to use language in the creative representation (and analysis) of the struggles their communities face is a testament to their own courage and dedication. Each could make a compelling memoir out of their own lives.

In an interview with Miguel Ruiz Gómez by Enrique Hidalgo Mellanes, titled "La literatura me ha permitido ver y entender a mi comunidad" (Literature has permitted me to see and understand my community), Ruiz comments that his life is a novel and he is the main character, citing the Spanish novelist Enrique Vila-Matas for the idea.[9] He includes William Faulkner, James Joyce, Julio Cortázar, Enrique Vila-Matas, Eduardo Antonio Parra, and others in his list of favorite writers. He says that while his mind and soul remain the same (in terms of his culture and identity), he credits literature for giving him the lens through which to analyze and reflect upon what he sees, especially regarding indigenous peoples in his municipality, in the state of Chiapas, and in the nation. Author of "In the Middle of the Desert" in this volume, he is also one of the emerging indigenous literary scholars of Chiapas.

In his fiction, Ruiz intentionally uses what he has learned from Western literature in his own work: flashback; colloquial or poetic language; first-, second-, and third-person narratives; use of the subconscious and interior voice, among others (interview). He says, "Cada historia que escuchaba de la gente en las calles las reconstruía en un cuento, modificaba el inicio, el final, agregaba personajes, o las cambiaba, primero sólo en la mente y después escrita" (Each story that I heard from the people in the streets I would reconstruct in a short story, I would change the beginning, the end, add characters, or change them, first in my mind and then in writing [interview]). His emphasis is on the reality of the lived experience of his community. He says, "La realidad en el que vivimos es tan crítica, para no decir criminal, que nos pasa cada cosa, y claro, muchos escritores se basan en eso, de su vida personal" (The reality that we live is so critically dire, not to say criminal, that things happen to us all the time, and yes, many writers base their works on these experiences, on their personal lives [interview]). In this respect, he notes that he is like many of the other writers. Certainly this is the case for Juan Julián Cruz Cruz and Alberto Gómez Pérez in terms of what they reflect in the stories in this collection.

The writers are influenced, as most writers are, by everything around them. A fundamental influence on their work is the oral traditions of their communities, because it is in these oral traditions that the stories of their

9. Enrique Hidalgo Mellanes, interview with Miguel Ruiz Gómez, "La literatura me ha permitido entender a mi comunidad," *Lengua y Literatura Hispanoamericanas*, Universidad Autónoma de Chiapas, Facultad de Humanidades, Campus VI, n.d., http://chacochis.blogspot.com/2011/03/la-literatura-me-ha-permitido-ver-y.html.

cultures are told, carried forward, sustained. Ochoa Nájera, in his essay in *El Mayoral*, writes that the work of cultural and linguistic revitalization, reflected in the different projects that CELALI engages in (like this volume), provides indigenous communities with the opportunity to see and reflect upon themselves in new and transformative ways: "Es así como el sujeto se puede dar cuenta de lo que es, de lo que puede ser y de la potencialidad de la historia; por ello mismo el sujeto no se debe permitir mutilarse, asimismo "mutilando su historia" (This is how the subject can realize who he or she is, what he or she could be, and the potentiality of history; for this reason the subject should not permit himself or herself to be mutilated, which would be 'mutilating his or her history'" [*El Mayoral*]).

María Concepción Bautista Vázquez's poem "O'on"/"Soy"/"I Am" provides the mirror for her community to see themselves:

> I am the hummingbird's song as the sun is rising
> I am incense on the altar of the gods
> I am the youthful sound of drums bringing joy to our lives
> I am a fresh season's fruit on an old tree
> I am the shadow that covers time
> I am the song of the cricket at night
> I am the spirit of our ancestors

The poet declares a certainty, a rootedness that is one with the generations from all time, with the earth, with the sounds and songs of the other beings from the natural world; the persona of the poem *is* the wholeness of her people. Furthermore, in a sense, the poem itself could be the "I"; the persona of the poem could *be* the poem. The poem, then, is "the incense on the altar of the gods," just as her people, too, are that incense. To the Tsotsil listener, the "I am" smoothly translates to the "We are."

Manuel Bolom Pale's poems address the many facets of silence, representing the *silencio sin frontera*, "silence without border," that was intended in the original title of the collection. In the case of Bolom Pale, and in the case of indigenous peoples (throughout the Americas—without borders) who have been thought to be dumb, somber, impenetrable, silence speaks wor(l)ds. In "Silence I," the persona of the poem, speaking generationally, tells us he is "in pain before [his] birth, / before taking a breath of life." The persona learns to "decipher the signs of night" that include the drops of blood on the earth, the blood that has been shed by himself, his family, his community. In "Silence II," the persona has become an oak that "destroys nostalgia"—he is not living in the past, even though there are still spiderwebs in his memory when he sleeps, but in the daytime, he is embraced by those memories; he is able to hear the "hummingbird's whisper," and a smile begins in his heart of his eyes and moves to his lips, lighting up his "sacred night." The transition is from the painful birthing to his finding and centering of himself. "Silence III" is the first of the three poems that has a reference to words, words threaded, woven. In these poems and in his others, silence is an awareness, of life, of death, of people, of words.

The poems of Adriana López reaffirm the power of silence as a heightened awareness, a consciousness, even of one's own birth, as in her "Metaphors of the Heart," where the persona of the poem is at one with her mother during the nine moons she is in the womb. She hears nature, "the cricket orchestra" is in rhythm with the "music of [her] body," and when she is born, she is a "plucked flower," nursed and caressed, and her "heart is born!" As she grows, she learns in silence, in a meditative silence, with finely attuned listening to the sounds of the earth, to her own spirit that speaks to her metaphorically. In her poem "Desolation," she speaks of another silence, the one that causes agony to her brother who is facing death and to herself. In "The Heat of the Heart," "[w]ords . . . silently invade the soul / that hide in a sinister song." Silence, even when meditative, even as an acute awareness, cannot ignore suffering or rage. The poet finds "joy of the heart," as the persona of this poem tells us, by "holding out a dark clay jug of verses / dressed of night, to catch metaphors in sleeplessness." These poems speak to the creative process, the entering inside the self, in silence, through reflection, to be able to see, to hear, to process, to be inspired, and then, to write.

Angelina Díaz Ruiz's poems also have a focus on meditative silence and a heightened awareness of the persona of the poems regarding the movements of the cosmos. "A god . . . / forms in the womb of Mother Earth; / in him is the beginning of life." This god is the one who moves and gives sustenance to the earth, the sky, the water. Sometimes he "dives into an abyss" in the "figure of a serpent"; he does so at festival time, which is when the work of the cosmos is in the hands of the people—it is his time of rest. In "Quietude," we are told that the "silent mist keeps secrets" and the "time of life" (the day) is announced by the "gods of the forest" each morning. The poem's persona says that "her mother taught her that the time before dawn / is the language of plants." There is a keen sensibility for time, a sensibility that comes from being quiet, listening, smelling, touching, seeing. In "Autumnal," the poet tells us that at the center of the home, the fire "bears witness to the grandfather's wisdom, / the father's counsel, / the mother's example." Díaz Ruiz's poems speak to the awakening and centering that occurs on a daily basis for each individual in an ever-expanding spiral movement.

Ruperta Bautista Vázquez's "Calling" brings us back to the other facets of silence. The poet writes of men without voice, women who hardly smile. "In the womb of tranquility / and the dancing heart / flows the blood of the ancients / pulsing through the skin of time." Sorrow runs deep, manifesting in the faces of the old ones whose "bloody memories" fill their thoughts. The cause of their pain is "[t]he scourge of humanity," as she says in "Cry." She bears witness to how the "[r]ed tears fall / boiling from the sky: / Cry of the people . . ." At the same time, in her poetry there is hope. "Spirit Descendants" affirms the strength of young girls who have always written in words, even though some "words sleep through the years." The girls persist, "[t]he words travel the universe, / . . . the words' wisdom distilled / takes shape in the faces of women." These women are the contemporary word-shapers in indigenous communities. She invokes the spirit of continuance in "Drummers," reminding us of the always present movement of spirit between worlds, of the sacred interrelationship of all life that goes back to the beginning of time, to the "[r]oots of the first men and women."

Andrés López Díaz's "Ojov" is a prayer that takes us into the heart of Tsotsil culture and cultural practices, to the sacred ceremonial mountain called Ojov. The persona of the poem says, "I summon your spirit / with the melody of my prayer / in the four corners of the earth, / as arrows of lightning flash / I awaken your heart." Ojov is a "[s]pirit summit," a "[d]welling of serpents, / jaguars, and quetzals, / glittering home of the naguals, / glittering, your deer and rabbits." The poem's persona says, "I long to meditate in this space, / shine light on my history . . ." "This space" is a Tsotsil place of prayer, ceremony, contemplation; the poet asks Ojov "to awaken our spirits, / beaten down for centuries, / and let wisdom blossom again / in the light of our ancestors." The speaker sees "spirals of words" in the incense; the request is also for a good harvest. Ojov is the guardian and protector of all of life; Ojov is the soul of the Supreme Being.

Juan Julián Cruz Cruz, in "Carnival Disaster," represents for us the chaos of carnival time: the outlandish costumes, the explosion of people, the sounds and tastes of the festival, and the narrator's sense, from the beginning, of foreboding, a feeling that intensifies as the day progresses. The narrator is filled with fright and confusion, moving back and forth between the actual goings-on and what he recalls from dreams that scare him. He is literally struck with fear, because "[a] vague worry, since my dream, stopped my tongue, tied up my words and my own *ch'ulel* [spirit]." The danger draws closer and closer, rapidly sending the men in the plummeting brakeless truck to an inevitable crash, ending in the horrible wreck, the unspeakable (apparent) death of the narrator's friend. Cruz Cruz is able to take us with the narrator on this journey that becomes a battle between life and death, a battle for the *ch'ulel* of each person in the truck, with many of the passengers being badly wounded, but the one who loses the battle is Carlos, and the narrator becomes speechless with sadness and a "sobbing that mixed with the murmur of the river that bordered the highway soaked in blood." This is another "silence without border."

Miguel Ruiz Gómez's story, "In the Middle of the Desert," also speaks to the dreaded silence that emerges from the battle with death as the migrants try to cross over into the land of promises. From the first line of the story, the narrator tells us of the smell of death in the unforgiving desert, his "body turns into ash," . . . and everything reminds him of death, including the "[s]keletons of bushes." He says, "silence becomes our prayer from this place. . . . [It is a] land without blood!" The movement across the desert is grueling, treacherous, and the opening passages of the story foretell what is to come: the truncated journey; the will of Mateo, the narrator, his uncle Manuel, and Pedro to try again, at the uncle's insistence; their terror-stricken discovery of the remains of those who have tried to make the journey and failed; the heartbreak of losing the uncle. During this journey, Mateo, in fleeting moments, recalls his home, the "mountain of candles and incense" he offered for the journey. And in the end, the uncertainty of what will happen next, and Pedro's silence.

Alberto Gómez Pérez's "I Never Knew Anything" is a story of two men, Manuel Kojtom and Pablo Wech, who are traveling home a long distance by foot, from El Campanario to Petalcingo. They stop at a shack where they meet an old man who allows them to spend the night. What ensues we are told in flashback, how the two traveled to El Campanario to deliver an official message, how they wanted to make it home that night but were slowed down by their age and by Pablo's "weak spirit," how Manuel "walks in the web of his memory" where Pablo appears to him later to accuse him of failing him. What happens on that dreadful night has to do with the *ch'ulel* (spirit): Pablo's *ch'ulel* and how it is taken by the old man, and Manuel's *ch'ulel* and how he is frozen with fright; "fear took over his soul, tangled his veins, squeezed his chest," and he can do nothing but barely see and hear. In this story, the silence of horror takes over and Pablo's words come only after he is gone.

A Note on Translation

We the readers have received the works of indigenous writers writing in their original languages of Tsotsil and Tseltal; the works appeared in those languages with an accompanying translation into Spanish (and sometimes the works were written in Spanish first and then translated to the indigenous languages); now this book presents the works in English as well. For readers who are bilingual in Spanish and English, they are afforded the opportunity to read the works in these two languages. For readers who are fluent in Tsotsil and Tseltal, there is another deepened level of reading that can take place. This publication is a step toward expanding the awareness of an ever-widening community of readers who are able to come to know the world of contemporary Maya literature from Chiapas.

Other Forms of Creative Expression

The renaissance that is occurring with the literature in Chiapas is also occurring in the fine arts, theater, and music. *Semblanzas de artistas plásticos mayas-zoques de Chiapas*, edited by Pedro Antonio Martínez Gómez (2002), includes the biographies of ten distinguished indigenous artists, one of whom is María Concepción Bautista Vázquez, whose poems are in this volume. *Sjalel stalel jch'ielaltik: Tejer nuestra historia* (2002), edited by Óscar Pérez Pérez, includes the stories of ten indigenous women weavers from Chiapas.[10] There are two well-known theater groups in Chiapas—Sna Jtz'ibajom, a writing collective (funded by Cultural Survival) composed mostly of men; and FOMMA (Fortaleza de la Mujer Maya; Empowerment of Maya Women). The founders of FOMMA, Isabel Juárez Espinosa and Petrona de la Cruz Cruz, were part of Sna Jtz'ibajom from 1983 to 1993, when they left to start their own women's group.[11] FOMMA is internationally known, and they are now also a member institution of the Hemispheric Institute of Performance and Politics in the Americas at New York University (http://hemisphericinstitute.org/

---

10. Both of these volumes were published by CELALI and CONACULTA. There is a fourth volume on potters.

11. For more information, see http://www.culturalsurvival.org/publications/cultural-survival-quarterly/mexico/la-fomma-la-fortaleza-de-la-mujer-maya-empowerment-m.

hemi/fr/modules/itemlist/category/69-fomma), which is directed by Diana Taylor. Both theater groups write and perform in their original languages as well as in Spanish. A new development in the music world in Chiapas is the annual Festival de Rock Indígena Bats'i Fest, where musicians from Chiapas, other Mexican states, and some from Guatemala meet to share their music (rock, reggae, blues) with enthusiastic audiences.[12] Pérez López comments that the musicians are engaging in the struggle to find new dignified spaces for the expression of their work, and that their artistic expression in their languages encourages a more profound understanding and use of those languages; again, the languages themselves are intimately intertwined with the creative process, and the subsequent works and creative expression promote language revitalization ("Rock 'Verdadero'").

The Maya Literary Renaissance

This literary and artistic renaissance is indeed occurring more broadly in the Maya world, in Mexico, in the Yucatán, and in Guatemala. In the Yucatán, some of the most recognized of the writers are Feliciano Sánchez Chan, Jorge Cocom Pech, Briceida Cuevas Cob, and Miguel May May. *In the Language of Kings: An Anthology of Mesoamerican Literature, Pre-Columbian to the Present* (W. W. Norton, 2002), edited by Miguel León-Portilla and Earl Shorris, includes the work of Sánchez Chan, Cuevas Cob, and May May. Carlos Montemayor and Donald H. Frischmann coedited *U Túumben K'Aayilo'ob X-ya'axché—Los nuevos cantos de la ceiba: Antología de escritores mayas contemporáneos de la península de Yucatán* (The new songs of the ceiba: Anthology of contemporary Maya writers of the Yucatán peninsula), published by the Instituto de Cultura de Yucatán, as a trilingual volume devoted to the works of eight Maya writers. In the chapter "New Songs for a New Millennium: Contemporary Yucatec Mayan Writers," Frischmann notes, "Contemporary Mayan writers take on their profession as heirs to a long tradition that includes pre-Hispanic texts replete with vivid narrative imagery and logo-syllabic glyphs, engraved or painted upon stone, ceramic, *ju'un* or ficus paper, and other media; and their colonial-period books, in

12. Sergio Alejandro López Ruiz, "Rock 'verdadero' en el Bats'i Fest," Todo Chiapas: En un mismo sitio, September 30, 2010, http://todochiapas.mx/chiapas/rock-"verdadero"-en-el-bats'i-fest/5852.

which the ancestral tongue acquires new form in Roman letters" (81).[13] In the Maya world, in Mexico and Guatemala, there is a sharing of this ancient heritage that produced the Dresden, Madrid, and Paris Codices; the *Annals of Chilam Balam*; the *Cantares de Dzitbalché*; *El ritual de los Bacabes*; and, of course, the *Popol Wuj*. These texts are the indisputable links to the contemporary *florecimiento* of Maya literature.

One of the most distinguished Maya writers from Guatemala is my colleague Victor Montejo, a Jakaltek Maya and professor emeritus of the Department of Native American Studies at the University of California, Davis. A prolific poet, novelist, essayist, author of children's books (including a children's version of the *Popol Wuj*), and eminent scholar, Montejo has contributed *Voices from Exile: Violence and Survival in Modern Maya History* and *Maya Intellectual Renaissance: Identity, Representation, and Leadership*, both with a focus on Guatemala, to the field of contemporary Maya Studies. Montejo says, "Our pride in our own heritage and our link with our ancestral past has reconnected the fabric of Maya culture, worn by centuries of neglect."[14]

The Importance of This Collection

This volume is a significant contribution to several scholarly fields, including Latin American and Latina/o Studies, Native American and Indigenous Studies, Comparative Literature, Chicana/o Studies, and American Studies, to name some. LASA, the Latin American Studies Association, has recognized the importance of addressing issues of race and ethnicity in relation to indigenous peoples in the Americas. The fiction in this collection takes up the theme of migration, crossing into the United States—the fact is that when indigenous peoples from Mexico or other parts south of the border arrive in the United States they become "Latinas/os," even when they bring their languages and modes of social organization with them. The term "Latina/o," generic as it is, is unsettled by the arrival of indigenous peoples, and this is a

13. Carlos Montemayor and Donald H. Frischmann, coeditors, *U Túumben K'Aayilo'ob X-ya'axché—Los nuevos cantos de la ceiba: Antología de escritores mayas contemporáneos de la península de Yucatán* (Mérida: Instituto de Cultura de Yucatán, 2009).

14. Victor Montejo, *Maya Intellectual Renaissance: Identity, Representation, and Leadership* (Austin: University of Texas Press, 2010), n.p., from introduction.

good thing. In the field of Native American and Indigenous Studies, the flagship association in the field, NAISA, is international in scope, yet the connections to Mexico, Central America, and South America are slower in being solidified because of the Spanish/English obstacles that must be faced (NAISA is much more comfortable strengthening linkages between the United States and other English-speaking countries like Canada, New Zealand, and Australia). This volume is one step toward bringing indigenous writers and intellectuals from the north and south closer to one another. In relation to the field of Comparative Literature, this volume will provide some much-needed attention to writers who are not likely even on the radar screen of those working in the field. Chicana/o Studies will benefit from this collection as well, since often when Mexican immigrant students come to universities in the United States, they find a kind of home in Chicana/o Studies because the field at least addresses Mexico, but most likely not the indigenous peoples of Mexico—this volume will therefore be a welcome addition. American Studies, with its intent to broaden and complicate what is known as "American," will find much to consider with the writers in this collection. And finally, this book will be an important connection to and with indigenous peoples wherever they are and wherever they may be from.

What Might the Future Hold?

Hermann Bellinghausen notes that contemporary indigenous literature is a new "verdadero" (true) chapter apart from the national literature of Mexico, and that the standard literary canon has lost its authority in the new millennium, yet at the same time this canon continues to ignore indigenous letters ("Hervidero"). He writes:

> Como si el "poder cultural" de ciertos grupos de intelectuales sustituyera el gusto, la inspiración y el duende de la literatura, algo que no amenazan las zancadas tecnológicas del siglo y las nuevas maneras de narrar. Los pueblos se han puesto a cantar, recuperar historias e inventarse nuevas, escribirlas, grabarlas. Y no sólo: los escritores indígenas se dan a la adicional tarea de describir y analizar el nuevo fenómeno desde dentro.

> [As if the "cultural power" of certain groups of intellectuals could substitute the taste, inspiration, and muse of literature, something that the technological strides of the century and the new ways of narrating do not threaten. [Indigenous] peoples have set them-

selves to singing, recuperating stories and inventing new ones, writing them, and recording them. And not only that: indigenous writers have given themselves the additional assignment of describing and analyzing the new phenomenon from within.][15]

Indigenous writers are in many ways highly, excruciatingly aware of how their contemporary songs and stories resonate in the world; they are clearly situated and, as Bellinghausen acknowledges, they are describing and analyzing their process from within; this is very much like the Zapatistas who go inside of themselves (personally and collectively) to have time for reflection so that they can come out again to express their *palabra florida*. There is a consistent approach to self-reflection and expression throughout the Maya (and the indigenous) world.

Natalio Hernández has noted: "In general we can say that the countries in the American hemisphere have engaged in dialogue with the West rather than with their own peoples. The relationship has been more one of confrontation rather than dialogue and *convivencia* [living together]. What is needed is to give life to cultural politics directed toward the development of a linguistic and cultural diversity with a focus on interculturalism" ("La voz indígena," 51; my translation). This is the ultimate goal of the writers in Chiapas as well. As they affirm their identities, languages, cultures, and cosmovisions, they are practicing a cultural politics that contributes judiciously and admirably to these goals.

Bibliography

Ma'yuk sti'ilal xch'inch'unel k'inal: Silencio sin frontera. San Cristóbal de las Casas, Chiapas: CELALI and Secretaría de Pueblos y Culturas Indígenas, 2011.

15. Hermann Bellinghausen, "En el hervidero de las letras indígenas" (In the hotbed of indigenous languages), *Ojarasca* 183, *La Jornada*, July 14, 2012. Bellinghausen is a distinguished Mexican journalist, poet, essayist, and medical doctor. Since 1994, he has resided in Chiapas; he has served as a correspondent covering the Zapatista Army of National Liberation, as well as editor of *Ojarasca* (a monthly supplement to the newspaper *La Jornada*) and *México Indígena*.

Translator's Note

Sean S. Sell

The writers in this collection were generally born between the 1974 First Indigenous Congress and the 1994 Zapatista uprising, as explained in Inés Hernández-Ávila's introduction. It was a time when indigenous people in Mexico were developing various ways to promote their languages and strengthen their presence in their ancestral land. Efforts to promote literacy in indigenous languages mostly failed to reach these writers during their childhood years, but for different reasons at different points they all decided for themselves to learn to read and write in their native languages. Eventually they connected with CELALI.

When translating these works, I seek always to emphasize the Tsotsil or Tseltal nature of the poem or story and its cultural context, yet I also want the English words to feel natural and pleasing, though not the same as if having originated in English. In *The Translator's Invisibility*, Lawrence Venuti criticizes translations that seek to present works as if they could have been written originally in English, so that people can forget a translator was involved: "By producing the illusion of transparency, a fluent translation masquerades as a true semantic equivalence when it in fact inscribes the foreign text with a partial interpretation, partial to English-language values, reducing if not simply excluding the very differences that translation is called on to convey" (16). I agree with Venuti's criticism, though not necessarily with how he uses the term "invisible." I want the Tsotsil or Tseltal origins of these texts to stand out, so I keep some "differences": some foreign words and some unusual, perhaps foreign-sounding English phrases. In Venuti's sense, this would appropriately make me as a translator more visible, as the reader can't help but see that the text has been translated. To my way of thinking, however, this strengthens the original author's voice and highlights the original source culture. That makes me less visible, not more.

With these works came the added challenge, or perhaps benefit, of the author's own decisions in creating their Spanish versions. I will call these versions "translations," although they do not necessarily fit that term. The authors here do not all follow the same process, and processes may vary even for individual authors. For example, the Tsotsil poet Manuel Bolom Pale says that for poetry he writes in Tsotsil first, then Spanish, but he uses Spanish first for academic writing. The Tseltal storyteller Juan Julián Cruz

Cruz says that when he first started writing fiction, it would be in Spanish first and then translated to Tseltal, and that was the case with his story "Carnival Disaster," but now he writes in Tseltal first. The Tsotsil poet María Concepción Bautista Vázquez says she usually writes in Tsotsil first, but sometimes she drafts and revises in both languages simultaneously. Should it still be considered translation if the two versions are crafted together? Of course, one sense in which all the Spanish versions qualify as translations is that the authors cross linguistic and cultural borders to bring their works and their worlds to a global language; however they crafted their Spanish versions, they did so with the idea of presenting their culture to the world. My coeditor, Nicolás Huet Bautista, director of research for CELALI and a published short story writer himself, sees this presentation of Chiapas culture as essential to the writers' literary project. He believes that literature helps show the spiritual essence and fortitude of the language, culture, and cosmovision of the Tsotsils—"*un pedazo de conocimiento*" (a piece of our consciousness) he called it in a discussion with me. By writing and promoting literature, he hopes to show the value not just of the Tsotsil language but of all languages. The values and consciousness of their traditions, he said, the essence of their children, can strengthen our understanding of living in this world.

These works, then, are pieces of their authors' consciousness presented to the Spanish-speaking world, and my role is to help take them to the English-speaking audience. Often the writers chose to leave some Tsotsil or Tseltal terms in their Spanish translations, and I saw no good reason to change those when I translated to English, though, as CELALI did in its bilingual version, I have included footnotes for clarification. Similarly, I sometimes retain Spanish words in my English translations, either because I think they're familiar to most English readers (*muertos, señor*) or because no workable English option exists (*huipil, petate*). In the latter case, footnotes are provided at the first appearance. We also decided on a glossary, and the various authors helped make sure it had the best terms. As those authors did, I have used italics to indicate foreign words, whether Tsotsil, Tseltal, or Spanish, at every occurrence.

Now, despite all these foreign words and indigenous cultural references, I do want these works to read well in English so readers with no knowledge of Mayan languages (likely the vast majority) and little knowledge of Spanish could still understand and enjoy them. Of course, with poetry and sometimes even fiction, ambiguity and opaqueness may be intentional and part of the appeal, but I want any such disorientation to be due to its presence in the original(s), not my choices as a translator. I will explain how that process applied to some specific works.

The poem "I Am," by the Tsotsil writer María Concepción Bautista Vázquez, is unusually individualistic for a Chiapas Maya. Communal identity runs through their cosmovision, so "we" statements might seem more likely. Yet the "I" statements in this poem have a distinctly communal character, as she finds her identity in visible and audible aspects of her native space. Only in the last line does she specifically look beyond the material world. Translating this line presented a dilemma, for the Tsotsil *totil me'iletik* did not seem to match so well the Spanish *los abuelos*, which in English would normally mean "the grandparents." Tsotsils commonly speak of *totil me'iletik* as important influences in their lives. Some have translated it as "fathermothers"—*totil* is "father," *me'il* is "mother," and the *-tik* makes it plural. I opted not to use this term here, as I wanted something more universal. Bautista celebrates her Tsotsil identity, but she uses words (such as *abuelos* in Spanish) that do not limit the interpretation. A mestizo Spanish reader may think, "*Sí, yo también soy el espíritu de los abuelos.*" Had she used the more literal *padresmadres*, it might have been off-putting, creating a barrier to connection. I feel "fathermothers" would have that effect for English readers. It is one thing to see a foreign word in an otherwise translated text; it is another to see a word that is in one's own language, but not really, and I feared it would sound like invented English in a way that would call attention to my translating choices. Yet "grandparents" in English too specifically means our ancestors of two generations back, without conveying the sense of our greater past. So while "ancestors" may not have the same ready connection to us as *totil me'iletik* does to Tsotsils, it seemed the best method for presenting the concept in a way we understand. And I used the possessive "our," unlike the Spanish *los*. Tsotsil has possessives, and Bautista did not use one here, but I did to reinforce the communal nature of the poem's individual identity, which I feel is implicit in the Maya cosmovision subtending her lines. The word "our" also has the advantage of a possibly inclusive interpretation: the "ancestors" are not just hers and those of her people; they may be "ours" too.

Now, I am willing to make choices that may not literally match the original(s) but present something appealing in English without changing essential meaning. One such choice was in the central line of this poem. Here is that line in three languages:

O'on satun li mol te' ta yech'el osil k'ak'al
Soy el fruto del viejo árbol en la estación
I am a fresh season's fruit on an old tree

The Tsotsil *mol te'* is *viejo árbol* is "old tree"; *yech'el osil k'ak'al* means roughly "that part of time" and is how they express "season," or *estación* in Spanish. Bautista's Spanish line works well, with *árbol* and *estación* almost rhyming, and a stressed syllable at the end. A direct English translation, "I am the fruit of the old tree in the season," has no music. "In the season" is not a phrase we use in English and is not interesting enough to count as useful foreignizing. Nor, since Tsotsil lacks a word comparable to "season" and thus uses a metaphor of the heart to express the idea, would this count as using English phrasing to approximate the style of another language. So I opted for the current version. Neither the Tsotsil nor the Spanish line has anything like "fresh" in it, but "fresh season's fruit" adds a nice alliteration, "on an old tree" finishes the line with two strong beats, and altogether I felt it created an inviting image for the poet and the literature Chiapas Maya writers are now creating.

Complicated choices like this did not arise much in translating Bautista's short poems, but they did with other pieces, such as Andrés López Díaz's long poem "Ojov," an ode to a Maya deity, a spirit of the Chiapas highlands. López did not try to translate the title to Spanish. The word *ojov* or *ajav* in Tsotsil (and, from what I understand, all Mayan languages) may translate as *señor* and "lord," and it is a word Tsotsils use to invoke God when they pray in Christian churches. Someone familiar with Tsotsil culture suggested I use "Lord" throughout the poem, as that is generally done in English translations of Tsotsil prayers. I disagreed, feeling that the deity invoked here is different and should keep the ancient Mayan name. But I also contacted the author to ask why he did not use Spanish for the title. He said he could not find an exact translation in Spanish, but that if I thought such a word existed in English, he was fine with my using it.

I don't. The Ojov of this poem lives in Chiapas and speaks a Mayan language. Ojov is intimately connected to the natural world:

> In the four corners of the earth
> I observe the colors that paint your language,
> see the geometry of your mountains,
> and feel the perfume of the trees
> that brings joy to my heart.

While these words might apply to a god of any region, at least any colorful, mountainous, tree-covered, nice-smelling region, other lines connect Ojov specifically to Chiapas, as in this stanza that names three mountains:

> You live in the number three,
> in three bosoms of the earth,
> Oxyoket, Tsonte'vits, Jmatsab,
> like the three brother villages.

Or this one that references three characters from Maya mythology:

> Ojov,
> guardian of earth and sky,
> protector of our spirit animals,
> Ojov, soul of Itsamná, Ixbalanqué, and Hunahpú.

I am glad López found no Spanish alternative for "Ojov," for it would not be the same poem. It would be taking a generic concept of God and invoking it around some Chiapas scenery, as if summoning the being to visit there for a tour. By using "Ojov," López reaches into the earth and sky around him to reintroduce this resident yet forgotten spirit to the people of the Chiapas highlands, and to introduce Ojov to the world beyond.

> Sacred Ojov,
> sacred hillside,
> here is your home,
> here your grandeur,
> here on my knees am I,
> here in reverence am I,
> to ask you, my lord,
> to awaken our spirits,
> beaten down for centuries,
> and let wisdom blossom again
> in the light of our ancestors.

Now Ojov and other ancestral spirits of the Chiapas Maya may cross the border into English and share their words and their consciousness with the spirits of worldwide humanities.

López's answer points out how the writers themselves have had to make translation choices for each work, and as far as I know, none of them had any sort of formal training in translation. Sometimes their choices were difficult, and sometimes that led to difficult choices for me in English. The Spanish version of "Desolación" by the Tseltal poet Adriana López opens:

> Vino la malicia que levanta el ojo,
> su coraje es un soliloquio de dioses:
> deseó chupar mi sangre
> desde la boca de mi choza.

A direct translation of the first line would be "Came the malice that raises the eye." So whose eye was raised? The eye of malice? If so, why not use the possessive? She does use the possessive in the second line with "*su coraje*," but that now creates ambiguity—*su* can be the second-person singular formal possessive, "your" for the "usted" form of "you," or the third-person possessive for "his," "her," "its," or "their." Since López did not use *su* before, can we be sure that this "su" refers to malice? Is the speaker perhaps addressing someone? The rest of the poem gives no indication of second person, so I eliminated that possibility. The third and fourth lines feature *mi*, so we have a first-person speaker, but if it's the speaker's eye in the first line, why did she not use *mi* there? I was able to present this question to López, and she explained that the Tseltal phrase "*slik sitil*," literally something like "eye shakes," is an expression for the feeling that someone is saying bad things about you. She told me:

> Es común que en los pueblos originarios se diga, que cuando una persona está hablando de otra pero en forma negativa, la persona de quien hablan lo siente o llega a saber porque el ojo brinca o hace ciertas palpitaciones en uno de los ojos, que tarda unos cuantos segundos o minuto.

> (It is common in the original villages to say, when a person is talking of another in a negative way, that the person being talked about feels or comes to know it because the eye jumps or makes certain palpitations in one of the eyes, lasting some seconds or a minute.)

So "*levanta el ojo*," while not a familiar idiom in Spanish, was her way of conveying this sensation. When I learned this, I considered some variation of the similar English expression "ears burning" but opted against it. For one thing, with ears burning the talk isn't necessarily negative, and also, since López did not use a familiar Spanish idiom, for me to impose an English one would be to inscribe my interpretation on her culture. As explained above, my decision not to do this fits with Venuti's ideas, if not his terms: the English idiom, while perhaps providing a comfortable familiarity for English readers, would make me more visible and exclude the evidence of López's choices in both Tseltal and Spanish. To convey the unease that malice brings, I chose "our eyes shuddered." The possessive "our" replaces the article *el*, and "eye" becomes "eyes" to indicate that this is a general sensation in the community. My English version became:

> Malice came, our eyes shuddered;
> it raged in a soliloquy of gods,
> wanted to suck blood
> from the mouth of my home.

One last point on these lines: The Spanish word *choza* would indicate a small rural dwelling like a hut or a cabin. The Tseltal word is *jna*, with the letter *j* indicating "my" and *na* the word for house or home. So López's use of *choza* makes the image in Spanish more Tseltal than the Tseltal word does. Perhaps the indigenous language writing requires less indigenous-oriented imagery. For English, however, I thought the general and rather emotionally intimate "home" seemed preferable to any more specific term like "hut," "shack," or "cabin" that might more likely evoke a particular image not fitting the Chiapas setting.

Another case where I sought help from the writer was with the Tsotsil poet Angelina Díaz Ruiz's poem "Ts'ijlej / Quietud / Quietude," which contains the following:

ta o'lol k'ak'al chlok' k'atinikuk	al mediodía emergen a solearse
li ts'i' ojovetike.	las serpientes de los *ojovetik*.

The word *ts'i'* in Tsotsil is "dog," but *serpientes* is Spanish for serpents or snakes. "*Ojovetik*," the plural of *ojov* as in Andrés López Díaz's poem, was explained in a footnote as "*guardianes ancestrales de las montañas*," ancestral deities who guard the mountains. Angelina Díaz Ruiz's explanation for the discrepancy between dog and snake was that "*li ts'i' ojovetike*" was a Tsotsil expression for the spiritual force of the mountains. She felt readers in Spanish would not understand it, and that *serpientes* would work better in that case as a more mythical, less commonplace animal. So here we see a case where the writer herself had to make decisions on how visible she would be as a translator. She opted against a literal translation of "*li ts'i'*," feeling that in Spanish the word *perro* (dog) would not convey the intended meaning, but she kept *ojovetik* without any translation, as an essential name. My English translation is:

> at midday the serpents of the *ojovetik*
> emerge to bask in the sun.

For both the Spanish and English, a footnote explains the meaning of *ojovetik*.

One last note on the spelling of the indigenous languages: the "Tz" spellings—Tzotzil and Tzeltal—are, I believe, still more commonly seen in the United States, but in Chiapas they are giving way to the "Ts" versions used by CELALI. In fact, the letter *z* does not appear at all in any of the Tsotsil or Tseltal texts, and so I use the "Ts" spellings.

Bibliography

Venuti, Lawrence. *The Translator's Invisibility.* 2nd ed. New York: Routledge, 2008.

Part 1

Poems

The poets here are fully aware that they speak for their communities. María Concepción Bautista Vázquez, Tsotsil, writes short poems about fellow residents of her native land, human or otherwise, and her poem "I Am" suggests that these honored subjects are herself, her community, and all people. The protagonists of the Tsotsil writer Manuel Bolom Pale's poems include a deaf man who is not trapped in silence, a girl who becomes part of a forest, and an old woman who weaves moon music. These characters' relationships with nature highlight connections the Chiapas Maya have with their environment. The Tseltal writer Adriana López offers us "Metaphors of the Heart," a heart that may give poisonous kisses but also knows a mother's caress, and reflects the heart not only of a person but of a community. It is worth noting here the importance of the heart as a metaphor among the Maya people. As Robert M. Laughlin explains in *Mayan Hearts* (2002), an unknown Spanish monk who prepared a Tsotsil dictionary near the end of the sixteenth century found an "infinite" number of expressions using the word "heart." "He learned that the heart was the seat not only of the soul and of emotion but also of thought, of judgment. Everything we call 'human' was there in the heart" (n.p.). Angelina Díaz Ruiz, Tsotsil, examines the spirits of the earth and their influence on the lives of her people, whether these spirits be recognized Maya entities, natural forces that underlie conscious routines, or both. The Tsotsil writer Ruperta Bautista Vázquez (no relation to María) explores how the identity expressed in music and weaving and cultivating corn may spread to the cosmos, and the Tsotsil writer Andrés Díaz López's long poem "Ojov" invokes an ancient Maya deity, forgotten today by many, to awaken his people to the divinity of the earth.

Los poetas aquí son plenamente conscientes que hablan para sus comunidades. María Concepción Bautista Vázquez, tsotsil, escribe poemas cortos sobre personas, animales y cosas de su tierra nativa, y su poema "Soy" sugiere que estos sujetos honrados son sí mismo y su comunidad y todas las personas. Los sujetos del escritor tsotsil Manuel Bolom Pale incluyen un hombre sordo que no está atrapado en el silencio, una niña que se vuelve parte del bosque y una anciana que teje música de la luna. Las relaciones entre personajes y la naturaleza ponen de relieve la conección que tienen los mayas de

Chiapas con su ambiente. La escritora tseltal Adriana López nos da metáforas del corazón, que puede dar besos venenosos pero sabe la caricia de una madre, y refleja el corazón no solo de una persona sino de la comunidad. Es notable aquí la importancia del corazón como metáfora para los mayas. Como explica Robert M. Laughlin en *Mayan Hearts* (Corazones mayas), un fray español desconocido que preparó un diccionario tsotsil hacia finales del siglo XVI encontró un numero "infinito" de expresiones que usan "corazón." "Aprendió que el corazón fue la base no solo del alma y la emoción pero además del pensamiento, juicio. Todo que llamamos 'humano' estaba allá en el corazón." (El libro *Mayan Hearts* no tiene números de página. La cita va de la segunda a la tercera página de texto.) Angelina Díaz Ruiz, tsotsil, examina los espíritus de la tierra y su influencia en las vidas de su gente, si son entidades mayas reconocidas o fuerzas naturales que subyacen las rutinas conscientes, o las dos. La escritora tsotsil Ruperta Bautista Vázquez (sin parentesco con María) explora como la identidad expresada por música y escritura y la cultivación del maíz puede extender a los cosmos, y el escritor tsotsil Andrés Díaz López con su poema largo "Ojov" invoca una deidad maya anciana, hoy olvidada por muchos, para despertar su gente a la divinidad de la tierra.

Ta sk'ob Yaxte' / En los brazos de la Ceiba / In the Arms of the Ceiba

María Concepción Bautista Vázquez

Mank'uk'

Ta xch'ut unenal Yaxte'
skux yo'onton jkot muk'ta mank'uk' ta o'lol smuil yok
nene'tik xchi'uk uch'al o' nichim.
Sk'ejinta slikben xch'iel jtotj jme'tik.
Xviletaj sjoyobta toketik;
ta vinajel, li ch'ul mute
a' st'ujumal syaxal ston jch'ultotik.

Quetzal

En el regazo de una Ceiba joven
posa un gran quetzal entre aromáticas bromelias y orquídeas.
Canta la historia de mis ancestros.
Revolotea surcando nubes;
en el cielo, el pájaro sagrado
es la esmeralda de los dioses.

Quetzal

In the arms of a young Ceiba tree
a grand quetzal perches among the fragrant bromeliads and orchids,
sings the story of my ancestors.
It swirls, plowing through the clouds;
in the sky, sacred bird,
emerald of the gods.

"Mank'uk'" / "Quetzal" / "Quetzal"
by María Concepción Bautista Vázquez

31

K'ak'al

Ta yolon xojobal
li sk'obe sjaxbe sat li jvok'-osile,
sk'eloj
xchi'in ta vok'-osil,
k'unk'un ch'anal xch'ay sba
ta sti' malom k'ak'al.

Sol

Su luminosidad
acaricia el rostro del campesino,
mientras lo observa
lo acompaña a labrar la tierra,
lento y enmudecido se oculta
en las puertas del ocaso.

Sun

Your brightness
caresses the campesino's face,
while you watch him,
go with him as he works the earth,
slow and silently you depart
through sunset's door.

◆

Ts'unun

Ta sikil ikliman,
ta yanal nichimal uk'um
slok'ta sat li ts'unune,
sk'opon t'ujumal
jpech'biljol ants.

Colibrí

En el fresco rocío,
en los pétalos del lirio
dibuja su rostro el colibrí,
saluda a la mujer
de hermosas trenzas.

Hummingbird

In fresh dew,
in iris petals
its face appears, the hummingbird,
greeting the woman
with the beautiful braids.

◆

Jbonolajelte'

X-ak'otaj ta sbon k'utik,
yik' lum ta sbon,
sbon xchi'uk snatil sjol
slo'il jme'tik u;
osil k'ak'altik yich'oj li sk'ope.
Sbon jujup'el sk'op unen bats'i ants.

Pincel

Danza en los colores,
pinta olor a tierra,
su cabellera traza
la historia de la abuela luna;
su palabra rostro del tiempo.
Pinta versos de la joven tsotsil.

Paintbrush

Dance in the colors,
paint the smell of earth,
with your mane you trace
the story of grandmother moon;
your word the face of time.
Paint verses of a young Tsotsil woman.

◆

Unen tseb

Sikil ikliman pixil ta tok
sk'eloj chanav unen tseb,
yunenal skuchoj ta sk'ob.
Jkuch si' unen tseb,
jkuch o',
xchi'uk smol k'ib
sk'opon ikliman.

Niña

Fría neblina
vigila el caminar de la niña,
en sus brazos carga su infancia.
Niña cargadora de leña,
cargadora de agua,
con su viejo cántaro
saluda a la mañana.

Girl

Cold fog
watches over the girl as she walks,
carrying her infancy in her arms.
Girl, bearer of wood,
bearer of water,
with her old pitcher
greets the morning.

◆

Nab

St'ujumal sakil skebal ya'bat jch'ultotik,
yak'ot tselobal na'b spok staki nukulel,
xchi'uk sk'unil k'ob
st'uxubtas sat k'ak'al,
sk'unil yik'al jch'ulme'tik,
stuxnuk'al ta stsob li jtoktike.

Mar

Encanto del esplendoroso ángel,
danza de olas baña su arena piel,
con sus delicadas manos
rocía el rostro del sol,
brisa de diosa,
que la nube con su algodón recoge.

Sea

Splendid angel's enchantment,
the dancing waves bathe your sandy skin,
with your delicate hands
you spray the sun's face,
goddess breeze,
gathered into cotton clouds.

◆

O'on

O'on sk'ejojun ts'unun ta sob ikliman
O'on pomun ta smexa jch'ultotik
O'on yunenal sk'ejoj jnitvaneb vob
O'on satun li mol te' ta yech'el osil k'ak'al
O'on nak'ombailun chispix ta osil k'ak'al
O'on sk'ejojun chilil ta ik'al ak'ubal
O'on xch'ulelun totil me'iletik

Soy

Soy el canto del colibrí en la aurora
Soy el incienso en el altar de los dioses
Soy el sonido joven del tambor que alegra la vida
Soy el fruto del viejo árbol en la estación
Soy la sombra que cobija el tiempo
Soy canto de grillo en la nocturnidad
Soy espíritu de los abuelos

I Am

I am the hummingbird's song as the sun is rising
I am the incense on the altar of the gods
I am the youthful sound of drums bringing joy to our lives
I am a fresh season's fruit on an old tree
I am the shadow that covers time
I am the song of the cricket at night
I am the spirit of our ancestors

◆

Jme'tik U

Ta k'ob chats'isbun
jvaech jujun ak'ubal,
chalok'ta ek'etik xch'iuk noetik
ta spok'lejal ak'u'.
Tsebal U jts'is vaecheletik.

Luna

Con tus manos bordas
mis sueños cada noche,
con tus hilos dibujas las estrellas
en tu manto.
Joven Luna bordadora de sueños.

Our Mother Moon

With your hands you embroider
my dreams every night,
with your threads you sketch the stars
in your cloak.
Young Moon, dream seamstress.

◆

Ch'anetel / Silencio / Silence

Manuel Bolom Pale

Jun vinik makal xchikin

Xchikinta ti ue,
k'analetik xchi'uk slajelal jujun k'ak'al.
Chk'ejin ti jujun ak'obal
xchi'uk sk'ejimol ulich mutetik.
Kuxul mu sk'uxubin sba,
mu xcham, makal ti ch'abetel.
Tsjal ak'obal stsotsil sjol.
P'aj ti sva'ech.

Ti pukujil xi'ele xchochoj skuxlejal,
xchamxa batel;
k'alal xchlaj ti sk'uxul skuxlejale
xcham ti jnene ok' xchi'uk ti ik'e tsjim batel
snopel yu'un sjunlej osil.

Un hombre sordo

Escucha a la luna,
a las estrellas y el tiempo que muere.
Oye desde la sombra
con música de pájaros nocturnos.
Vive sin vivirse atrapado en el silencio.
Teje la noche con su cabellera.
Cae de sueño.

La nebulosa angustia arrastra su existencia,
agoniza lentamente;
cuando desvanezca su dolor
el viento desplazará
su pensamiento hacia la órbita celeste.

A Deaf Man

He listens to the moon,
to the stars, and the dying day.
From the shadows he hears
music of night birds.
He lives in silence without being trapped.
He weaves the night with his hair.
He falls into sleep.

Cloudy anguish drags his existence,
slow as death;
when his pain fades away,
the wind will lift
his thought into heavenly orbit.

◆

Ch'anlan

Ti jsate chanav ta ch'ayem be,
ch'anal xliket ti snak'obal ak'obale;
jyakubel tsutal ti slajesel vayele,
tsjuch'ilan k'uxulil ta xch'ut ch'abetel;
ta jpajes k'ak'al jvaech.

Enmudece

Mis ojos viajan en el sendero perdido,
callados recorren la sombra de la noche;
vuelven borrachos desgastando insomnios,
moliendo dolores en el vientre del silencio;
en mis sueños detengo el tiempo.

Being Silent

My eyes travel the lost trail,
silently crossing the night's shadows;
drunk men return, wearing down sleeplessness,
grinding pain in the belly of silence;
in my dreams I hold back time.

◆

Jlajeletik

Skoj mu xa sutik tal ti jlajelaletike k'usi van tsnopik.
Te oyikxa ta xch'ut balumil,
k'atp'ujxa ta lun ti snopbenal yu'unike,
tsnochan sba ta svomolalik ik'liman,
tsk'an tsutik tal,
tsk'an sts'akliik ch'ul u.

Tsvachinik jujun ch'anetel be.
snopik k'uyu'un mu xchamik yanbelta,
tsk'uinik sts'ubil yanal te'.
Yu'un mu sk'an sk'elik vo'neal skuxlejalik.

Tsk'an xch'aniik,
mu sk'an xmakatik ta sna ob xchi'uk k'anal ta sbeik,
tsk'upinik ch'anal mutetik,
k'ux yo'ntonik chjelav k'ak'al;
xchik'ik ik' ta sk'opik,
tsmochik ta xabil ch'anetel ti sike.

Ta xchikin xik' sat,
tsmuk snak'obalik,
tsmalubesik ti vo'neal p'ine,
xkiletik k'uchel jkot chon
tsve' stanil snopbenal yu'unik.

Los muertos

¿En qué piensan los muertos?
Sus pensamientos son de barro
y de hierbas que reposan en el alba,
quieren regresar,
seguir la luna.

Sueñan pasos afligidos,
piensan por qué no morir de nuevo,
cobijarse en partículas de hojarasca
para ya no ver el pasado.

Ellos prefieren callar,
estar sin estrellas ni telarañas adheridas a su paso;
anhelan el silencio de pájaros invisibles,
dolientes al pasar los astros;
queman el viento con su voz,
enredan el frío al abismo del silencio.

A la orilla de sus pestañas
sepultan la simetría de su sombra,
arrugan la vasija añeja
y reptan como serpiente,
devorando el polvo de sus pensamientos.

Los Muertos

What do the dead think of?
Their thoughts are of dirt
and grasses that settle at dawn;
they want to return,
follow the moon.

They dream of mournful steps,
think why not die again,
cover themselves in debris of fallen leaves
to block out the past.

They prefer to be quiet,
without stars or spiderwebs in their way;
they long for the silence of invisible birds,
suffering as they pass the stars;
they burn the wind with their voice,
entangle cold in the abyss of silence.

At their eyelids' edge
they bury their shadow's symmetry,
wrinkle the aging coffin walls,
and slither like a snake,
devouring the dust in their thoughts.

•

Xmal

Jun p'ijilal tseb tsnak' sba ti yanal tulan
ti xik' sat te'tik,
tsmil ti tajimol ti k'ak'aletike,
tsnak' stanil ye ta ch'anetel
nichim cha'i sba.

Chk'atp'uj ta t'ujumal nichim ta sk'ob tulan jujun malk'ak'al.
Tstik' sba ochel ti svaech mol te'etik
vay jmuk'ta ok' yu'un muk' xcham.
Sk'an ch-an yu'un tsmoch sba ta bebetik,
chatintas sbek'tal ta ch'anetel.
Chik'tal jmuk'ta ok' ti lajelale
yu'un tsk'an ch-an yan belta ti bik'it tsebe.

Xmal[1]

Una niña numinosa se funde
en las pestañas del bosque,
juega a matar el día,
a esconder silencio entre dientes
para sentirse flor.

Al atardecer
se vuelve orquídea prohibida
y se sumerge en el sueño de viejos árboles.
Dormita una hora sin morirse,
se enreda en los caminos
y baña su cuerpo en el silencio.
Llama a la muerte un instante y vuelve a ser niña.

---

1. Tsotsil para el nombre "María."

Xmal[2]

A spirit girl blends in
with the forest's eyelashes,
plays at killing the day,
at hiding silence between teeth
to feel flower.

As darkness comes
she turns into a forbidden orchid
and dives into the dream of old trees.
She dozes an hour without dying,
entangles herself in pathways,
and bathes her body in silence.
She calls to death for an instant and then is a girl again.

"Xmal"
by Roberto Antonio
López de la Cruz

2. Tsotsil for the name "Mary."

Ch'anetel I

K'alal muto xi ane,
k'alal mu to jta xnichimaj jkuxlejale k'uxun.
Laj snak'batel jvaech ti ik'e.

Tsjovijes jnopbenal ak'obal mutetik,
tsjax batel pamlej ch'ich'etik;
ta yanal te'etik nochajtik ik'al pepen
kats'al ti snuk' ch'ul k'in
tsabe smelolal ti ak'obale.

Silencio I

Estoy adolorido antes de nacer,
antes de respirar la vida.
El viento ahuyentó mis sueños.

Hay pájaros nocturnos que confunden mi memoria,
sobre tierra rocían charcos de sangre;
mariposas negras sobre hojas secas
con rituales se anuda en la garganta,
descifran los signos de la noche.

Silence I

I am in pain before my birth,
before taking a breath of life.
The wind dispersed my dreams.

Night birds confuse my memory,
spray pools of blood on the earth;
black butterflies on dry leaves
with rituals tie up the throat,
decipher the signs of night.

◆

Ch'anetel II

Mol bochje te'un jlajes sk'uxul o'ntonal,
chivay ti sna ob snopelal,
ti skeval k'ak'al jmeyoj jba chivachaj.

Chka'i sts'ijts'un ti ts'unune
tspukbe stanil balumil.

Ta yut jsat
xta'et jun tse'ej
yu'un tsk'ixna ti sti' kee
xchi'uk skevta ch'ul ak'obal.

Silencio II

Soy roble que destruye nostalgias,
duermo en telarañas de memoria,
en luz del día sueño abrazado.

Escucho el susurro del colibrí
que agita sus partículas de polvo.

Al fondo de mis ojos
se ensancha una sonrisa
que abraza mis labios
y alumbra mi noche sagrada.

Silence II

I am the oak that destroys nostalgia,
I sleep in a web of memory,
in daylight's embrace I dream.

I hear the hummingbird's whisper
that stirs up the dust.

From the depth of my eyes
comes a wide smile
that embraces my lips
and lights up my sacred night.

◆

Ch'anetel III

Bak'intik

A' laj jchanbe ak'obal ti ch'anetele.
Oy yantik belta ti jvol k'opetik,
ta jal xchi'uk svolil k'ux o'ntonal
ja' spixob koltak.

Li' oyun xchi'uk spixjol kuxlejal,
ti jmak jba ta k'ak'al
sme'onal jkuxlejal.

Silencio III

A veces

A veces imito la noche a guardar silencio.
A veces hilo palabras,
tejo con la madeja de dolor
el abrigo de mis retoños.

Aquí estoy con el sombrero de la vida,
tapándome del sol de la indiferencia.

Silence III

Sometimes

Sometimes I imitate the night to keep silent.
Sometimes I thread words,
weave with the skein of suffering
a coat for my little ones.

Here I am under the hat of life,
shielding myself from the indifferent sun.

◆

Jchamel k'opetik

Jchamel chbatik ti k'opetike,
chlajik xa batel ta jamal mukenal,
tsukulin yakan ta snak'obalik
ti ak'obal xch'inet ch'ul u.
Jujun k'ak'al me'on tsutiktal.

Palabras enfermas

Las palabras se enferman,
mueren sobre tumbas abiertas,
tropiezan sus sombras
en las noches sin luna.
Los días retornan vacíos.

Sick Words

Words grow sick,
die over open tombs,
trip over their shadows
in moonless nights.
Days come back empty.

◆

Chvay ti olol tsebe

Ti tsebe
tsmeltsan sna'elal xchiuk spech' jol.
Xch'ay ta sat svaech,
ti'bat snichimal snopbenal ta ak'obal.

Ch-ok' ti olol tsebe,
chuch' ya'lel sat ti snichimal tseke,
xko'laj k'uchel nichim tstik' ti kuxlejalil.

Duerme la niña

La niña,
con sus trenzas recrea su memoria.
Desperdicia el sueño en su mirada
que devora la noche de su fantasía.

Llora, su enagua bebe las lágrimas
como si fuera pétalos succionando la vida.

Sleeps the Girl

The girl
re-creates memory with her braids.
She squanders the dream in her glance
that devours the night of her fantasy.

She cries, her skirt drinks the tears
like petals sucking in life.

◆

K'ejimol mukenal

Ti sbe jch'ich'el xko'laj k'uchel mokoch chon.

Jvaechta ti oy jkuxlejal ono'ox ti yan k'ak'al,
chkojtikin sbe ak'obal k'uchel j-almantal,
tsjam sba ti sti' vaeche, ch-och ta jsat ak'obal
xchi'uk skeval tan.

Ti yolon xik' jsat jmetsan ti ch'anetele
k'uchel sk'uxul yo'nton ak'obal.
¿K'usi chonal xt'aet ta yut jbek'tal tsti'un?
me avan ti ak'obale, bu yakil chanav k'usitik oy,
ti snuti'al vaech tsjombun snopbenal.

Ti jsate xvinaj k'uchel ch'anetel ch'ulelal, k'uchel chumante' slapoj snak'obal
xchi'un ti snopele xch'ay batel, tsjitun sba ti xchukulel jnuk'e, chlekub ti xi'ele,
chk'a' jnak'obal ta abiletik, a'me chopol, stsij ochel ti ko'nton, sak ch'ay batel ti
ch'abetel k'uchel svayeb olol k'uchel mesobil ti chak'bukutik iluk ti lekilale ti
chjelav snopbenal k'uchelk'anlajel.

Chvay ti ko'ntone, tsbon lekil kuxlejalil svaech ti ak'obale. Tspas yan belta ti k'usi
tspase, t'anal chanav ta jvaech, mu'yuk sk'oj xoyilan ti ak'obale: ja' tsti' nak'bal ti
ak'obale.

Ta yut jchinab oy jkot tobtob
sbon snak'obal
xchi'uk xch'ailal ch'anetel.

Canto en la tumba

Mi vena es una nauyaca debajo de mi piel.

He pertenecido a otro cosmos,
conozco los caminos de la noche como un presagio,
la puerta del sueño se abre, entra por mis ojos la noche
con relámpagos de polvo.

Bajo mis pestañas forjo el silencio
como angustia de la noche.
¿Qué animal se arrastra por mis venas
y me carcome?
Acaso la oscuridad,
donde andan los sonámbulos
con el equipaje de sueños,
atraviesa la vida.

Mi rostro es un fantasma, un tronco disfrazado de sombra; toda mi memoria
se desvanece antes del amanecer; deshace el nudo de mi garganta, desahoga
mi miedo; se oxida mi sombra en el tiempo, menos mal, la humedad escurre
sobre mi corazón y se diluye en el silencio como los recuerdos.

Mi corazón duerme, dibuja la forma del kuxlejal[3] y sueña la noche cubierta
de estrellas. Repite el gesto único, la humedad que viaja por mi cuerpo, a
través de los sueños sin abrigo, sin máscara que retuerce la noche: es la noche
que devora la sombra.

Dentro del pensamiento
un caracol dibuja su sombra
con el humo del silencio.

3. Vida.

I Sing in the Tomb

My vein is a viper under my skin.

I have belonged to another cosmos,
I know the night passages like an omen,
the dream door opens, night enters through my eyes
with lightning bolts of dust.

Under my eyelids I forge silence
like the night's anguish.
What animal drags itself through my veins
and eats away at me?
Maybe the darkness,
where sleepwalkers go
with the baggage of dreams,
crosses my life.

My face is a ghost, a tree trunk disguised as shadow; all my memory
fades before the sunrise; the knot in my throat melts, my fear eases; in
time my shadow rusts, less evil, the dampness drizzles over my heart
and is diluted in silence like memories.

My heart sleeps, draws the form of the good life and dreams the night
covered with stars.
It repeats the only gesture, the dampness that travels through my
body, across the dreams without cover, with no mask to twist the
night: it is night that devours the shadow.

Within the thought
a snail traces its shadow
with the smoke of silence.

◆

Ti xchikin vaechil

Tspik jvaech ti ak'obale,
chk'ot ti sbeyo'al ch'ayem o'ntonal;
li k'usi mu ojtikinbile chvok' ta jch'ich'el,
mu x-an ti ak'obale,
ti k'opetike mu xlok' xk'opojik
ta sbi ch'abetel.
Ti snopbenal ku'une
tspaj sba ta svaech ak'obal.

Los presagios del sueño

La noche palpa mi sueño,
llega al arroyo del olvido;
este dúctil enigma que me brota en la sangre,
no nace ni la noche,
y la palabra no consigue enunciar
el nombre del silencio.
Mi pensamiento se incrusta
en los sueños de la muerte.

Dream Omens

The night palpates my sleep,
comes to the stream of forgetting;
this shifting enigma that rises up in my blood,
not even night is born,
and words cannot speak
the name of silence.
My thinking encrusted
in dreams of death.

◆

Jalom

Ti jme'tik me'ele tsnit sjamlej skuxlejal.
Ti jme'tik u xchi'uk k'anal
tstus sna'omal stsebal,
chk'ejin.

Ti svobal arpa tslikes ti jalome,
chak'be sk'ejojal jalbilal u' ta ak'obal.

Tejedora

La anciana carda los surcos de su vida.
Entre la luna y las estrellas
peina sus recuerdos de niña,
y canta al tiempo.

Al son del arpa comienza su cosecha de huipiles,
y ofrece a la noche música tejida de luna.

Weaver

The old woman straightens the furrows of her life.
Between moon and stars
she combs through her girlhood memories
and sings to time.

To the sound of the harp she begins her harvest of huipiles,[4]
and to the night she offers music woven of the moon.

"Jalom" / "Tejedora" / "Weaver"
by Roberto Antonio López de la Cruz

4. Traditional blouses worn by indigenous women.

Slok'omba k'op o'tanil / Metáforas del corazón / Metaphors of the Heart

Adriana López

Slok'omba k'op o'tanil

Sjalbon jme' te sk'axel jk'aal
sok nichimetik soknix sk'ayoj baluneb u,
k'alal smaliyon ta sti'il k'aal.
Jt'ul ja'on le'a te yakal ta ch'iel
ta lejch'elejch' snichimal u.

Ta smajlib k'aal
stijik te chiletik
sonil jbak'etal;
speton te ajk'ubal,
xwijk' jsit,
ya jax te jts'unbal.

Xnijk'on yu'un sik,
t'anal nichimon;
xchu'unteson jme'
k'alal sjaxbon te k'ax k'un kelaw,
¡bejk'aj te ko'tan!

Slap k'ejluyel ko'tan
te ya st'anantes te ch'ulel;
jich jta ta ilel te skitsumal jbak'etal
ta sit xch'ababet k'inal.
Yujts'iyon te slok'mba k'op
ya x-aan sok te jch'ulel,
wususet ta ilel te k'opetik
ya smakbon ke.
Ka'iy muken k'op
ta smuxuk' lum k'inal,
ta xchumante'ul Yax te'
te ya smak'linbon kutsilal.

II

Sboltesba te ko'tan
sok sjijban slajelaltak ta sit sna,
stul ta jsit wojt' snich xch'ababet k'inal
te ya yejch'entes tse'ejetik.

Ayme ya x-ok' jich bit'il sloxoxil ik'
sok xk'opoj ta ijk'al k'opetik.
Te siknax yejk'ech xjayubteswan.
Ayme ya xch'ab k'alal xway te k'aal,
yelk'anbey skuxlejal te ch'ayel o'tanil,
ya sok sba ta ik',
smak k'ayojetik, yak' mel o'tan
sok spisil ora ya xcham.

Metáforas del corazón

Mi madre teje mi tiempo
con flores y cantos de nueve lunas,
mientras me espera en el borde del día.
Soy ahí una gota que va creciendo
en los pétalos de la luna.

En el ocaso
la orquesta de grillos toca
la música de mi cuerpo;
me abraza la noche,
abro los ojos,
acaricio mi origen.

Tiemblo de frío,
soy una flor desnuda;
mi madre me amamanta
mientras acaricia mi rostro frágil,
¡mi corazón ha nacido!

II

Se viste mi corazón
de miradas que desnudan el alma;
yo descubro las líneas de mi cuerpo
en el ojo del silencio.
Me besan las metáforas
y platican con mi ch'ulel,[1]
enjambre de palabras
que me cierra la boca.
Escucho un murmullo
en el ombligo de la tierra,
en el tronco de una ceiba
que alimenta mi esencia.

Mi corazón se cultiva
y cuelga sus muertos en su ventana,
deshoja ante mí una flor de silencios
que hiere las risas.

1. Alma.

A veces como rosa en el viento llora
y habla con palabras oscuras.
Sus heladas garras descarnan.
Por momentos calla mientras duerme el día,
le roba la savia a los olvidos,
se enreda en el viento,
encierra cantos, decepciona
y muere todos los días.

"Sk'ak'al o'tanil" / "El calor del corazón" / "The Heat of the Heart"
by Roberto Antonio López de la Cruz

Metaphors of the Heart

My mother weaves my time
with flowers and songs of nine moons,
while she awaits me at the day's edge,
I am here, a water drop growing
in the moon's petals.

In the sunset
the cricket orchestra plays
the music of my body;
night embraces me,
I open my eyes,
I caress my origin.

Trembling with cold,
I am a plucked flower;
my mother nurses me
while caressing my fragile face—
my heart is born!

II

My heart wears the gazes
that bare my soul;
I discover the lines of my body
in the eye of silence. Metaphors kiss me,
speak with my ch'ulel,[2]
a swarm of words
that closes my mouth.
I hear a murmur
in the navel of the earth,
in the trunk of a ceiba tree,
that feeds my essence.

My heart grows
and hangs its dead in its window,
strips petals from a flower of silences
that wounds the laughter.

2. Soul.

At times it weeps like a rose in the wind
and speaks with dark words.
Its frosty claws scrape off my flesh.
For moments it hushes as the day sleeps,
it robs the life force of my memories,
gets tangled in the wind,
subdues the singing, loses heart,
and dies all the days.

◆

Sk'uxul o'tanil

Tal te bolil ya slik sitil,
sk'op ajawetik te sk'ak'al yo'tan:
la sk'an snuk'bon jch'ich'el
k'alalto ta ye jna.
La yak' ta na'el yajk'ot k'alal k'ax ta sit jna,
och ta skaw ti' nail.
¿Bin yu'un kich'ojbey yik'al lajel?
¿Ta bin witsil tal te k'uxulil into
te la sjatsbon jsakil k'u' sok la yejch'entesbon te yet'al jch'ujt'e?
Le'aya, kajkonel ta kuxlejal,
ch'aben, stsak ya'tejibal
ma'yuk sk'uxul yo'tan smalbon jch'ich'el,
sok yuts'inbon jkuxlejal.

II

Ta ijk'-ijk'tik ajk'ubal into
xtil ta sts'ejel sjol kakan te ch'abajel,
sts'is pat o'tan te jti';
jok'ol ta xch'ulel jbankil te lajel.
Spetbey sk'ayoj xoch' ta amak' te ik'e,
k'alal te ijk'al Ajawetik
yotsesbonik sk'uxul ko'tan,
jich bit'il ajk'ubal te'tikal mutetik
te sk'ajinik yujk'il uts'inwanej,
sok yak' ta ilel axinal te ya stsuubtes xmal k'aal.
Yuch' xch'ababet k'inal te ch'aelal pom
k'alal te Ch'uy K'aal snamaltes te jowil wayichinel
sok te pox soknix te ch'ab.

Desolación

Vino la malicia que levanta el ojo,
su coraje es un soliloquio de dioses:
deseó chupar mi sangre
desde la boca de mi choza.
Enunció su danza que atravesó la ventana,
penetró las rendijas de la puerta.
¿Por qué huelo a muerte?
¿De qué montaña vino este dolor
que rompió mi túnica y lisió mi vientre?
Ahí está, trotando en mis horas,
callado, sujeta su arma,
violento me desangra
y corrompe mi existencia.

II

En esta noche gris
arden súplicas junto a mis rodillas,
una oración borda mis labios.
La muerte cuelga en el ch'ulel de mi hermano.
Afuera el viento abraza el canto de la lechuza,
mientras lóbregos dioses cimbran dolor en mi pecho
como aves nocturnas que cantan ecos de tormentos,
y muestran sombras que arrugan la tarde.
El humo del incienso bebe el silencio
mientras el ch'uy k'aal[3] aleja el delirio
con el pox[4] y los rezos.

3. Autoridad religiosa.

4. Aguardiente.

Desolation

Malice came, our eyes shuddered;
it raged in a soliloquy of gods,
wanted to suck blood
from the mouth of my home.
It declared its dance through my window,
pushed through the cracks of my door.
Why do I smell death?
From what mountain came this pain
that tears my clothes and rips my gut?
It's there, treading on my hours,
silent, baring its weapon,
it forcefully bleeds me,
debases my life.

II

I kneel on this gray night,
my fiery voice pleads,
my lips weave a prayer.
Death hangs in the ch'ulel of my brother.
Outside the wind embraces the owl's call
while gloomy gods beat pain in my chest
like night birds that sing echoes of storms
and bare shadows that furrow the night.
Smoke of incense drinks the silence
while the ch'uy k'aal[5] dispels delirium
with pox[6] and prayers.

◆

5. Religious authority.

6. Homemade liquor, usually a specific type prepared in Chiapas.

Sk'ak'al o'tanil

La yak' majtan te ko'tan
ta yelaw slab
jich amen k'opoj ta atojol.
Ma'yuk sk'uxul yo'tan la smajat.

Stse'en ta yejch'enul ach'ulel,
smil sba ta ok'el sok ta sk'anel wokol
te xch'eltesbat st'ujbilal anichimal
sok stakintesbat ach'ulel.

Sbultesbon jch'ich'el te sk'ak'al o'tanil,
kujts'iyat sok kak'bat jilel bolilal:
k'ajk'uben te ko'tan
ya yak'bey xchamelul ach'ulel.

II

Mukenal te lujben yo'tan xmal.

Te takin yo'tan la sk'atbunik,
ta snaul miltomba k'opetik
te stakintesbon jbak'etal.

Xch'ababet x-och ta jch'ulel te k'opilal,
snak' sbaik ta xibajsba k'ayoj,
ta sluchil kaxlan pak' te smukojon.
Ja'to abi ya yesmajtes te ajk'ubal,
labetik te xpaxaj ta jchial
sok sk'uxbonik jbakelal.
Ya sk'atbunon ta ak'al te k'ajk'e,
ya sti'bon jsit
sok sk'ak'al yo'tan ya yawtaon.

El calor del corazón

Ofrendó mi corazón
delante de su nahual
y conjuró en contra de tu nombre.
Te golpeó sin piedad.

Ríe sobre tu alma lacerada,
preñada de llantos y ruegos
que ensucian tus orquídeas
y secan tu alma.

El coraje hierve mi sangre,
te beso y te engendro veneno:
mi corazón es fuego
que enferma tu alma.

II

Es una tumba el alma fatigada de María.
Hicieron de su corazón marchito
morada de asesinas palabras
que secan mi carne.

Palabras que penetran en silencio el alma,
se ocultan en un canto siniestro,
en una bordada manta que me cubre.
Desde entonces la noche engendra
demonios que viajan en mis venas
y carcomen mis huesos.
Llama que me abrasa,
muerde mis ojos
y con furia me grita.

The Heat of the Heart

My heart submitted
before its nahual[7]
and conjured against your name,
hurt you beyond mercy.

It laughs over your lacerated soul,
fraught with tears and pleading
that soil your beautiful orchids
and dry up your soul.

The rage boils my blood,
I kiss you and spread venom:
my heart is fire
that sickens your soul.

II

The exhausted soul of María is a tomb.
They made of her withered heart
a dwelling for murderous words
that dry my flesh.

Words that silently invade the soul,
that hide in a sinister song
in a woven blanket that covers me.
Since then the night spawns
demons that travel in my veins
and eat away at my bones.
Flame that singes me,
bites my eyes,
and screams at me in fury.

◆

7. Nagual, a spirit guardian in animal form.

Slab o'tanil

Stoy sba moel te jch'ulel
ta yajk'lal yantik ch'uleletik,
sok stse'ej slabantey
te kuxlejalil yato xtal.
Tulan swajbael
te sk'ayoj lajel ta namey k'inal
te xbejk'aj ta k'atinbak.

El nahual del corazón

Se eleva mi alma
por encima de otras almas,
burlando a carcajadas
los destinos.
Arroja con fuerza
el canto cavernario de la muerte
que nace del inframundo.

The Nahual of the Heart

My soul is lifted
past other souls,
laughing at and mocking
the fates.
It casts out forcefully
the dreary death song
born of the underworld.

◆

Sbujts' o'tanil

Chikan yijk'al sk'ib te majk'amajk' nichimal k'op
sk'u'ilal ajk'ubal te yalajin lok'omba k'op yu'un wik'il sitil;
te site yak' bael xojobal ta sjok'il xch'ababet k'inal
k'alal ya sjuch'ik lum te t'anal tonetik.
Te sonil ja' snuk'ilal arpa sok sajlalul ajmay
te xch'i ta sbujt'emal ko'tan
sok xmo ta sk'ayoj sk'axel k'aal.
Ayme xch'uunik te ijk'-ijk'tik xmal k'aal yu'un lajel
sok te mel o'tantil k'ayoj te spetbon jbak'etal,
ayme yantik ya sch'albey slumil jijte'etik:
manchuk xyal koel te k'aal,
manchuk xyal koel te u
pajal sbujts' sok te ko'tan.

La alegría del corazón

Resalta su cántaro oscuro de los versos
vestido de noche pare metáforas de insomnio;
su ojo resplandece en el pozo del silencio
mientras las desnudas rocas muelen la tierra.
Su música es sonante arpa y flauta de astillas
que germina en mi corazón fecundo
y trepa el canto del día.
Unos alaban la tarde gris de la muerte
con cantos taciturnos que rodean mi figura,
otros adornan el campo de encinas:
aunque caiga el sol,
aunque caiga la luna
saben a mi corazón.

The Joy of the Heart

Holding out a dark clay jug of verses
dressed of night, to catch metaphors in sleeplessness;
its eye shimmers in the well of silence
while the bare rocks grind the earth.
Its music, sounding of harp and wooden flute,
grows in my fertile heart
and climbs up the song of today.
Some praise the gray afternoon of death
with somber songs that circle around me,
others decorate the forest groves:
though sun will fall,
though moon will fall,
they know my heart.

◆

Takinaltik / Otoñal / Autumnal

Angelina Díaz Ruiz

Yoxo'

Jtotik ch'abal stakopal, sik ts'ajan, sak pak'an
ta xvok'tal ta sk'unil jme'tik banomil,
tey chvok'tal kuxlejal ta stakopal.

Ta yavanel tstuki vinajel,
ta slambe stakiti' yanal te'etik
sjoyobal vitsetik ta smalk'in.

Ta skux yo'nton ta te'tik li vo'e,
steminoj takin yanal te'etik
vayal ta yolon syijil jch'ulme'tik,
ta taivtike ta syojbinsba ta j-ulel nats'il.

Oy j-alk'opetik ta xalik chbat xa.
Ta ch'ayk'in ch-ochbal ta xa'ab,
sbek'talinoj chon,
tsjatvilta jch'iel jk'opojeletik.

Yoxo'[1]

Un dios sin carne, frío, pálido
brota en el útero de Pachamama,
en él germina la vida.

Desordena el cielo con sus retumbos,
apacigua sedientas hojas
y alimenta el eje de las montañas.

El agua descansa en bosques,
en su cama de hojas secas
duerme bajo la luna llena,
y en invierno retorna en diamantes efímeros.

---

1. "Yoxo'" es el nombre para un tipo de "agua cristilina" de la región tsotsil, según la
autora.

Augurios presagian su ausencia.
En ch'ayk'in[2] se sumerge en un abismo,
figura de serpiente,
huye de las manos humanas.

Yoxo'[3]

A god not of flesh, cold, pale,
forms in the womb of Mother Earth;
in him is the beginning of life.

He shakes up the sky with his rumblings,
pacifies thirsty leaves,
and feeds the core of the mountains.

The water rests in the forests,
in its bed of dry leaves
it sleeps under the full moon,
and in winter returns in fleeting diamonds.

Signs foretell his absence.
In ch'ayk'in[4] he dives into an abyss,
figure of a serpent,
he flees from human hands.

◆

2. Días festivos en el calendario tsotsil actual.

3. "Yoxo" is the name for a certain type of crystal clear spring water of the Tsotsil region, according to the author.

4. Festival days on the modern Maya calendar.

Ts'ijlej

Tsk'ej mukbil k'op li ts'ijil lumal toke,
schijil ts'i'lal abnaltik.
Chjulavanuk yajvaltak li te'tike
chak'ik ta ilel sk'ak'alil kuxlejal.

Li cha'uke tslup xa muyel ya'al,
sujom xa xchi'uk sk'ib
yo xatintas li banomile.

Oy jun ants ta st'uj muikil vomoletik;
albat yu'un sme' ti ja' sk'opojelik
vomoletik li jujun sobe.

Ta te'etik, ta xvabajomajik xchi'uk yok'esik li mutetike,
ta o'lol k'ak'al chlok' k'atinikuk
li ts'i' ojovetike.

K'unil ik'etik tstaniik batel yik pometik,
ta xa spas ta yax uran, sakil ton li vinajele:
julav xa li osilal vinajele.

"Ts'ijlej" / "Quietud" /
"Quietude"
*by Roberto Antonio
López de la Cruz*

Quietud

La neblina callada guarda secretos,
abrigo de la montaña.
Despiertan los dioses del bosque
y anuncian tiempo de vida.

Un chauk[5] embarca agua,
se apresura con su cántaro
a bañar el mundo.

Una mujer traía hierbas aromáticas;
su madre le enseñó que la madrugada
es el lenguaje de las plantas.

En árboles, aves forman orquesta de flautas,
al mediodía emergen a solearse
las serpientes de los ojovetik.[6]

Vientecillos irrigan perfume de inciensos,
el cielo de ágata celeste y blanco se torna:
el universo ha despertado.

5. Rayo.

6. Guardianes ancestrales de las montañas.

Quietude

This silent mist keeps secrets,
the mountain's cover.
The gods of the forest awaken
and announce the time of life.

A chauk[7] loads water,
and hastens with its pitcher
to bathe the world.

A woman gathers aromatic herbs;
her mother taught her that the time before dawn
is the language of plants.

In the trees, birds form an orchestra of flutes,
at midday the serpents of the ojovetik[8]
emerge to bask in the sun.

Soft breezes irrigate the perfume of incense,
the sky turns celestial blue and white:
the universe has awakened.

◆

7. Lightning bolt.

8. Ancestral guardians of the mountains.

Takinaltik

Ta sluch xa ik'etik li ak'obale,
ta xvay ta sxonkolal tok li vinajele.

Ta xlik jun ants,
nak'obalil ta ik' osil yilel,
ta spech' sch'ut
k'ucha'al ta xich' yomel nichimetik.
Tey ts'ijil chmalavan li sve'ebal nae.
Ta sa' ta stanil sti' sk'ok' li ak'al ts'ik yu'un sikil ak'obale:
chk'elomaj li leb k'ok'e, ch-ak'otaj xchi'uk sob osil.

Chjatav lok'el ch'ail ta jol na;
li k'ok'e rextiko yu'un sbijil li muk'totile,
yu'un smantal li totile,
yu'un smantal li me'ile.
Ta xa xbaj snich takinal osil li ta panae,
yik' xa slikeb taiv li ik'e
ju ts'ub xa chuch'bal ik'loman osil li jtatatike

Otoñal

La noche borda vientos,
duerme el cielo en su almohada de nubes.

Una mujer se levanta,
es sombra en la oscuridad,
se faja la cintura
como se ciñe en ramos las flores.
Su cocina la espera taciturna.
Busca en la cal del fogón
la brasa que resistió el frío nocturno:
retoña la llama y danza con la aurora.

En el techo escapa humo;
el fuego atestigua sabiduría del abuelo,
consejos de un padre,
los ejemplos de una madre.
Afuera, caen pétalos de otoño,
el aire huele a helada
y el sol de trago en trago se bebe la aurora.

Autumnal

Night embroiders the winds,
the sky slumbers on a pillow of clouds.

A woman rises,
a shadow in darkness,
she arranges the folds in her skirt
like flowers in a bouquet.
Her kitchen awaits her in silence.
In the stove's cinders she seeks
the ember that resisted the night's cold:
the flame sprouts again and dances with the dawn.

On the roof smoke escapes;
the fire bears witness to the grandfather's wisdom,
the father's counsel,
the mother's example.
Outside, the petals of autumn fall,
the air smells of frost
and the sun, sip by sip, drinks up the dawn.

◆

Ch'iel k'opojelal / Vivencias / Life Lessons

Ruperta Bautista Vázquez

Sts'umbal ch'ulelaletik

Sluch sts'ibaik k'opetik ti tsebetike,
Ti k'opetike te snak'sba manchuk me x-ech' ti abile,
oy te xlajik te sik.
Ti tsebetike sloktaik ti k'opetike
te xcha'kux tal yo'ntonik ta sakubel osil.

Te xanav ta osil balamil ti k'opetike,
yicho'jik batel ta sti'il yeik ti osil k'ak'ale:
Ti yuts'il sp'ijil k'opetike
te xpas tal ta sat yeloval antsetik.

Descendencia de espíritus

Niñas escriben palabras,
pero las palabras duermen en los años,
algunas fallecen de frío.
Pero las niñas dibujan palabras
que despiertan con el amanecer.

En el universo viajan las palabras,
llevan en sus labios al tiempo:
la esencia sabia de las palabras
se forma en la faz de las mujeres.

"Sts'umbal ch'ulelaletik" /
"Descendencia de espíritus" /
"Spirit Descendants" *by María
Concepción Bautista Vázquez*

Spirit Descendants

Girls write words,
but the words sleep through the years,
and some perish in the cold.
But the girls draw words
that awaken with the dawn.

The words travel the universe,
carry time on their lips:
the words' wisdom distilled
takes shape in the faces of women.

◆

Xch'ulel vitsetik

Te snak'oj spetoj ti osil k'ak'ale,
xcha'bioj lekil yaxal p'ijil jol o'ntonal:
ti sp'ijil sjol yo'nton ti jbai jtotik jme'tike
te xvok' tal ta sk'ob muk'ta tok'oy.

Te ta sk'alk'al ch'ench'enetik skux yo'nton,
ti lu'benal sikt'ojan o'e.
Te skux yo'nton ti yech'omal ye
xch'ulel o'e.

Sk'an ta jmaltatik xchi'uk ti o' li'e
ti te' chak'be skuxlej jnaklejetik,
j-ak' na'el p'ijilal,
jchapanej jtusanej k'opetik.

Te' jsatinel ch'ul osil k'ak'al,
te' jsatinel ch'ul ya'lel vinajel,
te' jsatinel ch'ul o',
te' jsatinel ch'ul kuxlejal.

Espíritu de montañas

Esconde el tiempo en sus brazos,
conserva húmeda sabiduría:
viejo conocimiento brota
en manos del gran sauce.

Duerme lluvia cansada
en rincones y paredes de jícaras.
Reposa el eco sagrado
del espíritu del agua.

Y damos esa agua
al árbol protector de los pueblos,
constructor de saberse,
entablador de palabras.

Árbol con frutos de tiempo,
árbol con frutos de lluvia,
árbol con frutos de agua,
árbol con frutos de vida.

Spirit of Mountains

Hiding time in its arms,
it conserves moist wisdom:
the old knowledge sprouts forth
in great willow branches.

The tired rain sleeps
in corners and crevices.
There rests the sacred echo
of the spirit of water.

And we give that water
to the tree protector of the pueblos,
builder of self-awareness,
founder of words.

Tree with the fruits of time,
tree with the fruits of rain,
tree with the fruits of water,
tree with the fruits of life.

◆

Jtij vobetik

Xpipun yutsil yu'unik ti yamaike,
xjit'et yutsil yu'unik snuk' svobik ti viniketike,
skuxlej osil k'ak'al spatbe yo'nton jteklum.

Xch'ulel sp'ijil jol o'ntonal ta sp'ejlej osil k'ak'al,
k'ejbilal p'ijilal,
slikben xch'iel ach' talel ch'ielal.

Xnamamet batel stijel ti vobetike,
snichimtasbeik yo'nton xch'ulel ti kajvaltike.
Xch'uvil sots'il viniketik.

Svinajesobil k'in,
sk'ejoj ch'ul poko' te'etik
pasbilik ta nichimal o'ntonal.
Slup yibel jba'i totil me'iletik.

Tamboreros

Deletrean sonidos de flautas,
hombres tejiendo la voz de tambores,
vibraciones del tiempo que viajan al pueblo.

Ángeles del pensamiento a través de los siglos,
sabiduría guardada,
germinación de nueva descendencia.

Aplausos de música vuelan
besando espíritu de dioses.
Plegaria de hombres murciélago.

Mensajero de la fiesta,
eco de milenarios árboles
forjados en las sonrisas.
Raíces de los primeros hombres.

Drummers

They spell out sounds of flutes,
men weaving the voice of the drums,
vibrations of time that travel to the village.

Angels of thought across the centuries,
wisdom preserved,
seeds for the new generations.

Applauses of music fly
kissing spirit of the gods.
The men of bats send prayers.

Messenger of the fiesta,
echo of millennial trees
forged in smiles.
Roots of the first men and women.

◆

Yip skuxlejal jlumal

Ivok'ik ta stsuk' ch'ul ixim,
ta syol ixim ipas tal ti yo'ntonike,
tsatsubtasbatik tal stakopalik ta chan tos sbontak ixim,
te ii'bilajik ta smiyik ti osil k'ak'ale.

Ta vinajel skap svots' sbaik xchi'uk yip svu'el jch'ultotiketik,
ta sts'uts'unbeik yip osil k'ak'al,
ta spukik komel p'ijil jol o'ntonal ta osil balamil.

Likbil ta tok ta ik' xanav ti sts'umbal jtsajal tsuk' ixime,
ta xk'atajik ta ya'lel vinajel.
Ants viniketik chapanbilik tal ta sjol yo'nton vinajel.

X-epaj sve xch'ich'elik, spixbeik slekil tse'ej ti jch'ulme'tike,
ta jik'jik' o'ntonal xlo'ilaj skixnal ti kuxlejale,
xyal tal ta tselab ti slo'il sk'opike.
Jnaklejetik tsatsubtasbilik ta yip sjol yo'nton osil balamil.

Esencia de mi pueblo

Nacieron del *tsuk'*[1] de maíz,
la pulpa de granos formó sus corazones,
cuatro colores fortalecieron sus cuerpos,
el tiempo echó raíces en sus ombligos.

En el cielo se enredan con esencia de dioses,
beben gotas que caen del tiempo,
sembrando sabiduría en el universo.

Morenos *tsuk'* de maíz caminan con el aire,
fluyen en metamorfosis del agua.
Hombres y mujeres formados en núcleo celeste.

Sus arterias se extienden, acarician la risa de luna,
fuego sagrado comunicándose en suspiros,
en palabras llegan sus rayos.
Un pueblo con pensamiento de cosmos.

---

1. Cabellos de maíz.

Essence of My People

Born of the *tsuk*[2] of corn,
the pulp of grains formed their hearts,
four colors fortified their bodies,
time put down roots in their navels.

In the sky they entwine with the essence of gods,
drink drops fallen from time,
sow wisdom in the universe.

Swarthy *tsuk'* of corn walks with the air,
flows in the metamorphosis of water.
Men and women formed in the heavenly kernel.

Their arteries spread out, caressing the moon's laughter,
sacred fire communicating in sighs,
lightning flashes in their words.
A people with awareness of the cosmos.

◆

2. Corn silk.

Ik'vanej

Ti viniketik buch'utik oy svokolike,
a' no'ox sk'elojik ti ach' osilk'ak'ale.
Jsaklikan k'ob antsetik
sloktabik stse'ej lekil kuxlejal.

Ta yut svinkilel ti lametel osil balamile
xchi'uk snichimal o'ntonal,
te xlok' tal skuxlej xch'ich'el ti mol me'eletike,
spuk sba ta svinkilel ch'ul osil k'ak'al.

Xbaletik no'ox ta sat yelovik xchik'ik
ti j-ich' mul me'el antsetike;
yakal xt'ab ta yut sjol yo'ntonik
tsajal ich'mul.

Luben xa yok'el xtavan ta ik'el ti ch'ul chone,
xtulajan no'ox x-ik'vanik yok'el ti ch'ul xulub vakaye,
xpujlajet no'ox x-ik'vanik ti ch'ul vobetike.
X-ik'vanik xch'ich'elik ti me'onetike.

Llamamiento

Ojos de hombres sin voz,
con el sufrimiento tocan el crepúsculo.
Pálidas manos de mujeres
dibujan sonrisa de esperanza.

En el vientre de la tranquilidad
y el corazón danzante,
brota la sangre de ancianos
regándose en la piel del tiempo.

El sudor acaricia rostros destruidos
de ancianas entristecidas;
mientras sus pensamientos acarrean
ensangrentados recuerdos.

Cansado sonido de caracol llama,
palabras de cuernos sagrados llaman,
golpes de fuertes tambores llaman.
La muerte llama la sangre de olvidados.

Calling

Eyes of voiceless men,
suffering, touch the twilight.
Pale hands of women
sketch a smile of hope.

In the womb of tranquility
and the dancing heart,
flows the blood of the ancients
pulsing through the skin of time.

Sweat caresses the ruined faces
of sorrowful old women,
while their thoughts harbor
bloody memories.

Tired sound of the conch, it calls;
words of the sacred horn, they call;
beats of the heavy drums, they call.
Death calls the blood of the forgotten.

◆

Jluchomajeletik

Ti tsebe xchi'uk sk'ob
sluch slok'tabe sp'ijil sjol yo'ton mol me'eletik
yu'un sk'u'iltas ti slumale.

Ti me'ele xchi'uk sp'ijil sjol yo'nton
sluch stsatsubtasbe yip tsajal o'ntonal,
sluch ta yaxal kuxlejal ti ach' jnaklejetike,
sluch ta k'anpomanil no ti lamentel sikil osil k'ak'ale.

Sluch slok'ta ta lajelal
ti stsatsal yip ach' jch'iele,
ta ik'mach'an no ti slajeb skuxlej ti me'ele.

Ta spixbe sbek'tal stakopal
chavo' antsetik ti osil k'ak'ale
ta xlikatik muel ta ik' ta tok
xtoyatik batel ta yoxlajun kojal osil balamil.

Bordadoras

Con sus manos la niña
borda el conocimiento de sus abuelos
para el vestuario del pueblo.

Con su pensamiento la anciana
borda en hilos rojos el corazón,
la descendencia en azules hilos,
el silencio en hilos color sepia.

Borda hilos quemados
los latidos de una joven,
hilos grises la palpitación de una vieja.

El tiempo entra con tranquilidad
a los cuerpos de dos mujeres
y se lleva a cabo en ellas la asunción
hacia el decimotercer escalón del infinito.

Embroiderers

With her hands the girl
embroiders the knowledge of her ancestors
for the raiment of her people.

With her wisdom the woman
embroiders the heart in red threads,
the children in threads of blue,
the silence in sepia.

She embroiders burnt threads
the heartbeats of a girl,
gray threads, an old woman's pulse.

Time tranquilly enters
the bodies of two women
and completes in them the ascension
to the thirteenth step of the infinite.

◆

Ok'el

Xpuk batel epal ants viniketik,
jmulavil k'obil,
xules slajesik ti pat o'ntonal
chapanbil ta tip svokol jkoltavanejetik.

Tsajal k'ak'al ya'lel satil,
xyal tal ta vinajel:
Ya'lel sat yok'el jnaklejetik.
Ya'lel sat yok'el jnaklejetik.
Ok'el.

Llanto

Se expande plaga de hombres,
de asesinas manos,
acaban con la esperanza
moldeada en grito de mártires.

Lágrimas rojas bajan
hierviendo del cielo:
Llanto del pueblo.
Llanto del pueblo.
Llanto.

Cry

The scourge of humanity spreads,
murderous hands
finish off hope
molded in shouts of martyrs.

Red tears fall
boiling from the sky:
Cry of the people.
Cry of the people.
Cry.

◆

Ojov

Andrés López Díaz

Ojov

Ch'ul muk'ul jch'ultotik ta vits,
yo'nton xch'ulel ch'ul vinajel,
yo'nton xch'ulel ch'ul banomil.

Slikebal slajebal vinajel,
sk'ejimolal mut ta ik',
nichimal ch'ul xojobal.

Ch'ul xojabal,
sjamlej vinajel,
j-almantal jch'ultotik,
jts'un kuxlejal ta banomil.

Ta sk'ejimolal kee,
ta jta ta k'oponel ta ch'ulele
ta xchanjotal xchikin ch'ul banomil,
xchi'uk sk'uykinajel jyolon k'ok'
ta jk'uxubtas ta jole, ta vo'ntone.

Kuxulot ta oxib ch'ul vits,
ta oxib ch'ul muk'ta abnal,
Oxyoket, Tsonte'vits, Jmatsab,
jech k'ucha'al oxib lum kuts'kalaltak.

Toylejal ch'ul ch'ulelal,
ak'u'inoj xojobal bijilal:
cha-avan, chanik ta ak'ol,
chbak' chnik la ch'ulele.

Ch'ul Ojov,
chul vits la bek'tale,
la ch'ulelal ja' yavanej chauk ta vinajel,
la ch'ich'ele ja' vo', chakilo', uk'um;
la sate ja' snichimal vits.

Tsonte'vits, xch'ulna jtsatsakil jchi'laktik
yu'un bats'i viniketik bats'i antsetik;
snail taival ch'ul ik', taival ch'ul sik,
snail chukulal ch'ul toketik, snail ch'ul xojobal.

Snail ch'ul chonetik, ch'ul bolometik,
snail ch'ul yaxal mank'uk'etik,
jcha'biej ch'ulelaletik, vayijeletik
jcha'biej t'uletik xchi'uk te'tikal chijetik.

Ch'ul Ojov,
mukul ta sakil toketik la ch'ulele, pixil ta yaxal abnal la nae,
muk'ot, tsotsot, tsinilot k'ucha'al avalab anich'nab;
ti svulel ti ko'ntone ja' ta k'oponele, ja' ta ti'inele,
xojobanukme ti yech'omal kuxlejale ta ok'ome, ta cha'eje.

Li' kich'ojtal avuni moton: oxlajunbej sakil nichim,
oxbej kuni pom xchi'uk kuni ts'unobal te',
jkilon, xchi'uk jtilil,
ta jnichimtas la vo'ntone.

Ch'ul Ojov,
ch'ul vits,
li' ta nae,
li' ta k'ulebe,
li' kejelun tale,
li' patalun tale,
ta sk'anbelot kajval svulesel jch'ulelkutik:
ti majbilunkutik ti tenbilunkutik ta epal a'vile
ta jk'anbot kajval ti k'uxi xcha'kuxiuk tal,
ti xcha'nichimajuk tal ti jbijilalkutike
ta xojobal ba'yel jtot jme'kuti ta vo'nee.

Oxbej sat kuni pom
ta xkak' ta yav ch'ul ak'al,
xjobanuk batel ti jk'opojele, ti ka'yeje,
xojobanuk ta vinajel ti kee ti jch'ulele,
ta sk'oponelot xchi'uk jch'ulel.

Ta xlamlunel svaklajunebal yak'il j-arpa vob
xnichimaj no'ox sk'ejimol k'ucha'al uni ch'ixtot,
ta sk'anbe ya'lel vinajel yu'un uni ts'unobaletik,
xchi'uk lek xbitbun ch-ak'otaj ti ko'ntone ta tojolale.

Toj alak' sba sbon li ach'ul k'opojele,
xlap'lajet ta xchanjotal xchikin ch'ul vinajel,
toj alak' sba la vitstake, yalel toyol smuk'tikil,
xlaet, xmuet ch-och ta ko'nton la ts'ilele, la vabnale,
ja' smuyubtasobil, ja' snichimtasobil ko'nton.

Ch'ul Ojov,
muk'ul ch'ul Jxun, sbanomilal tsajal tsonte',
sbanomilal oventik, sbanomilal tsij-uch
snail ch'ul k'anal pepen, snail ch'ul sak isim mut,
yosil Tsonte'vits.

Ch'ul Ojov,
chaukil Ojov,
k'inobal Ojov,
satvo'al Ojov.
Joybijemot ta nichimal vo',
joybijemot ta yoxo'al kuxlejal.

Ch'ul Ojov,
yajval ch'ul banomil, yajval ch'ul vinajel,
yajval jch'ulelkutik, yajval jchonkutik,
ch'ulelal Itsamna, ch'ulelal Ixbalanke xchi'uk Junajpu.

Ojoval ch'ul vits,
Ojoval ch'ul kajval,
nichim ch'ul Ojov.

Vo'ot ch'ul k'ak'al,
vo'ot ch'ul osil,
vijbenal yanalte'ot
uninal nichimot.

◆

Ojov

Dios supremo del cerro,
esencia y corazón del cielo,
corazón y espíritu de la tierra.

Principio y fin del cosmos,
música al viento de los pájaros,
luz al brote del día.

Luz,
universo,
fuego predictor,
sembrador de la vida.

Llamo tu espíritu
con la melodía de mi rezo
en las cuatro esquinas de la tierra,
con veloces flechas de relámpago
despierto tu corazón.

Vives en el número tres,
en tres senos de la tierra,
Oxyoket, Tsonte'vits, Jmatsab,[1]
como los tres pueblos hermanos.

Vértice espiritual,
vestido de sabiduría:
ecos, alturas y sonidos,
vibra tu esencia.

Ojov,
tu cuerpo es montaña,
tu alma es relámpago al universo,
tu sangre es agua, lluvia, ríos;
tus ojos, flor de la mañana.

Tsonte'vits, morada
de tsotsiles de la voz ruda,
Tsonte'vits de vientos helados,
de espuma pesada, de luz ardiente.

---

1. Nombres de montañas en Chiapas.

Morada de serpientes,
jaguares y quetzales,
centellean el corral de los naguales,
centellean tus venados y conejos.

Ojov,
nubes blancas guardan tu espíritu,
verdes plantas decoran tu casa,
sereno, fuerte como tus pueblos;
mi deseo es meditarte en este espacio,
alumbrar mi historia más allá del presente.

Traigo trece llamas blancas para ofrendarte,
tres granos de incienso y plantas,
de ts'unobalte', kilon y tilin,[2]
perfuman tu corazón.

Sagrado Ojov,
sagrado cerro,
aquí es tu casa,
aquí es tu grandeza,
aquí hincado estoy,
aquí reverenciado estoy,
para pedirte, mi señor,
el despertar de nuestros espíritus
golpeados por muchos siglos,
y nuevamente florezca la sabiduría
en la luz de nuestros antepasados.

Mis tres granos de inciensos
pongo en la brasa del fuego sagrado,
se desprenden espirales de palabras,
eleva mi voz al espacio cósmico
para dialogarte con mi alma.

El sonido de mi arpa de dieciséis cuerdas vibrantes
como el melódico canto del pájaro ch'ixtot,[3]
suplica sangre del cielo para la milpa
y mi rítmico corazón suplica en tono alto.

2. Tipos de plantas usados para incenso.

3. Pajarito.

En las cuatro esquinas de la tierra
observo los colores que pintan tu lenguaje,
veo la geometría de tus montañas
y siento el perfume de los árboles
que alegra mi corazón.

Ojov,
San Juan Mayor,
tierra de laureles, musgos y oventik[4]
tierra de mariposas amarillas,
aves de barbas blancas
sobre el techo de Tsonte'vits.

Ojov,
Ojov rayo,
Ojov lluvia,
Ojov manantial.
Lluvia que se vuelve flor,
agua que se vuelve vida.

Ojov,
guardián de la tierra y del cielo,
protector de nuestros espíritus animales,
Ojov, alma de Itsamná, Ixbalanqué y Hunahpú.[5]

Ojov es Montaña,
Ojov es Sol,
Ojov es Flor.

Es tiempo,
espacio,
hoja caída y flor al brote.

◆

4. Fruta nativa de Chiapas.

5. Personajes de la mitología maya

"Ojov" *by José Osvaldo García Muñoz*

Ojov

Supreme god of the highlands,
essence and heart of the sky,
heart and spirit of the earth.

Beginning and end of the cosmos,
music of birds on the wind,
light at the break of day.

Light,
universe,
predictor of fire,
sower of life.

I summon your spirit
with the melody of my prayer
in the four corners of the earth,
as arrows of lightning flash
I awaken your heart.

You live in the number three,
in three bosoms of the earth,
Oxyoket, Tsonte'vits, Jmatsab,[6]
like the three brother villages.

Spirit summit,
clothed in wisdom:
echoes, heights, and sounds,
your essence vibrates.

Ojov,
your body is mountain,
your soul is lightning to the universe,
your blood is water, rain, rivers;
your eyes, morning flower.

Tsonte'vits, dwelling
of Tsotsils with rough voices,
Tsonte'vits of frozen winds,
heavy mist, burning light.

---

6. Names of mountains in Chiapas.

Dwelling of serpents,
jaguars, and quetzals,
glittering home of the naguals,
glittering, your deer and rabbits.

Ojov,
white clouds guard your spirit,
green plants decorate your house,
serene, strong like your people;
I long to meditate in this space,
shine light on my history beyond the present.

I bring thirteen white flames to offer you,
three grains of incense and plants,
ts'unobalte', kilon, and tilin[7]
perfume your heart.

Sacred Ojov,
sacred hillside,
here is your home,
here your grandeur,
here on my knees am I,
here in reverence am I,
to ask you, my lord,
to awaken our spirits,
beaten down for centuries,
and let wisdom blossom again
in the light of our ancestors.

My three grains of incense
I place in the sacred fire,
they come away as spirals of words,
lift my voice to the cosmic sphere
to commune with my soul.

My harp with sixteen vibrating chords,
like the song of the ch'ixtot[8] bird,
begs the blood of heaven for the milpa,
my rhythmic heart pleads loudly.

7. Types of plants used for incense.

8. Little bird.

In the four corners of the earth
I observe the colors that paint your language,
see the geometry of your mountains,
and feel the perfume of the trees
that brings joy to my heart.

Ojov,
San Juan Mayor,
land of laurels, moss, and oventik,[9]
land of yellow butterflies,
white-bearded birds
over the roof of Tsonte'vits.

Ojov,
Ojov lightning,
Ojov rainfall,
Ojov flowing spring.
Rain becoming flower,
water becoming life.

Ojov,
guardian of earth and sky,
protector of our spirit animals,
Ojov, soul of Itsamná, Ixbalanqué, and Hunahpú.[10]

Ojov is Mountain,
Ojov is Sun,
Ojov is Flower.

Is time,
space,
fallen leaf and flower in bloom.

◆

9. Fruit native to Chiapas.

10. Characters from Maya mythology.

Part 2

Stories

The stories in this collection address aspects of modern Maya life in Chiapas. The desire to proclaim an indigenous identity must coexist with the necessities of survival—and the realities of death. Juan Julián Cruz Cruz, Tseltal, shows how a traditional festival can combine joy with disaster. Miguel Ruiz Gómez, Tsotsil, takes us on a journey with Chiapas men who, due to limited opportunities, have undertaken the dangerous journey to the United States to look for work. Finally, the Tseltal writer Alberto Gómez Pérez looks at the consequences of mistrust and desperation among people whose connection to the land is powerful but still unsettled. Though fictional and at times fantastical, all three stories draw from the realities and challenges that face indigenous people in Chiapas today.

Los cuentos en esta colección abordan aspectos de la vida moderna para los mayas en Chiapas. El deseo de proclamar una identidad indígena tiene que coexistir con las necesidades de la supervivencia—y las realidades de la muerte. Juan Julián Cruz Cruz, tseltal, muestra como un festival tradicional puede combinar alegría con desgracia. Miguel Ruiz Gómez, tsotsil, nos lleva de viaje con hombres de Chiapas que, debido a sus oportunidades limitadas, han emprendido el paso peligroso a los Estados Unidos para buscar trabajo. Por fin, el escritor tzeltal Alberto Gómez Pérez considera las consecuencias de desconfianza y desesperación entre personas cuya conexión a la tierra es poderosa pero todavía inestable. Aunque ficcional y a veces fantástica, todos los cuentos parten de las realidades y retos que enfrentan la gente indígena de Chiapas hoy.

Wokolil ta tajimal k'in

Juan Julián Cruz Cruz

Ma'yuk bin xchi ko'tanyotik, te sbujts'il k'inal ta slapel jk'upak'yotike ya xk'ot sok ya bajt sok te yik'al sakubele; aynix ya xmajliwan jichnix bin ut'il te sjep'el jsitik te ayto swayel ae, sut'ubento yu'una te yakubele. K'ajonax ay binti la yabonyotik jna'tik te k'ajk'al ine maba ku'untikuka; melel, te k'alal och yich'cholel ta jujutujl bin yipalel ay ku'untik ae, ja'nax la kak'tik ta ilel sma' bujts'il k'inal. Jtukel, k'ajonax ay jun xi'el och ta sk'ubulil ko'tan, k'ajon ta sikilel xi'el; ja'wan yu'un te ayto xchamelal jajchonyotike sok mijnax ja'al ae, ja' yu'un ma'yukix bin xchi ko'tanyotik yu'un te ayinel jpisiltik ta parkee. Patil te wayonyotik yantikxan orae, ja' la sjachonyotik te sikil yik'alel stibiltayel k'inal och ta wentanae. Te ja'ale ch'ayixbael ta banti x-och te k'ajk'ale, ja'to jich la yich' chapel ta oranax te jk'opyotike. La jk'ejlutik te ch'ujlchane, k'epelixa, ja' la yotsesix stse'elil ko'tanyotik ta slapel te jk'u' jpak'yotike, tey-nixa ta banti jpasojyotikix te wakax pojpe. Xojetxanix yik' ta ajch'em lum te ik'e, sok chikanxanix och ta esmajel tokal ta ajch'em karetera, te jtebnax k'ix-najtesbil yu'un k'ajk'al ta stibiltayel k'inale. Ja' nail k'ajk'aletik yu'un pebre-roa, te ja' slajibalix u te yato yil ya xyal ja'al, jich bin ut'il ya spisil jabil, ja'me k'in, sk'ajk'alel sk'atbuneljbatik, sk'ajk'alel tse'elil o'tan.

Te Jkarlos sok jo'one ayotik ta jun tsoblej yu'un tajimal k'in tey ta balioe. La jchapyotik stsobel jbatik ta stibiltayel yu'un xchan lajunebal k'ajk'al u ta sna, jpisiltik k'oonyotik. Tey ayotika jichnix bin ut'il ta yantik jabil talel, ta spasel te ja'nix talelile. Te Jkarlose smulanej euka te ixta'e, ma'yuk sti'il yu'un te sba-jk'ele. Ta k'ajk'al ine la kak' ko'tanyotik ta spasel te wakax pojpe; melel ayix ku'untika spisil te binti ya yich' tuunele, la yich'leel ta yu't ja'mal: lajchayeb set'bil ajb soknix te spat bate. Ja'to jich lijkonyotik ta spasel te k'alal ch'ayon-yotikix-a ta sit te k'ajk'ale, ta skaj te la snak'ix sba ta spat Bajwits. Nail la yich' pasel xchanul te wakaxe, jichnix bin ut'il jun jol wakaxna, patil la yich' ts'isel te pojp ta yajk'olal te xchelchel bak pasbil ta ajbe; ta patil la yich'pasel sit, yu'un jich ya xju' k'ejluwanej lok'el teyto ta yutil ae; la yich' namijtesel sik ta sk'ajk'alel pox, jich sok yakubelil la yich' majliyel te sakubele, ja'to jajchonyo-tik te k'alal k'axemix ta yojlil ch'ulch'ana te k'ajk'ale.

Yakaltonax jlok'esbeltik xchamelal pox ta sikil ja' pajwuchila te bin ora te k'a' "bocina" yu'un kabiltoe, la sbeentes ta ik' te son "Quereke" sbiile, ta yoxebal ora stibiltayel k'inal. Wen t'ujbil te sone, te ja' cheb oxeb k'ajk'al nail ya stijik yu'un ya yich' ak'el ta na'el te k'ine. Jich abi, x-och xchajpanixsbaik te jujutsojp tajimal k'inetike, jich te jtsobojeletike maba smajliyikix k'inal, ya x-och tsobik ta oranax te winiketik mach'atik ya slap te tsekele. Yo'tik ini, te sbujts'il te sone la yak' yipalel sok la syajltes o'tanil ta parke, ta yilel ajk'ot, ya'iyel awetik, slach'el k'abal; smulanel te yik' chabe, chicha sok yalel nants te ya x-ik'awan teyto ta p'olmaletik ta sti'il te parkee. Ta oranax la jeltajbaj-yotik. K'ax mijnax la smulan bin la jpastik te sme' Jkarlose sok k'ax t'ujbilnax la yil te sujtemonyotik ta ants te jajtalal chikan te bak baktik ka'yotike; ja' yu'un la sjaponyotik jtsima mats', sakmolte ich sok ats'am ta jujutujl, yu'un jich ay yipalel ku'unyotika ta ajk'ote. La jmakjbajyotik ta na banti k'ejel ku'unyotika te spojtsil sitil sok te jk'u' jpak'yotike. Ja'teya te banti nailto lok'tal ta aw te tse'elil o'tane, melel la kiltik te jujutujl la snak' sit ta xibajem sba pojtsil sitile-tike. Sole ja'nax tey aya te ixta'e, tse'elnax ko'tanyotik ta xch'ojel tep ta bayuk-nax jbak'etalyotik; jo'one yajl ta kjol, ¡k'ux la jak'i! K'alal chapalonyotikix ae, la jamyotik te tsajal tak'in ti'nae, ta nawtamba lok'onyotik, xch'ikch'un jk'abyotik ta banti ma xpas ta pikel; lok'onyotikta muk'ul be te aynax ta sti'il te nae, jo' tejk'wan snamalil, banti tey tek'ela te xme' Karmelae, la yilon-yotik sok slab yo'tan, teynix banti la kil ta jwayich te yakal xch'akesbel-a te binti ixta' ya jpasyotike. La yabon xi'el spasel bitik bajk'el ta stibiltayel k'inal ine. Ay binti chopol tal ta ko'tan sok la yabon xi'el, axan maba stukel, maba ju'ku'un sujtel sok maba ju' yijkitayel ku'un te kjoyotake; ja' yu'un stsajyalel la kjach jk'ab, la jnik kok ta jwa'el sok ta jk'exan bael, jichnix euk te kjole xtal xbajt, k'ajonax ta wen tse'el ko'tan. Spisilik yakal spasbelik te binti yakal jpasbel ejk ae, bayuknax ya x-ajnumajonyotik bael, te sone ja' yakal yak'bel sbujts' o'tanil; nopijonyotik bael ta yojlil tejklum. Kuxu k'ojelonyotika ta yawil ixta basketbol, te ay ta ojlil yu'un kabilto sok te parke, k'alal toj chikna-jel sk'op jtujl ach'ix:

—Tey xtalik te "bojluben keremetike".

Spisilik la sut'pin sitik ta banti yakal jnikbelyotik sujtem ta chopol yilel sok yauben antsetike; la kjamyotik be ta yojlil ch'ich'bak'et te bin ora bayuknax ya xboonyotike, yantikxan ya sjip k'axel ujts'iyel ta sk'abik sok te yantike wen ya snik xcho yitik; ta nail, cha'tujl tulan yak'oj sba keremetik la sjamik be sok te wakaxpojpe, yakal sp'isbelik yok'el: "uuuuuuuu". La kich'yotik majliyel ta xuxub sok ta slach'lunel k'abal, ta patil, te in stse'elil o'tane t'ojm ta muk'ul tse'ej k'alal la yilik te wen komnax sk'u spak' slapoj te antsetike; yu'un t'ujbiluk-nax ya yilika te j-il k'inetike la sjach spak'ik, la yak'ik ta ilel te bakbaktik ya'ike sok te tsajal sok sakal wexal slapojik cha'tujle. Jo'otik te patil julotik ta plasae: "Bojluben keremetike", wen kolemnax ijk' ts'ijbabil ta spat te wakax yakal sjoyobtabelonyotik ta ajk'ot sok te ya sp'is skujel te ants winiketik ya xk'axik ae.

La ka'i yakalonyotik ta ilel sok ta tuchk'abtayel ta banti ochonyotik ta ajk'ote; la jsut'pin jsit ta kjojyobal: te stsek sok sk'u' antsetike wen t'ujbilnax

ta ilel te bayelnax sbojnile, cha'oxtujl mamaletike sak sk'u'swex slapojik, spi-
sil te keremetike slapojik ach' k'u'uletik sok meskliya wexal; ta k'in ini ja'
yorail te syajltesbeyel yo'tan ach'ixetike. Te xchanul tejklum xbajt xtal yu'un
yo'tan yilel te slekil j-ixta'etike, machuk maba yich'ojbeyik sbelal te son kapal
xa'alix ta awetike; te alnich'anetike la sle k'axel sbeik ta yojlil niwak kristiano,
ma'yuk ta sjolik te p'e'tamba nawtambae, yu'unax te yakuk sk'ejluyotik ae.
Wen t'ujbilnax jayal sonil lok'tal ta kitara, ta biolin sok ta mandolina, jajchem
tal ta jun sti'il parke, banti yakal stijbelik te mamaletike; jich ya xyajl ko'tan-
tik ajk'ot sok te yantsileletik, te ja' winiketik slapojik stsek antsetike. Ta yojlil
te kjoyotake, te mach'atik chopol yakalik ta k'ope, k'unk'unax la kijkita yilel
sok ya'iyel; ja' och ta kjol te yantik cha'tsojp j-ixta'etik jich ayik ta jts'ejlyotike;
te junxan yakalik ta nopijel talel ae, t'uninbilik tal ta alnich'anetik. Ta par-
kee chantsojpix j-ixta'onyotika. Te mach'atik slapoj pasbil stsotsil sjol antse,
k'ajonik ta melel ants sok ya sk'ajk'ubtes te keremetike; yantikxan, jich bin
ut'il te pukuje, chopol yilel sit yelaw. Te j-il k'inetike ya xt'ojm stse'ej k'alal ya
yilik te me'el tulan sok ma'yuk sbelal ya sniksbae; te xchopolil pox sok te sonil
te k'ayoj "Moño colorado" sbiile ya xsujawan ta snikel jk'abtik ta bayuknax
sok smujtesbeyel stsek te yantike.

Te Jkarlose wen lek ya snik te sjayal sok k'ixin bak'etal ay ta yutil te jchajp
sok chopol yilel te xchik'inem sk'u spak'e; stukel yuch'ojtowana, k'axem-
towan ta syakubelil-a, ja' ya xbujlantesbot xch'ich'el yu'un te k'ajk'al sok te
pox jujuts'in yakal yuch'bel jasal ta sakubel ae. Ora ini, k'alal wen yuch'ojix
ae, jujuts'ijn ya sjach te spojtsil site, jich ya yak' ta ilel te yijk'al yelawe. Te
mach'atik nabot sbae mukenax ochik ta tse'ej sok och yalik ta chikinil te ja'la
te Jkarlose snak'o sba ta stsek tujl lujben ants. Sna'oj te yakal ta k'ejluyele, ja'
yu'un wen sak' itnax och snik sba xchajk'ole.

K'alal och kak' ta ilel euk te yipalel ku'une, yu'un la jk'an ak'a sk'ejluyonik
te j-il k'inetike, tojlijkelnax k'ajon la ka'i jun namal k'op, kapxatiksbaxanix ta
kjol, maba la jnabe swenta; ch'abon sok och ka'ibe sbelal ta lek, axan jichnix
maba la jnabe swenta te bin yakal yuts'imbelon ae; ja' te k'opetik ine te ya'kal
sututetel ta kjole. Tulan la kak' jba sok la jtejk'an ta jsit te lok'ombail k'ax ta
kjole; ja' jun lok'ombail te k'unk'un la stsakbael sk'ejlal jun sakaluben elawil.
Tejk'ajon, ja'to jich la kilbe sit ta lek te Xkarmelae; ¡maba la jch'uun! Ja'mati, la
jcha'a'ibe te sk'op jajchemtal ta jwayiche; k'ajonax ta jchikin la sk'oponon, jich
laj te yipalel ku'une. Jul ta kjol te ja'chiknaj ta jwayich te bin ora wayon ta sna
te Jkarlose. Sojkem sjola; axan te sk'ope chukul ajil ta jch'ulel: "Ch'ayemex,
ma x-ana' te bin ka pasike. Te pukuje ay sok ja'ex. Swentame ya xchamex
apisilik". Machuk wayichilnax, stukel te yipalel ajk'ot ku'une namij k'axel,
ajn bael sok och xi'el ta jbak'etal. La jk'ejlu kreloj, sjo'ebalix ora stibiltayel

k'inala. Teyto k'alala, k'ajon k'ax k'un ak'axix ora la ka'i, najtub te oraetike. Lijk yuts'inon, k'unk'un och swojlan sba ta jnuk' te xi'ele, jijtson bael ta jun tak'in najktajib, ma'yuk mach'a la sna' yilel te jwokole, ja'wan yu'un te bojluben sit smajkil jsite, jich te kjoyotake lajwan skuyik lujbenon o te wen kuch'ojix ae.

Maba sujten jpensar yu'un te xi'ele, la jlok'es ta jchojak' xujt'xan pox ta slimiteal, la jlajin ta uch'el. Tejk'ajon k'alal la jka'ibe sk'op te jtsobojel ta jtojolyotike.

—Yorajilix ya xbootik.

Jkojt sakil kamioneta yu'un Tumbala, muk'nax yilel, nopij tal ta k'un ta muk'ul be sok choxaj ta sti'il te parkee, yu'un ja' ya yik'onyotikix bael ta tsaltomba ajk'ot te tey ya spasik ae.

K'alal muonyotik ta k'aal ch'ich'uben kamionetae, te kjoyotake ochik ta aw sok lek xuxub bael: "Xboonyotikix, k'anayik kutsilalyotik", xchi jtujle; te jtsobojele la yalbonyotik: "Muanik, ta ora jtsa' atetik". Te kristianoetike tulan la slach' sk'abik, te sk'op ach'ixetike la sjachtiklabe yipal yo'tan te kjoyotake, yu'un jich ya tsalika te Tumbalae sok jich ay jmajtanyotik ya sujtonyotik talel ta Petalcingoe.

La jlajmanyotik ta lek te cheb wakax pojp ta yutil yit te kamionetae yu'un machuk mach'a xmua. Wen tse'elnax yo'tanika, ja'nix jich te yelaw ch'ulchane tse'elnax sit yelaw euka, jich la sk'upinonyotik ta bajk'el ayinel: la jmaj jbajyotik ta jujutujl ta jpatyotik o ta jolol sok lom chopol k'opetik la kawtayotik ta alel: "Akay ke, ma' abi pendejo"; yan stukel te Jkarlose sok te mach'atik sjoyuk tey ta yajk'olal te kamionetae, yakal slajimbelik junxan limite "quetzal", te ja' wen lekil trawoe.

Te jo'one maba xk'opojona. Maba chikan ta lek bintia, ta namal, ta jwayichto, te yakal yuts'imbelone, ya xch'abtes kak', ya xchuk jk'op sok jch'ulel; la jtup' jsit sok la kutjba sok jpensarnix: "¡Xch'enal yit sme'!", teme xk'opojon ta swenta jwayiche, xba skuyonik ta antsilwinik, ja'wan lek te ma'yuk binti ya kale".

K'ax mijnax binti maba lek chikan sk'ejlal och ta talel ta kjol, ta yalel jun wokolil te nopijem tale, te snak'osbae. Te xi'ele k'unk'unax och stsalon la ka'i; ch'abal te jk'ope, mijnax ochon ta chik'inel. Aynix mach'atik la sta yawilik ta yajk'olal slonail te karoe, te t'imil ta stak'inal k'atabule, yantik lajto sle yawilik ta kanastiya banti ayixa te yantike, yu'un jich ya smulanik bael ta leka te sikil sok te syaxal k'inale.

K'alal jil ku'unyotik te ch'ulna ta nail weltae, te karoe k'unax yakal ta beel bael ta jun stojil be, jich nopij bael ta yan sweltail be. Te tulan ik'e ya skup ik'ta te tse'elil awetike; jpisiltik, tujlutujl, lijk xcho'ik te spojtsil sitike, k'ixinax sok ajch'em jilel te yelawike, t'ujut'uj yajlel te xchik'ik yumoj te spojtsil sitike; chikanax tulan lijk sjik'yo'tanik sok la yak'ik lok'el te spisil lujbelil ay ta sot'ot'yu'unike. Te ealetike chikan sjam smak sbaik bayel welta ta yalel bime jejchukil, maba la kabe smuk'ul ko'tan; ja'nax la ka'i cha'oxp'ajl k'opetik: "Yakal ak'ajk'ubtesbelon, ja'ma aba, ajch'emonix". Te yajnumal karoe toj miubel. K'alal la sta te xchebal sweltail bee, toj miubel te yajnumale; k'ajonax ta ay binti jajk' yo'tan la snawonyotik; k'alal la sutp'in sba ta jun swa'ele, och ta juxuxetel te syantae; k'alal mabayix toj yakal ta beela te karoe, la jnamijtes jbajyotik sok la stsakonyotik xi'el. Mabayix tejk'aj te karoe; te koele yakalix ta ik'aw bael k'alal ta ch'en; la jka'i xlok'ix ta jabk'etal te jch'ujlele; k'ajonax ya xbojts'ix jsit, la sjujch'iyon jun xiben sba sikil lajel. Xibajen sba ochik ta tulan ok'el; te pukuje yakalix spit'bel jch'ulelyotik, yakalix ta wijlel ta kojlil-yotik, yo' tanix ya sk'ux te jch'ulelyotike. Maba la jna' bin yu'un, toj lijkelnax la ka'i jba ta yutil sikil mukenal; ay mach'a yakal snitbelon ta kok, tey yakalix ste'ubtesbelona te ta xiben sba xch'enal mukenale. La kawtayotik te mach'a yakal snikbele yu'un ak'a stejk'an te karoe, axan tojolxanixa.

Tulanax och ta tijtinwanej te karoe sok maba la jna'yotik binti la jpasyotik yu'un, teme sjipeljbayotik o smajliyel ta kawilyotik te yajlele. Ja' jich la jpasyotik: smajliyel te k'ojele; la jk'ejlu te kjoyotake; jujutujl ochik ta yajlel ta snajtil te sweltail muk'ul bee. Yantikxan, yajlik ta yutil te karoe, ta jujun te k'ojele la spas ejchenil ta yelawik sok ta sk'abik.

K'alal la sutp'in snikujibal karo te mach'a yakal snikbele, la xchuk sba te syantail ay ta sni'ile, lijk ts'o'etel, la sk'ajtan sba ta karetera; te yalal yijkats sok te stulanil sbeele la snaw sok botk'ij oxeb welta ta ik', la sjochinsba k'alal ta sti'il muk'ul be, jaysajltik jilel.

Te ka'e maba la yak'on jajchel, potsoben la jka'i te jabak'etal balal ta ake, ta lajunebwan okol snamalil banti pak'al te karoe. Sok ya'lel jsit la jk'ejlu atinemik ta ch'ich'te kjoyotake, pujkemik ta sti'ti'il te kareterae, sultch'ich'tikxanix, maba ya snikix sbaik. Ta k'ax yutilto te jk'ejlujelike yakal sk'ambelik koltayel, te k'uxul o'tane yanax yabe mel o'tan xch'ulelik; lok' tal ya'lel jsityotik; ma'yukix yipalel la jochin jbayotik ta sts'ejl te yantike, ma'yukix binti ju' spasel ku'unyotik.

Tey balalonyotika, ta muk'ul be te maba la xcholonyotik bael ta Tumbalae. La jlej ta sit te Jkarlose, te ja'k'uxnax ta ko'tan kjoye. Maba la jta ta ilel. La sut'pin jsit, te lajele k'ajonax la sjuch'iyon sok te kik'e maba k'an sujtuk, la jk'ejlube ta lek sjol te Jkarlose, ijk'nax yilel puk'bil ajil te sbak'etale.

K'an ka'i aw, maba ju' ku'un; te mel o'tane k'ajonax ta bak la sk'ajtan sba ta jnuk' sok k'atpuj ta ok'el te la skap sba sok te sk'op muk'ul ja' ay bael ta sti'il karretera bejk'em ta ch'ich'ele.

Carnaval de desgracia

Estábamos indecisos, el ánimo de disfrazarnos llegaba y se alejaba con el viento del amanecer; a veces aguardaba, como las pocas ganas de abrir los ojos con sueño, sazonados aún por la borrachera. Un presentimiento nos prevenía que ese día no era para nosotros; pues, tras comentar qué tanto de entusiasmo disponíamos cada uno, sólo manifestábamos inseguridad. Pero a mí algo más íntimo me incomodaba: era una sensación de miedo; quizá porque despertamos muy crudos y además con un aguacero que terminó de nublar nuestro afán de estar ahí todos juntos, en el parque. Después de dormirnos otras horas, nos despertó el viento del atardecer que entraba por la ventana. La lluvia se había alejado por el horizonte, eso hizo que tomáramos una decisión inmediata. Vimos el cielo, ahora despejado, y eso animó a disfrazarnos, ahí mismo donde ya teníamos hechos los toritos de petate. El aire despedía un olor a tierra mojada y veíamos elevarse lentamente el humo de la carretera húmeda, apenas calentada por los rayos del resplandeciente sol de la tarde. Eran los primeros días de febrero, el último mes que despide la lluvia del invierno; y como todos los años, son días de fiesta, disfraz y alegría.

Carlos y yo formábamos parte de un grupo de payasos en el barrio Grande. Habíamos acordado reunirnos la tarde del catorce en casa de él, y nadie faltó. Estuvimos ahí como en los años anteriores, renovando la misma tradición. A Carlos también le gustaba el desorden, su temperamento no tenía orillas. Ese día nos preocupaba hacer el torito de petate, pues ya teníamos los materiales que habíamos conseguido en el monte: una docena de bambú de dos metros y corteza de corcho. Comenzamos a trabajar cuando el sol nos perdió de vista, guardándose detrás del cerro Bajwits. Primero hicimos la estructura del torito con varas de bambú en forma de techo de dos aguas y más tarde costuramos el *pojp*[1] sobre su esqueleto; luego formamos con delicadeza una ventanita triangular por la parte de enfrente para ver la intemperie desde adentro; alejamos el frío con el calor del *pox* y recibimos a la madrugada lluviosa con una borrachera, hasta que despertamos cuando el sol estaba más allá de medio cielo.

Estábamos tratando de quitar el efecto del aguardiente con un baño de agua fría en el río Pajwuchil,[2] cuando escuchamos que la vieja bocina de la

1. Petate.
2. Lugar de ámbar.

agencia municipal desplegó al aire la primera canción de "El querreque", en punto de las tres de la tarde. Era una música alegre, que desde unos días antes se comenzaba a escuchar para anunciar la fiesta. Entonces, los grupos de payasos comenzaban a organizarse; y los *tsobojeletik*[3] no perdían tiempo de nombrar a los señores que se vestirían de *yantsileletik*.[4] Ahora, el ritmo de la música infundía más júbilo y arrancaba desde muy dentro de uno las ganas de bajar al parque y ponerse a ejecutar la danza, escuchar los gritos, los aplausos; saborear el olor a dulces, chichas y curtidos de nance que nos conquistaba desde las garitas de las orillas del parque. Corrimos a disfrazarnos. La mamá de Carlos admiraba nuestro relajo y le causaba mucha gracia vernos convertidos en mujeres mostrando las huesudas piernas; por eso nos ofreció enseguida un guacal de pozol, chile blanco y sal para cada uno, y así tener energía nueva para la danza. Nos encerramos en uno de los cuartos donde guardábamos las máscaras y las vestimentas. Ahí florecieron nuestros primeros gritos de regocijo al ver que cada uno escondía su semblante tras horripilantes antifaces. Todo era un desorden, nos divertíamos tirándonos zapatos viejos en cualquier parte del cuerpo; a mí me calló uno en la cabeza, ¡sí que dolió! Una vez listos, abrimos la puerta roja de metal y empujándonos uno contra otro, metiendo mano por donde no debíamos, salimos a la carretera que está enfrente de la misma casa, a unos cinco pasos, en cuya orilla doña Carmela nos miró con odio, justo en el mismo lugar donde la había visto en sueños una noche, maldiciendo nuestras travesuras. Sentí desconfianza de hacer locuras esa tarde. Un mal presagio me causaba titubeos, pero no, no podía retroceder ni quedar mal con mis compañeros; por eso me vi obligado a levantar la mano, a mover los pies de izquierda a derecha y la cabeza de un lado para otro, aparentando una diversión total. Todos hacían lo mismo que yo: movían su cuerpo, corrían sin sentido, la música nos motivaba; así nos dirigimos al centro del pueblo. Apenas íbamos llegando a la cancha de basquetbol, entre la agencia municipal y el parque, cuando se dejó escuchar una voz femenina:

—Ahí vienen "Los Rebeldes".

Todos voltearon la vista hacia nosotros que meneábamos con ímpetu nuestros cuerpos disfrazados de mujeres mal vestidas y desnutridas: abríamos camino entre la gente al ir de un sitio para otro, mientras algunos aventaban

---

3. Organizadores del carnaval.

4. Hombres vestidos de mujeres tseltales.

besos con la palma de la mano a las muchachas y otros hacían movimientos sensuales con las nalgas; por delante, dos apuestos jóvenes abrían paso con el *wakax pojp*[5] sobre ellos, imitando el lenguaje propio del animal: "uuuuuuuu". Fuimos recibidos con aplausos y silbidos, luego esa emoción descargó carcajadas al ver mujerzuelas con apasionantes minifaldas; que para atrapar más la atención del público mostraban sus flacas y peludas piernas alzándose las faldas hasta dejar al descubierto el bikini rosado y blanco que dos de ellos llevaban puesto. Éramos los últimos en llegar a la plaza: "Los Rebeldes", escrito en letras grandes de color negro sobre un torito que danzaba alrededor nuestro, fingiendo cornear a las personas que atravesaban su camino.

Sentí que las miradas se fijaban en nosotros y señalaban con los dedos en donde nos concentrábamos a danzar; miré a mi alrededor: las enaguas y los calados de las mujeres tenían floridos colores, algunos señores vestían de blanco, la mayoría de los jóvenes se engalanaba con ropas modernas, pantalones y camisas de mezclilla; estas fiestas era el momento de ponerle ojo a las muchachas y quedar bien con ellas. La gente se movía buscando el lugar perfecto para ver al mejor grupo de disfrazados, que bailaban sin llevar el ritmo de la música mezclada con bulla; con tal de vernos, los niños rompían paso entre los adultos, sin importarles empujones y apachurrones. Un delgado y cautivador sonido producido por la guitarra, el violín y la mandolina provenía de un lado del parque, donde los ancianos músicos ejecutaban sus instrumentos despertando la sensación de danzar con los yantsileletik. Estando en medio de mis compañeros, entre sus gritos obscenos, poco a poco dejé de verlos y oírlos; ganaban lugar en mi atención los otros dos grupos de enmascarados que bailaban cerca de nosotros, mientras uno más venía acercándose, perseguido por montones de niños. En el parque éramos cuatro conjuntos de payasos. Los que tenían pelucas parecían mujeres de verdad y hasta excitaban a los chamacos; otros más como el mismísimo diablo con los rostros deformados. El público prorrumpía en carcajadas al ver a la anciana que se movía con arranque y sin sentido; el efecto del *pox* y la música de "La del moño colorado" que reproducía la grabadora vieja nos forzaba a lanzar las manos por todas partes y mover los cuerpos mientras faldeábamos a los demás.

Carlos movía su delgado y caliente cuerpo dentro de ese traje exótico, ridículo, sucio y con olor a sudor; de seguro seguía borracho, tal vez más borracho de lo que parecía, pues le hervía la sangre el calor y el aguardiente

5. Torito de petate.

que sorbo tras sorbo se empinaba desde la mañana. Ahora completamente inconsciente, levantaba una y otra vez su máscara, dejando al descubierto su moreno rostro. Los que lograban reconocerlo reían en secreto y comentaban de oído en oído que Carlos se tapaba en la vestimenta y antifaz de una mujer extenuada. Sabía que las miradas se dirigían a él y eso lo motivaba a mover sus nalgas más ridículamente.

Cuando comencé a mostrar mi carácter y quise que la gente aguzara los sentidos, en un instante creí haber escuchado una voz lejana, como un confuso eco que se repetía en mi mente, sin que yo entendiera nada; guardé silencio y me concentré, aún así no supe qué me inquietaba; eran palabras que merodeaban en mi imaginación. Hice un gran esfuerzo y congelé esa imagen que atravesó mi memoria; sí, una imagen borrosa que poco a poco fue adquiriendo la forma de un rostro pálido. También detuve mis pasos y vi claramente a doña Carmela, ¡no puede ser! Sí, era ella, escuché nuevamente su voz que provenía de mi pesadilla; me susurraba a los oídos, calando así mis últimas fuerzas. Recordé que ella había aparecido en mi sueño la noche que dormí en casa de Carlos. Estaba enferma de la mente; pero sus palabras quedaron atrapadas en mi alma: "Están perdidos, no saben lo que hacen. El *pukuj*[6] está con ustedes. Todos deben morir". A pesar de que sólo había sido un sueño, mi gusto por bailar se alejó, escapó y un susto aprehendió mi cuerpo. Vi mi reloj, marcaba las cinco de la tarde. En adelante sentí el tiempo avanzar más lento que nunca, se alargaban las horas. Mi saliva ligosa y amarga comenzó a disgustarme y poco a poco el miedo empezó a formarme un nudo en la garganta, me arrinconé en un asiento de metal del parque; nadie se dio cuenta de mi situación, porque de seguro la máscara de diablo que tenía reflejaba agresividad e imaginé que mis amigos pensaron que estaba agotado o que el *pox* me mareaba.

Confundido por el pavor, saqué del *chojak*[7] una botella todavía con un cuarto de aguardiente, me lo tomé de un sorbo. Me puse de pie al oír la voz del representante del grupo que nos daba el aviso:

—Es hora de irnos.

Una camioneta blanca de Tumbalá, de tres cuartos, avanzaba lentamente por la calle central y se estacionó a un costado del parque, dispuesta a llevarnos al concurso de disfraz que allá estaba por realizarse.

Mientras subíamos a la camioneta vieja y oxidada, mis compañeros se despidieron de la gente con gritos y silbidos: "Ya nos vamos, deséennos suerte",

6. Demonio.

7. Red de henequén.

decía uno, y el representante nos gritaba: "¡Súbanse rápido, cabrones!". Las personas aplaudían con fuerza, las femeninas voces despertaban el ánimo de mis compañeros para ganarles a los de Tumbalá y así regresar con el premio sorpresa a Petalcingo.

Acomodamos cuidadosamente los dos toritos de petate en el interior de la redila para que nadie se encaramara sobre ellos. Estaban contentos, la misma cara del enorme cielo azul irradiaba alegría contagiándonos de locura: nos dábamos de manotazos uno al otro por la espalda y la cabeza, dejábamos escapar palabras obscenas acompañadas de gritos: "Ay güey, órale pendejo"; mientras Carlos y los que se hallaban en la canastilla de metal terminaban una botella más de "Quetzal", aguardiente del bueno.

Yo no hablaba. Una vaga inquietud, lejana, desde mi sueño, callaba mi lengua, amarraba las palabras y mi propio *ch'ulel*; cerré los ojos y discutí con mi pensamiento: "¡Chingada madre! Si hablo de mi sueño dirán que soy puto, mejor no digo nada".

Imágenes borrosas comenzaron a rondar en mi cabeza, presagiando un peligro cercano, oculto. El susto comenzaba cada vez más a atacarme; callada mi voz, sudé miedo en abundancia. Algunos habían ganado lugar sobre la lona sostenida por los fierros atravesados y otros más se acomodaban en la canastilla con los que ya estaban ahí, para disfrutar el aire fresco y el paisaje durante el recorrido.

Tras dejar la iglesia en la primera curva, la camioneta avanzaba lentamente en una recta no muy larga, para luego aproximarse a otra curva. El viento fuerte ahogaba los gritos festivos; todos, uno por uno, fueron descubriéndose el rostro caliente y mojado, gota tras gota caía el sudor contenido en las máscaras; se oyeron hondos suspiros de alivio y los pulmones dejaron salir el cansancio contenido. Las demás bocas se abrían y cerraban muchas veces charlando no sé qué, no le puse la menor importancia; sólo escuché pedazos de palabras: "Me excitas. Ábrete, estoy mojado". La velocidad de la camioneta aumentaba. Al aproximarse a la segunda curva la velocidad aumentó, como si una desesperada prisa nos empujara; y justo al virar por la derecha, comenzaron a rechinar las llantas: un zigzagueo distanció a mis amigos de la alegría y nos aprisionó el terror. Los frenos no respondieron; la inclinada pendiente facilitaba camino abajo hacia el abismo; sentí que mi alma abandonaba mi cuerpo; mis ojos salían de sus órbitas, me soplaba un escalofriante olor a muerte. Los gritos se transformaron en llantos aterrados; el pukuj apretaba nuestras almas, flotaba entre nosotros; esperaba ansioso triturar nuestro ch'ulel. No sé por qué, de repente me sentí en el interior de una tumba oscura y fría; alguien me jalaba de los pies, petrificándome en aquella celda fúnebre. Gritamos al chofer que controlara su volante, pero fue en vano. La camioneta nos sacudía con fuerza y entre tambaleos no sabíamos qué hacer, si aventarnos al monte o permanecer en nuestros lugares, eso fue lo que hicimos: esperar los chingadazos; miré a mis compañeros; uno por uno fue despegándose de la camioneta en el trayecto de la curva, rodando en el pavimento; algunos, en el interior de la redila. Cada golpe en la madera abría una herida en sus caras, en sus brazos.

El chofer, al darle un giro completo a su volante, hizo que la llanta delantera se trabara, comenzó a rechinar y la camioneta se atravesó, el peso de su carga y la fuerza de la velocidad la empujó dando tres vueltas en el aire, arrastrándose hasta detenerse fuera del pavimento, hecha pedazos.

Mis piernas fracasaron al querer levantarme, sentía entumido el cuerpo; tirado en el zacatal, como a diez pasos de la camioneta. Con los ojos llorosos vi a mis compañeros empapados de sangre, dispersos por la orilla de la carretera, ensangrentados, inmóviles. Desde muy profundo de cada mirada imploraban auxilio, el remordimiento únicamente provocaba dolor en el alma; nos brotaron lágrimas; débiles y heridos nos arrastramos hacia los demás sin que pudiéramos hacer nada.

Estuvimos ahí, tendidos en el camino que nunca nos condujo a Tumbalá. Busqué con la vista a Carlos, mi mejor amigo. No lograba identificarlo. Volteé la vista, la muerte me sopló su aliento y la respiración no me quiso responder; fijé mis ojos en la cabeza de Carlos, la llanta trasera del carro pasó sobre ella convirtiéndola en una oscura masa deforme.

Quise gritar, no pude; la tristeza se me atoró como un hueso en la garganta transformándose en llanto que se mezclaba con el murmullo del río que orillaba la carretera salpicada de sangre.

"Wokolil ta tajimal k'in" / "Carnaval de desgracia" / "Carnival Disaster"
by José Osvaldo García Muñoz

Carnival Disaster

We couldn't decide, the mood to dress up came and went like the wind at dawn; sometimes we waited, like the reluctance to open your weary eyes when they're still seasoned with drunkenness. A presentiment foretold that this was not to be our day; well, after discussing how much enthusiasm each of us had, it seemed we only felt insecurity. But something more private was discomforting me: a sensation of dread; maybe because we awoke so hungover, and in a downpour that washed away our eagerness to be here together, by the park. We slept some more hours until the afternoon wind woke us up as it blew in the window. The rain had left for the horizon, which meant we would make our decision immediately. We looked at the sky, now clear, and that encouraged us to get our costumes on right there; we already had the *petate*[8] bulls prepared. The air smelled of wet earth, and we could see the steam rising from the moist highway, just heated by the resplendent rays of the afternoon sun. It was the first days of February, the last month of the winter rains; and like every year, they were days of fiesta, costumes, and revelry.

Carlos and I were part of a group of clowns in the barrio Grande. We had agreed to meet the afternoon of the fourteenth at his house, and nobody had missed it. We were there as in the years before, renewing the same tradition. Carlos also liked the disorder, his temperament having no boundaries. That day we'd concerned ourselves with making the petate bull, since we had finished collecting the materials for it in the mountains: a dozen two-meter bamboo sticks and some bark from a cork tree. We began working as the sun went out of view, taking itself behind Bajwits hill. First we made the shape of a small bull from bamboo sticks in the form of a double-gabled roof, and later we sewed the *petate* over its skeleton; then we carefully formed a little triangular window in front to be able to see the outside from within; we had warded off the cold with the heat of *pox* and received the predawn rain with drunkenness, then we awoke today with the sun past the middle of the sky.

We were trying to lose the effects of the *pox* with a cold-water bath in the Pajwuchil River when we heard the old municipal agency horn sounding out the first song of "El querreque," right at three o'clock. It was a happy music, which we had begun hearing a few days before to announce the fiesta. At that time, the groups of clowns had begun organizing; and the *tsobojeletik*[9]

8. Mat made of woven straw.

9. Organizers of the carnival.

had lost no time in naming the men who would dress as *yantsileletik*.[10] Now the rhythm of the music brought more joy and pulled up from deep inside the desire to go down to the park and do the dance; hear the shouts and applause; savor the smell of the sweets, corn drinks, and *curtidos de nance*[11] that conquered us in our huts on the park's edge. We quickly got costumed. Carlos's mother admired our silliness and got a lot of pleasure from seeing us change into women showing our bony legs; for that she offered each of us a gourd of *pozol*[12] with chile and salt, and that gave us new energy for the dance. We shut ourselves in the room where the masks and costumes were kept. There we shouted out our first sounds of rejoicing as we each saw the others hide their faces behind hideous masks. Everything was in disarray, we had fun throwing old shoes at every part of our bodies; one hit me in the head—that hurt! Once we were ready, we opened the red metal door and pushed ourselves out, sticking our hands where they didn't belong, heading for the highway, about five steps in front of the house, at the edge of which Doña Carmela looked at us with disgust, at just the same place where I had seen her in my dreams one night, cursing our pranks. I felt unsure about getting crazy this afternoon. The worried feeling was bothering me, but no, I couldn't back down or upset my companions, so I just had to lift my hand, move my feet from left to right and my head from side to side, pretending it was great fun. Everyone did the same: moved their bodies, ran around senselessly, the music moving us; and so we set off to the center of town. We had just arrived at the basketball court, between the municipal agency and the park, when we heard a female voice:

"Here come 'The Rebels.'"

Everyone turned to look at us as we wiggled our bodies vigorously in costumes of badly dressed, underfed women. We opened a path through the people as we moved from place to place, while some blew kisses to the girls and others playfully shook their butts; up front, two handsome young men opened a path with their *petate* bulls above them, imitating the animal's language: "*uuuuuuu*." We were received with applause and whistles—later the emotion changed to guffaws at seeing us loose women with extreme miniskirts; to get more attention from the public, we showed off our skinny, hairy legs, lifting our skirts to uncover the pink and white bikinis that two of us were wearing. We were the last ones to arrive at the plaza: "The Rebels,"

10. Men dressed as Tseltal women.
11. Pickled nance fruit, which is a tropical yellow berry.
12. Cold drink made from tortilla dough and water.

written in large black letters over a bull that danced around us, pretending to gore any person who would cross his path.

I felt that the people were staring at us and signaled with my fingers where to concentrate our dance; I looked at my surroundings: the women's skirts had flowery colors, some men were dressed in white, most of the young men adorned themselves with modern clothes—blue jeans and shirts; these fiestas were the chance to have a look at the girls and get in good with them. The people moved around, looking for the perfect place to see the best group of performers, who danced without carrying the rhythm of the music mixed with the noise. In order to see us, the children broke through the adults' paths, shoving and smashing without care. A thin, captivating sound from the guitar, violin, and mandolin came from one side of the park, where the old musicians played their instruments, waking up the dancing feeling in the *yantsileletik*. Standing in the middle of my companions, among their obscene shouts, little by little I stopped seeing and hearing them; my attention turned to the other two musical groups who were dancing near us, while one more approached, followed by a large crowd of boys. In the park we were four groups of clowns. Those who had wigs really seemed like women and got the kids worked up; others looked like the devil himself with their deformed faces. The public broke out laughing to see the woman who moved in a senseless outburst; the effect of the *pox* and the music of "La del moño colorado," played on an old tape recorder, forced us to throw our hands all around and move our bodies while skirting around the others.

Carlos was moving his skinny, hot body behind his exotic, ridiculous, dirty, sweaty suit; he was drunk for sure, maybe more drunk than he seemed, from the boiling blood, the heat, and the *pox* that had been filling him up, sip by sip, since the morning. Now completely unself-conscious, he kept lifting his mask, uncovering his brown face. Those who recognized him laughed in secret and passed word from ear to ear that Carlos was covered in the clothes and mask of a worn-out woman. He knew the glances were directed at him, and that motivated him to shake his butt more ridiculously.

When I started showing my face, too, and wanting people to sharpen their focus on me, in an instant I thought I heard a faraway voice, like a confused echo repeating in my mind, without my understanding anything; I kept quiet and concentrated, still not knowing what was bothering me, words prowling in my imagination. With a great effort I froze the image that crossed my memory; yes, a blurry image that bit by bit was acquiring the form of a pale face. I stopped short and clearly saw the face of Doña Carmela—it can't be! Yes, it was she, I heard her voice again from out of my nightmare, murmuring in my ears, penetrating there my last strength. I remembered that she had appeared in my dream the night I slept in Carlos's house. She was sick in the head, but her words stuck in my soul: "You're lost, you don't know what you do. The *pukuj*[13] is with you. You must all die." Even though it had only been a dream, my taste for dancing left me, escaped, and a fear took over my body. I checked my watch and saw that it was five in the afternoon. From this point it seemed time moved more slowly than ever, the hours dragged. My sticky, bitter saliva began to disgust me, and little by little the fear formed a knot in my throat. I removed myself to a metal seat in the park; nobody noticed my situation, because for sure the devilish mask I wore reflected aggression, and I imagined that my friends thought I was exhausted or that the *pox* was making me dizzy.

Confused with dread, I took from the *chojak'*[14] a bottle that was still a quarter full of *pox*, and I drank it all in one gulp. I got to my feet when I heard a voice from our group saying, "It's time for us to go."

A white box truck from Tumbalá drove slowly along the central street and stopped beside the park, ready to take us to the costume competition.

As we climbed into the old, rusty truck, my friends said good-bye to the people with shouts and whistles: "We're going now, wish us luck," said one, and the one trying to get us on the trucks shouted, "Get in quick, *cabrones*!" The people cheered loudly, the female voices rousing my companions' spirits to win in Tumbalá and then return with the surprise award to Petalcingo.

We carefully found room for the two *petate* bulls so that nobody would climb over them. We were happy, and the enormous blue face of the sky radiated a crazy, contagious happiness: we slapped each other on the back and head and let fly some obscene words and shouts: *"Ay güey, órale pendejo"*; meanwhile, Carlos and those who ended up in the metal bed finished another bottle of "Quetzal"—good-quality *pox*.

I didn't talk. A vague worry, since my dream, stopped my tongue, tied up my words and my own *ch'ulel*; I closed my eyes and argued with my thoughts: *"¡Chingada madre!* If I talk about my dream, they'll call me a *puto*, better I say nothing."

Blurry images began going round in my head, foretelling a danger dark and close. The dread began to attack me again; my voice silenced, I was sweating in my fear. Some of the men stood up where the canvas crossed the metal,

13. Demon.

14. Bag made from agave fibers.

and others found room in the truck bed with those who were already there, to enjoy the fresh air and scenery during the trip.

Leaving the church behind at the first curve, the truck moved slowly down a straightaway, not very long, to approach another curve. The strong wind drowned out the shouts from the festival; everyone began to uncover their hot, wet faces, drop after drop of sweat fell from the masks; deep breaths of relief could be heard as our lungs let go of their exhaustion. The other mouths opened and closed, chatting about I don't know what, as I didn't give it much importance; I only heard pieces of words: "You turn me on. Open up, I'm wet." The truck's speed increased. Approaching the second curve, it increased more, as if a desperate hurry pushed us; and just as we veered to the right, the tires began to grind: a zigzagging ripped my friends' happiness from them and terror gripped us. The brakes didn't respond; the steep slope meant our path led toward the abyss; I felt my soul abandoning my body; my eyes left their orbits, I sucked in a bone-chilling odor of death. The shouts transformed into terrifying sobs; the *pukuj* squeezing our souls, hovering among us, anxiously waiting to crush our *ch'ulel*. I don't know why, but suddenly I felt like I was in a dark, cold tomb; somebody pulled at my feet, scaring me stiff in that gloomy cell. We yelled at the driver to control his steering, but it was useless. The truck shook us violently, and in its lurching we didn't know what to do, throw ourselves to the mountain or stay in our places. That's what we did: wait for the impact; I looked at my companions; one by one they were being thrown from the truck as it went around the curve, rolling on the pavement; some were being tossed around inside the truck. Every strike against the wood opened a wound in their faces, in their arms.

The driver, with a sharp turn of his steering wheel, made the front tire jam, and it began to grind, and the truck to turn over; the weight of its cargo and the force of its speed propelled it through three turns in the air, then it dragged along the ground until it stopped off the pavement, left in pieces.

My legs failed me when I tried to get up, I felt entombed in my body, thrown into a pasture, about ten paces from the truck. Through my crying eyes I saw my friends soaked in blood, spread out along the edge of the highway, bloody, not moving. From deep down, every look begged for help, the remorse only provoking pain in the soul; the tears flowed out; weak and wounded, we dragged ourselves toward one another without being able to do anything.

There we were, stretched out on the road that would never take us to Tumbalá. I looked for Carlos, my best friend. I couldn't find him. My view turned, and death sucked me into its breath so that my own breathing would not respond; as I fixed my eyes on Carlos's head, the car's rear tire passed over it, converting it into a dark, contorted mass.

I wanted to scream, but I couldn't—sadness clogged me up like a bone in the throat, transforming itself into sobbing that mixed with the murmur of the river that bordered the highway soaked in blood.

Ta o'lol takin osil

Miguel Ruiz Gómez

Stuil anima. Chtuch'bun kich'ob ik' ti yik'e, chchik'ilanbun sbek' jsat. Ti jch'ulele chk'unibxa ta yeloval l sat li jtatatike, muxa xkuch yu'un. Stuil anima. Chtuch'bun kich'ob ik' ti yik'e, Chjo'bin xa ti jch'ich'ele. Ti banumile tsk'ak'esvan k'ucha'al semet, chi-ul ta ju tek'el ta sba. Ti pukuke chtajin xchi'uk sk'ob ti ik'e, yantik spas ta stanil ti' k'ok' ti jbek'tale.

Chajchajbak te'etik chk'ak'ik yu'un ti sle'bal vinajel chbajtalele. Ti ta jlumale yaxal te'etiketik, yaxaletik; sikil ik', lek sikiket. Mechuk li jtatatik li'e tsjiptalel xupite'al k'ok', ja' no'ox xupite'etik. K'uk to yelan yu'un chixanav to ech'el, xtijlajet julikel ti si'baketik ta jti'bae, ti jchinabe tstsin xa sba ya'luk, jk'el muyel syax-elan pix ti vinajele, yax-elan k'ucha'al nab. Jtsop xulemetik xjoylajetik, jun yutsil k'in, nakastal chyalik talel. Mu'yuk buch'u chk'opoj. Tspas ta kilolkutik ti ts'ijlejale. Li' toe, ta o'lol takin osil, xka'itik chlik uts'intael. ¡Mu'yuk xch'ich'el ti banumile!

Skoj xa lubemal ya'luk me ti ch'ayele. K'uksiuk xk'ot ta pasel yu'un sk'an to ti beinale. Ti Petul xchi'uk juntote sjelubtasojikun lajunebuk okilal. Chkich'bekutik ech'el yok ti namal vaechile.

—¿Ke asen aí, kabrones? ¡No se keden atrás! —xka'itik tsatsal eal, xbejlajet, jpasvanej ta mantal ti xchavlajet yok ch-och ta jchikin ku'chik jmilvanej ome.

Ja' ti Maryo chkoltavan yo' xijelavkutik ta takin osile. Jelavem to'ox ech'el xchi'uk smuk'tikil ok, pe laj xa spajesan yo' smalaunkutik. Mu xka'itik mi oy slubemal ta yee: naka no'ox chal svo'lajunebal xcha'vinik syijil, yipal ta ch'iel; yisimtake chak'an xa ta ilel syijubelal.

—Batanik, muxa jk'an xixanav —chkalbe pe mu'yuk no'ox k'usi ya'binoj spasojsba, lik sjet batel ti yoke.

Ti bee la slajesbun xa ti yatel ko'nton chibat ta Neva Yorke. Mu xch'ay ta jol k'u xa sjalil, yoxvinikal k'ak'al jlok'elkutik talel ta jlumaltik yo' jtuch'kutik ti ts'ake, mu'yuk to kuchem o; ta chib enero li lok'kutik tal, ach' ja'vil, ti li'ni xchibal xa yu'un marso: yoxvinikal k'ak'al. K'alal chvul ta jol ti jtot jme'e chinoj ta at o'nton. Alal jik'o'nton tslajesbe yip ti kakantake. ¡Slam xa ka'i yu'un ti xanobal, anilajel, nak'bail yu'un ti jtsakvaneketike! Xi'elal. Taki ti'il. Ch'abal xa jts'ujuk ya'lel ti jbek'tale. Xt'elajet ti kok jk'obe, baketik ta k'ixin ik'..., chkomkomajan ti koke. ¡Mu jk'an xiok'! ¿K'usivan chalik ti yantike? Tsnopik van ti ko'chik olol chixi' yu'un ti banumilal li'e: ch'abal polbil be ta nutsel, ja' no'ox ti yav yok Maryoe. Sbe xch'ich'el ti banumile ts'uts'bil ta k'ak'al, ta sokem ak'obal, chlok'an tal yisimtak te'etik tsa'ik ch'iel, tsa'ik ik' ta jik'el.

—¿Pe bu li jlok'utik talel, me ta snamal Jlumaltik chi-jlajotik? Mo'oj, kak'betik xa yipal, chijelavotik. ¡Sobanikme! —tak'av ti juntote, malubem skoj abtelal ta banumil, slamoj xa xa'i ti me'onale.

—Li Maryoe li' tsjipotik ya'i komel ta chopolal osile, xka'i jutuk ya'luk. Mu xa sk'an smalaotik. K'elo avilik, chanav k'ucha'al to'ox jmol muk'tot, mu sventa k'usitik skomtsanan ta spat.

—Ts'ijlanik xa, mu li'uk xkutjbatike, ba jtatik ta be, xchi'nojotik Jtatatik. Ti koyote le'e chbat yak'otik ti bu kalojbetike —sk'optak li juntote noch'ajtik kom ta yutil jchinab.

Cha'vul no'ox ti ts'ijlejal xtoke, syak to chixanav.

Tsk'anik vo' ti yanaltak kee. Ti snopbenal jole tspas ta lum, k'unk'un chyal ta jnuk'. Ta namal osil, ch'ulch'ul vitsetik tstsajub ti maleb k'ak'ale. Ti mastroe yaloj uno'ox ti xko'laj k'ucha'al lajebal me li takin osile; mu'yuk vo', uk'um, mu'yuk k'usi. Li ak'obaletike mechuk, pe ta sakil osile chchik'van. Xvokvun ti jch'ich'ele, chtakij xa.

Ch'abal chkoman yav yok ti jchi'iltake, stukik chanavik, ch'ayemik ta namal banumil.

—Chilaj ta uch' vo', ta vi'nal, ta vayel —xi ti Petul Ariase, "kamkutik", k'ucha'al chkalbekutike, xchi'uk sk'unibel sat, xt'elajet ston sat, sakch'ayan tok sbek'sat, sakvajan sjol. Slajunebal xcha'vinik xa sja'vilal ta ilel me ti ta slekil lok'ol vinik pasbil yu'un jtatatike. Yoxibal xa k'ak'al ti chlaj xa ya'i la jtakutik ta xokon bee, yich' komtsanel yu'un ti yits'inabtak ta spat vitse. Skoj ti tsk'unajes ti yok xchi'iltake yich' jipel komel, ti vu'unkutike la jkoltakutik ta yutsilal ko'ntonkutik ili' jchi'nojkutike, xkoxkun xch'ulel. Ja' tsujunkutik ta sts'ikel ti xk'ixnal lum chch'i ta xanaveb jtatatike.

—Epal viniketik xanavemik me li'e —xi ti Maryo mu'yuk xjoybij, sk'unajes yok, li' xa nopol jchi'uke, pe ep xtok ti komemik ta bee —lik no'ox yal xtok—, ta lubel mi mo'oje ta lo'lael, ti'bilik ta k'ak'al, ta banumil, xchi'uk jti'val chon bolometik.

Li chotikutik ta yolon yanal te'etik, ta syaxinal yo' jkuxkutik jlikeluk xchi'uk jmalakutik x-ik'ub ti osile. Xko'laj jlik takin yanal te' bajtalel ta sba jol ti lik jna' ti jbats'i lumale, Chik'obtantik, jlumaltik xtok Chamula. Jechuk ti mu'yuk xa chak' ti isak'e, chenek'e, iximе, mu'yuk jech li' chkil jvokol jechuke. Ti avonoe, ti likiroetik chak'batel ti ajvalile mu'yuk xa xtunan. Xch'ulel ti banumile xko'laj yich' elk'anbel yu'un jtotiketik. Ti juntot Manvele ja' la yak'bun jch'un skomtsanel ti vitse.

Te kom smalaik tak'in ti jtot jme'e, ti lekilal la jkalbike. ¡Kabron, sna'ikuk ti k'u kelan ta orae! "Mu xa vat avo'nton, chibat ta nom ba jsa' talel tak'in, li'e muxa xtun, mu bu jtatik lekil abtel, ti jchanune mu xak'bun kabtel ta muk'ta lum, ti mu'yuk la ta jnoptik k'ucha'al ti jkaxlanetike . . . , jeche', ja' lek chibat, te ta jk'el k'u chkut", xi la kalbe ti jtot k'alal jkuchoj xa'ox kikats ti mu'yuk xa li'e. Ta spech' sjoltak ti jme'e skus xa no'ox ti ya'lel sat yokel to chch'aubtasbun ti ko'ntone.

—¡Sta xa ora, likanik xa, sk'an xa me xi jbatotik, ch-ik'ub xa me ti osile, ep me chi-jxanavotik! —xi ti Maryo, tsojik xa sbek' sat k'uchal ch'ich'e. Chotol ta muk'ta ton la jkil tstok'ilan jun sik'olal ti yik' chik'bil vomol ya'luke. Jtsop ch'ailetik, tsmak jnuk'tik, lok'anuktalel ta ye, ta sni', pere ti yane tsjik'anuk batel. Ti ta xch'in mochilae, lek xokxun, la sutesan ch'inik sbalikil vunetik sts'ililet ta xojobal jtatatik. Li'e xi choletkutik ech'el ta spat, sak skoton, pim xvex, nukul xonob. Chkap sjol me xi k'opojkutik ta bats'i k'ope. Mu xa'iunkutik.

Xi xanxunkutik ta o'lol votsvots k'ak'etal te'eteik, ti maryoe paj ta anil, ja' jech ta anil xtok la slok'es yuni kuchilu ta sch'in yikats, la sjam, xchi'uk ti xibalsba ye ti xu' sk'ok ti vaechil laj sk'okbe ta jsetel no'ox, mu'yuk xk'uxul yo'nton skob jtek' ch'ixal te', ti bu ta anil xchororet lok'talel vo'e, ak'o mi jun xch'ail te laj ta uch'el ku'unkutik ti ja' xa ta jk'ankutike. Ch'ay ta ko'nton jlikeluk me ti vi'nal xchi'uk taki ti'ile. Laj ta o'lol be me ti k'oxox kich'okutik to'ox talele, kuxinem, mu'yuk xa ta jak'el.

—¡Kon esta akua échenle kanas, en un tos por tres estaremos con nuestros "amikos krinkos" kanando tantos lólares! Aí es otra kosa—. Slo'il ti Maryoe chkuxesunkutik.

Lajun mil la jtojkutik jujuntal ti Maryo yo' xjelavesvan ta namal osile. Ka'iojkutik ti ta Jobel stak' jsa'kutike, ja' to tey la yik'unkutik talel li'e. Ju batele chlik lo'ilajuk stuk. Xlararet xa ye tk'ejimol ti mu xka'i k'usi ja'e.

—¿K'usi la chaval, Maryo? ¿Nopol xa van ta ti' be karo oyotik?
Chibat un.

Chanav to'ox ta sikiket beal ti karoe. K'unk'un chjoybij, chkomanan ta spat li te'etike, tonetik xchi'uk chon bolometik tsnak'anansbaik. Muk'ta jal xa kom ti takin osile. Jk'elkutik yaxaletik, yav ts'unobaletik.

Naka to'ox jech mechuk la kak'kutik jtek'el kakankutik ta be karo k'alal sts'u'et talel ti jtsakvanejetike . . . , ti jech ta aniluk kotie la snet'unkutik. Chkale, yu'un muxa stak' xicha'sutkutik. La xchukbun kokkutik ti xi'elale.

—Oh mai kad, ya los cojimos . . . , —xi talel ti jun sakil natil mole, yij, xi'bal sba ta ilel ti sat lok'talel ta sbats'i k'ob ta sti' skaroe. Stuktuk.

—Albo ak'u yak' ech'kutik, Mach, k'opono, vo'ot xa va'i jutuk ti kaxlan kope. Albo k'usi —xi tsk'an ti Petul ta bats'il k'ope, xi'el ta jek.

Ja' xa ta jk'an ya'luk me xet' ti banumile, ta jipjba ochel ta spajeb to. K'alal jal xa ti xanvile, sts'ikel vi'nal, vayel . . .

Syak ta jch'un ya'luk me ti Jtatatike la stenunkutik xa ta yo'nton. Ti ch'ul San Juane mu'yuk chkoltavan. Jeche' me la jk'opontik ta resku', ta pox, ta kantila xchi'uk jun yepal pometik k'alal li lok' talel ta sna jtot jme'e. Jechuk ni, ti Maryoe bat, ¿buy to? Na'tik. Ja' no'ox jna' ti sakil mol sna'oje. Te xa bat o k'alal la sk'opon sbaike. Laj to jk'elilan mi oy bu jta pe mu'yuk xa o. Te tso'bol li skomtsanunkutik ta xokon be karo k'ucha'al nene' ch'oetik lok'esbil ta sta-sik. Jech to xchopolil.

—Mu xapas jech, ak'o jelavkunkutik, avokoluk, mu chopoluk avo'nton —kejelun jech la kalbe ti k'a' mole, jech k'uchal la jk'opon komel ti muk'ulil San Juane, cht'om xa ox ti kok'ele. Tey sak ch'ayanuk ti jk'optake. Te oy ta jpat li juntote. Kuji, la stsak jp'ej ton.

—Ti tsajal tsone chich' un, chil buch'uotik, li lub xa ta yok'itael. ¿Me te no'ox kan jk'elojba? Koltaun, Mach —xi la yalbun.

Liva'i ta anil ek, lik kalbe: —Juntot, mo'oj, mu jechuk xa pas, ma'uk xa te chkuch ku'untik me la jmiltike.

—Pe k'ajom k'o stuk chkil ti vinik ni, chu'ku'untik. La aval chka' ti chamil ava'ek ni.

—Ja' lek la jk'opontike, a ti me sjelubtasotik ni. Ak'o mi stuktuk.

—Loj xa riox, abolxa jbatik, k'elavil lek k'u kelantik, sjayibalxa tak'in la jiptik komel ta bebetik —xi tak'av ti juntot sk'eloj muyel vinajel xchi'uk takin xa snuk'e, sbik' batel skapemal sjol, ta nakastal la syales li tone.

—¡Metense kabrones, si no me los chinko! —xi la yalbunkutik ti krinko xtuchoj stuk'e, la stik'unkutik ta sba skaro. Ip me k'alal la slikunkutuik ta tek'ele. Balchik' ta skapemal jolkutik la jts'ikutik ti yipale. Xt'elajan me li koktake. Ti yik' yut karoe to j-alak'sba ya'luk, to jmu, sikiket.

Li vulkutik ta yut iktabil k'a' na li'e, ta Nokales ti ja' jech chalbike. Ta xujel ta tek'el li stik'unkutik ochel xtok, k'uchal ts'i'etik. ¡K'u xa uno'ox sle-kil ti jtalelkutike! Jechuk ti yantike tsk'elunkutik, sjelsba satik, sk'opik va'e tsts'ijik. Yipal ti majeletike chk'atbuj ta at o'ntonal me li' ta xi'balsba nae. Ta yutile chlok'tal stuil yik'. Mu'yuk buch'u chch'uba yiluk. Ti bu jomajtik sba ti nae chjelavantalel xojobal k'ak'al yo' svu'lanunkutik. Ch-ochesik pato'bil o'ntonal, ti nae jun smuk'ul noj ta tenbil vaechiletik. Xi xach'etkutik no'ox ta banomil. Vayel. Vaechinajel. Li jtote la xa yich' xvaxton sventa paxional ta jlumaltik. Tsk'oponan jtotiketik, kolyal yu'un ti Jtatatik oy to xch'iele, ch-abtej ta yok sk'ob xchi'uk ti yalab xnich'nabe. Kejel ta yichon epal nichime-tik xchi'uk yik' pometik chyakubtasvane, chk'opoj xchi'uk ti Yajval vinajele.

—¡Rekresen a su tiera, larkense diuna vez, *pinches indios*! —xi yalbunku-tik ti jchabiej na kapem no'ox sjole, noj ta il k'op. Ech' xa vo'lajuneb k'ak'al ti la sbajunkutik li' ta yut me'onal nae. Ti muk'ta mol le'e, ik'yaman, kom-kom, xchi'uk xchi'iltak tsnutsunkutik lok'el ta tek'el, xko'laj k'ucha'al ts'i'etik mu'yuk yajvalik.

Mejiko xa me jk'elojkutik un. Te xa jujuntal xbat ta sna. Jvok' chamel tavi'naletik li lok'kutik ta yut ch'en, bu ti ve'lile ma'uk ve'lil. Ti jvaechkutik eke te bajajtik komik ta yut li muk'ta ch'en snail ometik xchi'uk ch'oetike.

Taj toe x-avet ch-ok' jkot ok'il. Sne k'analetik tstuk'ibtas ti jbekutike. Ta yolon sakilal stse'etel sat jmeme'tik, jtambekutik xanobal ta sob ik'luman osil, ch-ech' stusbun jol sni'tak sk'ob ti siketel ik' ta ik'luman osile. Tstsatsajes kok me ti yuninal sakubel osile. Ak'o mi jech, ti pukuk chmuytalele tsmak ti jni' ta xanobale.

K'alal li lok'kutik ta Nokalese la jch'akjbakutik xchi'uk ti jchi'laktak ta cha-mo'e. Stukike batik ta Mejiko, jechuk ti oxibunkutik uno'oxe li cha'batkutik no'oxtok, ba jtuch'kutik yan velta li ts'ak xtoke. Ti jvaechkutike mu'yuk bu xkomik ta jpatkutik, yanuk ni, lik tsatsajikuk k'alal yilik slekilal ti k'ak'ale, yech'oxal li' xi lok'kutike, ta jxanviltakutik yan k'opiletik. Jna'ojkutik ti ta to xi k'otkutike, jelavel to ta stakinal banumil Sonorae, ti ja' jech sbi ti lum li' xi tamlajetkutike.

—Ti jnich'nab te oyik ta nome la stakbikun talel tak'in yo' xi jelavotik, batik uno'ox. Chijk'ototik ta sk'ob Ch'ul San Juan. Vi le'ike ak'u batikuk, yan vo'otike chijelavotik, ja' ti k'u xkutike.

Ti yo'nton juntote ja' tstsatsubtasunkutik ek. Kerem to no'ox cha'i me yo'nton ta jeke. Yu'un ja' la yik'un talel. A ti jechuke, yiloj ti San Juane, vu'ne muxa ox jk'an. Mu jna' me vu'un to'ox lek jtuk ti tik'ilun ta yut jbek'tal ol ta vokolil, ch'abal xa ti jch'ulele. Li' ni to jven xa jich'ilun, mu'yuk xa yan jbek'tal ti ja' xa no'ox jnukulil xpixoj ti jbakiltake. Vuklajuneb ja'vil kochel ta slajesel ti svokol jtot jme'e.

—Chkuch ku'untik tana un, vo'oxuke keremoxuk to, mechuk li vu'une molun xa jutuk, pe ta to xibat ka'i ek. Chijbat —xi chal k'u uno'ox yelan sna' xk'opoj ti juntote.

—Jech xaval ava'uk mol Manel, batik —xi laj yal ti kamkutike, ak'o me mu sna' lek xk'opoj. Ja' jechun ek lik ka'i ti yu'un sk'an to xi tsatsub leke, yu'un chibat j-ich'el xtok. Mu uno'ox sna'ik ti kuts'kalaltak buy oyune, k'u kelan. ¿K'usi van tsnopik ta jtojolal taje?

Ja' jech li cha'likutik ta xanvil xtok, pere xi'elunkutik xa ta yok'el skaro ti jtsakvanejetike. Chapalunkutik ta uts'intael yu'un xnich sk'ok'il ti vitsetike, ti lume, ti jtatatik mu xa jaluk sk'an xlok'tale.

Lajuneb ora sob osil. Chk'ak' xa ti jol yu'un stsatsal xk'ixnal jtatatike. Ta staylej sjol vitsetike jtsop xulemetik chyaliktal ta banumil. Ti takin osile, snakleb ch'ayemal ch'ulelaletik, nakastal chlik julavuk ti banumil k'uyelan chiech'kutik ta sba.

Tsk'elikun ti jchi'iltake, oy k'usi tsjak'bikun ya'ik pe mu'yuk bu ta jtak'bik. Chlik jvules ta jol ti k'u xa yepal xanavemunkutike, muxa jna' bu chibat un. Mu jna' bu jotukal xchi'uk k'uxi ta tael ti bee. La yalbun jchi'iltak ti mu xch'ay ta jol ko'nton bu xanavemunkutik xchi'uk ti Maryoe. Jech li vu'une mu jna' k'uxi laj yut yo' la jyik'unkutik to'ox tale, mi oy van k'usi ta k'elel batel. Mu xa jna' k'usi ta jpas, ti jchinabe ch'ayem skoj ti xk'ixnal osil, li' ta yolon t'anal te'etike.

—Ja'lek batik xi ta jote, jk'eltikik bu chijk'ototik ta lok'el —xi ti juntote. Ja' te xi lok'kutik. Ja' no'ox oy to k'usi chopol. Xbitbun ta jyalel ti ko'ntone. Sts'ininet ti jchikine. Tsikub xa ti jch'ich'ele. Jeche' te' vach'an ti kok'e, mu stak' jbak'es yo' xi k'opoj jbeluk. Tstik'sba ta jbakiltak ti ch'ulele.

—¿Me jech me xavalik ti lekil be li'e? —jech lik kalbik ti jchi'iltak ta sjalil toe. Mi ja'uk ik' li stak'bun. Jech xa no'ox xi tamlajetkutik ech'el, ja' ti bu x-ik'van ech'el ti yok k'ak'ale.

—¡Malaik to, k'elavilik k'usi oy li'e!—, la svok' ts'ijlejal ti tsatsal avetele. Lik jtoy ti jole ja' to chkil ja' Petul ti x-avete, li bat ta anil ti bu oye. Li sate to jxi'em ta jek, ku'chik me pojbat xch'ulel yu'un junuk pukuj. Chk'opoj to ya'i pe mu xa xlok' yu'un. Xmaklajet. Ja' to t'olanuk lok'el jay beluk sokem k'opetik ta yanal ye. La jyak' iluk ta pat xulub tontik, lek no' sba smuk'tikil, skomelal kotoniletik kilajtik ta lumtik. Yo' xkilkutik lek ti k'usi oy teye li ochkutik ech'el ta yut chajchaj vomoletik ti bu la jtakutik ta ilel mol xonobiletike k'ak'emik xa ta k'ak'ale, ch'abal yak'il. ¡Yansba stuil!, mu xa no' ja'uk xak' kich'tik ik'. Chjemya'lukme jole. Chixanavkutik to o jech. Malaik to, ¿k'usi ja' le'e? ¿K'usi oy ta spat li te'etik le'e? Ja' to melel un ti ko'ntone paj ta abtel, muruch'tik xa ti jbek'tale, ti jsate chch'inub ya'luk. Baketik. Jun sbakil risano, oy no'ox yan xtok. Chlok'anuktal xuvitetik ta jbej sbakil jolal, oy to jujuti'uk sbek'talil xchi'uk stsotsil. Stsoplajet syaxal joval, xtal to smuk'tikil k'uchal akovetik, xturlajetik lok'el ta xi'el ta ye ta xch'ut ti baketike, ech'anuk ta jsatkutik. Te no'ox nopole xpochlaj xa lok'el jkot nak'obalil tsti' ti sbek'tal baketike. Xkilet lok'eltal jkot sotchon ta jpoch xonobil. Jelav ta xokon juntot. Xta'aet to tslukbinsba ech'. Vu'un xchi'uk Petule ts'ijil li komkutik, mu xi bak'kutik ta xokon ti juntote.

—So'banik, anilajanik —nom xa xka'betik ye ti Manele, nom to bu oyun-kutik ya'luk.

Mu jna'kutik lek k'uxi li jatavkutik lok'el teye, skoj ti xi'elale. Yokel to xbit-bun ti ko'ntone. Chutilanikun ti k'usi chvulan ta jole, ta jujulikel ku'chik xa

ek'el chet'bun ti jchinabe: Xuvit, vov, sot chon, xulemetik, stsotsil jolal. Ti
stuilale tsnutsunkutik to. Ti yoktake xko'laj k'uchal muk'ta votaetik.

—¡Malaikun to, mu xa xi xanav, chik'unib taj yalel! chka'ibe sk'unil e, cha-
mel juntote. Chipaj, chisutbatel li bu kome.

Chotol ta jbej ton la jta, x'i'et yu'un k'usi yipal. Sts'ujlajet ya'lel sti'ba k'u
yepal sk'ejoj ti sbek'tale. Jun spok'lej ta at o'nton, ta ok'el xchi'uk xi'el sat,
chlaj xa ya'i. Kol yalel jay ts'ujuk ya'lel sat. Vul ta jol ta anil k'alaluk to'ox chi-
batkutik ta kuch si' jchi'uke.

—¿K'usi chapas ya'luk? xut li Petul, xi'el to tsjak'bee.

—Mu jna', te lik k'unibuk stuk li kakantake. Mu stak' jik' lek ik'. Mu xa xu'
ku'un ti va'leje, ¡aay!

—Muxavat avo'nton. Ta jkuchotkutik batel. Chijbatotik uno'ox, mu'yuk bu
chijpajotik —xi chkalbekutik, xi'eltikun jutuk me vu'une. Ch'abal xa lek ta ilel.

Xchi'uk ti malk'ak'al ta jbakutike, ta sba jnekeb chlaj xa ti juntote. Jujulikel
chalanan jitunbil k'opetik. Jal tsjik' yo'nton ta sts'el jchikin. Ch-ok' xtok, to
j-ip ta jek ti yok'ele. Takin vinik, baketik xa no'ox mukbil ta k'u'il, la jelaves
ta jpat, chkalbe ti tsotsuktoe, ti jutuk xa sk'an, ti be karoe xvinaj xa. Ta namal
osile xvinaj xa chjelavan jaykotuk karoetik. Ta jol vits xa oyunkutik xtok.

—Keremetik, ¡jipikun komel li'e! —mu xa k'opoj, ich'o no'ox ik', xkut, ta
pujlajetel xa chixanav.

Jun yalal ti jol skoj ti baketik la jkile.

—Ich'o to ti ik'e, muxa xa jik' avo'nton —kalbe yan velta. Sk'anuk ti mu
to xchame, mu stak' jech spas. Ti Ch'ul San Juane mu stak' sten komel ta
yo'nton snich'on ta namal lum ch'abal yajval, ch'abal xch'ulel.

—Komtsanikun li'e, li' bu ti xulemetik stak' ta jujuti' st'olikun batel ta vilele
—jutuk xa xka'ibe yik'al ye ti juntote. Jlikel xa sk'an. Ak'u xa smala jlikeluk.
Ta xa xi jk'ot. Jlikeluk xa no'ox, va'e ta jpoxtatik. Ta x-ech' yu'un.

—Mu xa-ok' Manel, mu xa-ok', po'ot xa sk'an, chk'ot ta ko'nton ti k'u
yelan chka'i chaok'e, —k'un chkalbe ta xchikin, muts'ajtik xa sat, k'okaj-
tik xa chich' ti ik'e, ta snekeb xa ti Petul yik'oj ech'ele. Jlik no'ox level sk'u'
ts'ibarontik, sakil manta xvex, jlik xchuk ch'abal xa sbon, ta to skolta jts'uj
cha'ts'ujuk ya'lel sat chch'ay ta xk'ixnal ik'. Ta x-ok' ya'i ti Petul eke, ¿pe k'u
yu'un ti chi j-ok'otike?

—Jlikel xa no'ox, juntot, ti be karoe nopol xa ta jek, ich'o to ti ik'e —xi
chkalbe ta xchikin yo' stsatsub ti yo'ntone. To j-ech'em xa jal li xanavkutik.
Ch'abal xa chk'opoj, och ta vayel skoj ti slubemale, ta ok'el, ta ijetel. Ti bee to
j-ech'em lubesvan. ¡Pe mu to me xvay un! Ta jbak'es, lik jtoybe sjol, mu'yuk
xa k'usi. ¡Mu spas jech! Ti sk'obtake jeche' xa no'ox xjiplajet ta spat ti Petule,
ti sjole ts'ukul ta banomil.

—¡Mala to, Petul!

La jyaleskutik, jk'elkutik me stak' to xchoti, mu xa xbak'.

—¿K'usi ta jpastik?, ¿k'usi ta jpastik Petul? Alo ka'tik, ¿mu'yuk chamem jechuke? Vay no'ox ta slubemal, mu xa xbak', k'elo avil, ak'o k'opojuk.

—Ch'ul tot, ch'ul me' . . . —Kejel, ti Petule skoskun ta k'opojel sk'eloj muyel vinajel.

Kom xa ku'unkutik. Ta sjunul xk'uxul ko'ntonkutik, k'alal sk'an to'ox xi k'otkutik ta sbelil Altar Sonora, jech mechuk laj mukkutik komel ti juntot Manel yo' mu xich' ti'el yu'un ti xulemetike. Te la jkomtsankutik yo' xkux xa o yo'nton: abolsba. Mu'yuk xa xu' jsuteskutik batel ta sna. ¿K'uxi, k'u yelan? Ti sbek'tale yantik sok ta jujulikel ta jek. Chib k'ak'al la jkuchilankutik, jun k'ak'al kuxul, ti yane, la yik' xa komel ti kits'anbake, ti lajele. Laj to kil ta yanal ye, ta sat ti chkuxi to ya'ie. Mu'yuk xa jal laj kok'itakutik, ja' ti chbat ti k'ak'ale. Ti jtatatike xkuchoj xa yalel ti malk'ak'al ta jpatkutike. Ja' to chkil-kutike te xa uno'ox xtal jkot karo, ¡va' to yelanil un, ti li' ni ma'uk xa jtsak-vanejetik!, lek xa no'ox ik'van talel.

Ta sjalil ti xanvil ta karoe, li ch'aykutik ta yo'nton ch'iel yu'un ti vayele. Jechuk ti vi'nale eke mu'yuk xi sjulavesunkutik ja' to k'alal li k'otkutik oe. Mu jna' sjayibal k'ak'al, sjalil: xchi'uk buy li talkutik.

Li ik'yaman xchi'uk komkom vinike, la jyalbunkutik ti chi-abtejkutik xchi'uke. Ti Petul xchi'uk vu'une chlik abtejkunkutik ok'om ta skoltael jpas na, k'alal sk'an to'ox xlik ta beinel ti jtatatike, xchi'uk mu jna'tik k'usi yan, pe li'e ja' to no'ox ta jkoltakutik ti jpas nae. Lek la tstojunkutik, ta lolares jna', yu'un nan lek. Mu'yuk xa tostonuk ta jvolxakutik ni. Mu'yuk k'usi.

—Lek oy, ana'ojik xa, ta sob ok'me cha-abtejik xa —chal jech.

—¿Buy chivaykutik chive'kutik taj ni patron?, ep xa kich'ojkutiktal vi'nal, jal xa mu'yuk jve'ojkutik junuk vaj —ta jk'anilanbe.

Ta sjunlej sts'ijlejal xchi'uk stakinel yo'nton laj yal:

—Le'e te jk'eltik ok'om —jech ta slok'esunkutik ta sna.

Ti karoetike mu xak'ik xanavkutik lek ta bebetik. Ja' to melel yan-o ban-umil kak'tik un. Ti yik' viniketik li'e mu xko'laj k'ucha'al jlumaltike. Jk'el ta jxokontake yansba jxanviletik. Jelel ta k'elel stekel, oy jutuk xi'elal. Jun smuk'tikil ti naetike xchi'uk yax-elan jutuk ti vinajele. To j-ech'em k'ixin. Li' jchi'uk ti Petule. Ja' no'ox k'alal cham ti juntote mu xa xka'itik k'usi ti chale, mu xjalij chok'ita ta jek, mechuk ti vu'une.

—Petul, mu xa sts'ik ku'un ti jch'ute. K'elo avile, oy le' yav k'aepe, ba jk'el-tikik mi oy k'usi stak' jlajestik.

—Mach, mo'oj, ta jnatike oy o mats' chava'i.

—¡Ilo, lajeso ava'i li'e!, ak'o me yik' tso'. Ja' ti k'usi jtatike lek no'ox yo' jlo'latik ti vi'nale, mu'yuk sk'oplal, ok'ome lek chijve'otik. Tanae jve'tik no'ox ti li'e. Ok'ome yanotik xa o. Pe muxa xa-ok' un. Li' xa oyotike, ja' Neva Yor.

—Ti li'e Mach ma'uk ti k'u yelan ka'iojtike. Buy chal mi ja'e. Nopol ech'emotik tal ta muk'ta nab. Buy oyotik, ¿buch'uotik?

—Mu jna', Petul, ve'an no'ox jutuk ava'e. Me chak'ane chotlan lek ta lumtik, pe mu xa vay. ¿K'usi chapas? Totsan, Petul.

En medio del desierto

Me pica los ojos. Mi *ch'ulel* agoniza conmigo bajo el ardiente sol, ya no resiste. La sangre se huele a muerto, ese olor me corta la respiración, me evapora y el suelo es un comal abrasante, a cada paso siento derretirme en él. El polvo juega con las manos del aire, mi cuerpo se convierte en ceniza.

Arbustos esqueléticos parecen arder por la lumbre caída del cielo. En mi pueblo hay árboles, pastos verdes; aire fresco, bien fresco. Y aquí el sol deja caer brasas, solamente brasas. Aún así tengo que caminar, en mi frente chocan rescoldos de leñas invisibles y mi mente oscurece, observo el manto azul del cielo, azul como el mar. Zopilotes en movimientos circulares, rito en perfecta armonía, bajan lentamente, nadie habla; el silencio se convierte en nuestro rezo desde aquí, en medio del desierto se advierte la maldad. ¡Tierra sin sangre!

El cansancio es cómplice de la derrota, hay que seguir caminando a pesar de todo. Pedro y mi tío me adelantan, seguimos los pasos del futuro soñado.

—¿Qué hacen ahí, cabrones? ¡No se queden atrás! —se oye una voz fuerte, clara, imperante que entra en mis oídos como pasos de araña. Es Mario, él nos guía para cruzar el desierto, siempre avanza seguro, pero esta vez detiene sus pies para esperarnos, su voz no muestra ningún cansancio: indica treinta y cinco años de dureza, de fortaleza; bigotes, barbas intercaladas dan señal de madurez.

—Sigan, yo ya no quiero caminar más —le digo, y sin regresarme respuesta alguna decide alargar el paso.

El camino ha consumido mis anhelos de ir a Nueva York, la cuenta no se me olvida: sesenta días fuera de Jlumaltik[1] para cruzar este desierto, y no lo hemos logrado; salimos el dos de enero, año nuevo; y hoy ya es dos de marzo: sesenta días. Los recuerdos me llenan de tristeza al acordarme de mis padres, recuerdos que pesan y debilitan las fuerzas de mis pies. ¡Estoy fastidiado de caminar, correr, esconderme de la policía! Miedo, sed, mi cuerpo sin una gota de agua, mis manos y mis pies temblorosos, huesos al aire ardoroso . . . mis pasos se acortan. ¡No quiero llorar! ¿Qué dirían los demás? Pensarán que soy un niño que teme caminar en tierras extrañas: sin huellas que seguir más que los pasos de Mario entre las venas de la tierra absorbida por el sol, por las noches imperfectas, las raíces de los árboles salen a buscar vida, aire que respirar.

---

1. San Juan Chamula, pueblo nativo del narrador; con minúscula significa "nuestra comunidad/tierra".

—¿Pero dónde salimos, moriremos lejos de Jlumaltik? No, echemos muchas ganas, vamos a pasar. ¡Apúrense! —responde mi tío, hombre consumido por el trabajo en el campo, cansado de soportar su pobreza.

—Ese Mario quiere dejarnos en este malcarado lugar, lo presiento. Ya no nos quiere esperar. Mírenlo, camina como mi abuelo cuando era joven, sin importarle lo que deja atrás.

—¡Ya! No peleemos aquí, vamos a alcanzarlo, Jtatatik[2] está con nosotros y ese coyote nos llevará hasta donde le pedimos —las palabras de mi tío se encierran en mi mente.

El silencio otra vez, sigo caminando. Mis labios piden agua, mis pensamientos se convierten polvo y bajan por mi garganta; a lo lejos, los cerros despoblados, el horizonte enrojece. Bien decía el maestro que tuve en la escuela: "El desierto es un infierno". No hay agua, ríos, nada, no así las noches; pero el día quema la sangre, y ésta, hierve y se marchita.

Los pasos de mis compañeros no marcan huellas, avanzan solos y perdidos en el mundo.

—Me muero de sed, hambre, sueño —dice Pedro Arias, de Chenalhó, "el Pedrano", como le decimos; con el rostro desfallecido, mejillas temblorosas, ojos de nubes esfumadas, cabellos despintados, su imagen de hombre pensado por un buen Tatatik muestra tener veinticinco años de edad. Hace tres días que lo encontramos a medio morir por el camino, sus hermanos lo dejaron entre la espalda del cerro porque aminoraba el paso de sus compañeros, y nosotros le hemos entregado confianza en su corazón y va con nosotros, disparejo del alma. Nos obliga a aguantar esta lumbre, creciendo con los pasos del sol.

—Muchos hombres han pasado por este camino —dice Mario sin voltear la mirada ni disminuir su andar, ahora que va cerca de mí—, y muchos han quedado —continúa—, ya sea por cansancio o por traición, devorados por el calor, la tierra y los animales carroñeros.

Por fin nos sentamos debajo de unas ramas, buscando la sombra para descansar y esperar a que oscureciera un poco. Una hoja seca cae sobre mi cabeza y me hace recordar mi tierra natal, Chicumtantic, luego Jlumaltik, Chamula. Si no fuera por la siembra de papas, frijol y maíz que ya no dan resultados, no estaría sufriendo aquí. Los abonos y los fertilizantes que nos mandaba el gobierno ya no funcionaron. Pareciera que el espíritu de la tierra fértil haya sido robado por los dioses. Mi tío Manuel me convenció de dejar ese cerro.

---

2. Nombre honorífico; la *J* de "Jtatatik" significa el posesivo de la primera persona, usado cuando se le hable a alguien.

Mis padres se quedaron esperando el dinero, el bien que yo les prometí. ¡Carajo, si supieran cómo estoy ahora! "No se preocupe, voy a ir lejos a traer paga, este lugar ya no sirve, no hay dónde encontrar buen trabajo, mis estudios no dan para trabajar en la ciudad, no pensamos como ellos . . . para qué, mejor me voy, a ver cómo le hago", le dije a mi papá ya listo con la mochila que ya no traigo. Con el listón de sus trenzas mi mamá se secaba las lágrimas que siguen amargando mis recuerdos.

—¡Vámonos, levántense, tenemos que seguir nuestro camino, la noche se acerca, caminaremos más! —dice Mario, relumbrando los ojos de color de sangre.

Sentado sobre una piedra lo vi fumar un cigarrillo que olía a hierba quemada, bocanadas de humo asfixiante salían por su boca, por su nariz; pero la mayor parte lo tragaba. En su pequeña mochila, casi vacía, guardaba rollitos de papel que reflejaban la luz del sol. Ahora en fila vamos detrás de él con su playera blanca, pantalón de mezclilla, zapatos de cuero, se enoja que hablemos en *bats'i k'op*,[3] no nos entiende.

Luego de avanzar entre arbustos, de repente Mario se detiene y de su pequeño equipaje saca una navaja con rapidez, con ese filo capaz de cortar hasta el sueño, corta de un solo tajo el brazo de un árbol con espinas de donde brota tantita agua; la hemos bebido ansiosamente, sabe amarga. La sed y el hambre se me olvidaron por un rato, las tostadas se terminaron por el camino, enmohecidas, sin importar nada.

—¡Con esta agua échenle ganas, en un dos por tres estaremos con nuestros "amigos gringos" ganando dólares! Ahí será otra cosa —las palabras de Mario nos reviven.

A Mario le pagamos diez mil pesos cada uno para que nos ayudara a pasar. Habíamos escuchado que en Jobel lo podíamos encontrar y desde ahí nos trajo. A veces habla consigo mismo, tararea una canción que desconozco.

—¿Qué dices, Mario? ¿Que estamos cerca de la carretera?

Ora sí, me voy.

La camioneta que corría al aire fresco curveaba lentamente, dejando atrás los árboles, las piedras y animales que se escondían detrás de éstas. Dejamos el desierto hacía tres horas, veíamos pastos, lugares de siembra.

Apenas alcanzamos a poner el primer pie sobre la carretera e inmediatamente el chirrido de las camionetas, que al estacionarse con brutalidad casi nos aplastaba. Digo, ya no había forma de retroceder, el temor nos había amarrado los pies.

---

3. Tsotsil.

—*Oh my god*, ya los cogimos . . . —dijo el güero alto, rígido, de aspecto malvado que salió por la puerta derecha de su carro.

—Dile que nos deje pasar, Mateo, háblale, tú entiendes mejor el español, dile algo —aclamó Pedro, en *bats'i k'op*, sorprendido.

Yo quería que la tierra se abriera y tirarme hasta lo más hondo, después de caminar bastante, de aguantar hambre, sueño . . .

Más me convenzo que Jtatatik nos había olvidado. Ch'ul San Juan no ayudaba. En balde le había rezado con refrescos, *pox*, velas e inciensos de a montón antes de salir de la casa de mis padres. En cambio, Mario sí se fue ¿a dónde?, quién sabe. Sólo el güero lo sabría, hablaron y se fue, todavía quise buscarlo con la mirada, no lo hallé. Amontonados nos dejó a la orilla de la carretera como ratas recién nacidas sacadas de sus nidos, así de feo.

—No haga eso, déjenos pasar, por favor, no sea malo —le supliqué, hincado bajo sus pies, al güero malvado, tal como recé al Jtotik[4] San Juan, casi llorando. Mis palabras se desvanecían; mi tío estaba atrás de mí, se agachó, levantó una piedra.

—Ora si el *tsajal tson*[5] va a ver quiénes somos, me cansé de llorarle. ¿Acaso me quedaré así nomás? Apóyame, Mateo —me dijo.

Inmediatamente me puse de pie y le dije: —No, tío, no lo hagas, de nada nos servirá matarlo.

—Pero viene solo, le vamos a ganar, tú decías que lo querías matar.

—Mejor le hablemos bien, qué tal nos deja pasar aunque esté solo.

—Ch'ul San Juan, pobres de nosotros, mira bien cómo estamos, cuánto dinero hemos gastado, desperdiciado —dijo mi tío mirando al cielo con su garganta seca, tragando su coraje, contra su voluntad dejó caer la piedra.

—¡Métanse, cabrones, si no me los chingo! —el gringo, pistola en mano nos metió en la camioneta. Sus patadas dolían mucho, sudados de coraje soportamos el dolor de los golpes, mis pies temblaban. Dentro de la camioneta comencé a sentir un olor tranquilizante, rico y fresco.

Llegamos a esta casa vieja y abandonada de Nogales, que así le dicen, otra vez nos metieron a golpes, a patadas como perros. ¡Qué suerte la de nosotros! Y los otros nos observan, intercambian miradas, algunas frases y se callan; el dolor por los golpes cambia a tristeza en esta horrible casa. Respiramos un olor fétido, nadie hace aseo aquí. Por los pequeños orificios del techo hilos de luz entran a visitarnos en la oscuridad, nos iluminan gotas de esperanza; la casa es grande y llena de sueños abandonados. Permanecemos tendidos

---

4. Nuestro padre.

5. Barba roja.

en el suelo, dormir, soñar. Mi papá acaba de recibir el Bastón de Pasión en el pueblo, está rezando a los santos, agradeciendo al Señor por seguir con vida y servir bajo sus pies al lado de su gente. Hincado enfrente de mil flores encendidas, con el olor embriagante del incienso, platica con el Señor del cielo.

—¡Regresen a su tierra, lárguense de una vez, pinches indios! —nos dice el encargado con palabras ardorosas, lleno de furia. Hemos permanecido quince días en esta pocilga. Y ese gordo, piel morena, chaparro, con otros de distinto tamaño, nos retira a patadas, otra vez como a perros sin dueño.

El destino ahora es México, que cada quien se vaya a su casa. Montones de muertodehambres salimos de la caverna, donde la comida no es comida. Nuestros sueños también se quedan encerrados en esa horrible casa de arañas, de ratas.

Allá, a lo lejos, se escucha el aullido de un coyote, caminamos de madrugada bajo la claridad de una luna sonriente; el viento fresco del alba pasa sus dedos entre mi cabello, sentir, respirar. Pasan horas y la ternura de la mañana fortalece mis pasos, aun así el polvo me ahoga la respiración.

Después de Nogales nos separamos de nuestros paisanos de Chamula, ellos se fueron a México y los tres que vamos decidimos hacer otro intento, cruzar de nuevo la frontera. Nuestros sueños no se han quedado atrás, al contrario, han recobrado impulsos al observar la pasividad del día, y seguimos aquí, recorriendo una historia más, aún tenemos la esperanza de llegar hasta allá, después de la frontera de Sonora, que así se llama este lugar que vamos pasando.

—Mis hijos que están allá en el norte me mandaron algo de dinero y podemos pasar, lo arriesguemos, en manos de Ch'ul San Juan llegaremos. Aquéllos que se vayan, pero nosotros pasaremos a como dé lugar.

El deseo de mi tío nos impulsa también; tiene un corazón bastante joven, él nos ha convencido en realidad, por mérito San Juan, yo ya no podía, ya no quería ser el mismo, el que estaba dentro de mi cuerpo pesado de sufrimientos, sin conciencia. Ahora voy más delgado, sin más carne que el pellejo envolviendo huesos. Diecisiete años de haber consumido la ilusión de mis padres.

—Esta vez vamos a poder, ustedes están jóvenes, en cambio yo ya estoy un poco viejo, pero quiero pasar todavía. Nos vamos —afirma con la seguridad de siempre mi tío.

—Tiene razón, don Manuel, vamos —agrega "el Pedrano", de milagro porque nunca habla. Algo dentro de mí comienza a decir que también hay que luchar, ir otra vez, de todas maneras mi familia no sabe dónde estoy, cómo estoy. ¿Qué estarán pensando de mí?

Así retomamos el camino, temerosos pero atentos del chillido de los carros, dispuestos a las llamas crispantes de los cerros, de la tierra, del sol que no tarda en salir, por supuesto.

Diez de la mañana, me arde la cabeza por el intenso sol, en lo alto del cielo unos zopilotes bajan el vuelo. La tierra desierta, poblada de almas extraviadas, comienza a despertarse conforme avanzamos.

Mis compañeros me interrogan con la mirada, nada les contesto. Me pongo a pensar lo que hemos caminado, ya no sé a dónde ir, no sé a dónde o con qué ubicar el sitio; antes me decían mis compañeros que a mí no se me olvidaba el rumbo por donde Mario nos trajo la vez pasada, el caso es que yo no sé cómo lo hizo y ahora estamos perdidos, ninguna huella de zapato aparece, o algo que nos indicara el paso a seguir. No sé qué hacer, mi mente está derretida por la hirviente llanura, entre estos arbustos desnudos.

—Mejor sigamos de este lado, a ver hacia dónde llegamos —propone mi tío. Y por ahí vamos. ¡No todo está resuelto, claro! Mi corazón salta con mucha rapidez, un zumbido retumba mis oídos, mi sangre se enfría, mi lengua está tiesa y no puedo doblarla para pronunciar palabra alguna, mi alma se sumerge entre mis huesos.

—¿Están seguros que es éste el camino? —por fin pregunto después de tanto esfuerzo. Ni el viento me contesta, seguimos avanzando sin rumbo fijo, hacia donde las horas nos lleven.

—¡Esperen, miren qué hay aquí! —gritos desesperados rompen el silencio, volteo la cabeza, es Pedro, su rostro está pálido, como si algún fantasma le robara el alma, quiere hablar nuevamente y no puede, tartamudea, palabras sin sentido escapan de sus labios, nos muestra detrás de unas piedras rugosas no muy grandes, restos de playeras sobre el suelo. Nos adentramos un poco entre los pequeños montes, por la curiosidad, vemos zapatos despintados, sin cordones. Algo me sacude el cuerpo, la pestilencia impide nuestra respiración, siento un derrumbamiento en mi cabeza, seguimos avanzando a pesar de todo. Esperen, ¿qué es eso? ¿Qué hay detrás de esos arbustos? Ahora sí mi corazón se paraliza, se me enchina la piel y mi rostro se encoge. Huesos, un esqueleto humano, y otro, de uno de los cráneos salen gusanos, aún conserva un poco de carne y pelos, montones de moscas verdes, más grandes que las avispas, salen asustadas de la boca y estómago y pasan sobre nosotros. Más adelante sale volando una sombra que carcome la carne sobrante; de uno de los zapatos emerge una cascabel, pasa cerca de mi tío, se arrastra haciendo curvas, Pedro y yo nos quedamos sin palabras, inmóviles, a un lado de mi tío.

—¡Vamos, corran! —los gritos de Manuel se escuchan desde lejos, muy lejos.

De tanto espanto no supimos a qué horas huimos de ahí, mi corazón sigue latiendo sin medida, los recuerdos me atormentan, a cada momento un hacha de imágenes aniquila mi cabeza: gusanos, moscas, cascabel, zopilotes, pelos. El hedor nos persigue, sus pasos suenan como botas de hule.

—¡Espérenme, ya no puedo caminar! —escucho la voz frágil y enfermiza de mi tío. Me detengo y regreso por donde se ha quedado.

Lo encuentro sentado sobre una piedra gimiendo de dolor, en su frente surgen las últimas gotas de agua que su cuerpo esconde, empapado de tristeza, de lamento, con el rostro muy pálido, languidece. Suelta algunas lágrimas; rápidamente me acuerdo de cuando íbamos a cargar leña juntos.

—¿Qué te pasó? —le pregunta Pedro, también asustado por el quejido.

—No lo sé, mis pies se doblan, no puedo respirar, quiero descansar. Ya no puedo seguir de pie, ¡aay!

—No te preocupes, te cargaremos, a fuerza nos vamos, nada nos detendrá —le digo lleno de incertidumbre, se ve muy mal.

Caminando con la tarde a cuestas, en mi hombro derecho mi tío delira a cada rato, pronuncia palabras destejidas. Cerca de mis oídos suelta largos suspiros, también llora, solloza lastimosamente. Hombre seco, huesos cubiertos de ropa, lo paso a mi espalda, le digo que aguante, ya falta poco, la carretera es visible. Desde lejos se ven pasar algunos carros, por fin llegamos a las lomas.

—*Keremetik*,[6] ¡déjenme aquí! —no hables, solo respira, le digo, y sigo caminando, tambaleando.

Mi cabeza pesa por las imágenes de los esqueletos.

—Sigue respirando, ya no suspires —le pido otra vez, ojalá no se muera, no puede hacerlo, Ch'ul San Juan no puede olvidar a su hijo en este terreno sin dueño, sin alma.

—Déjenme aquí, aquí donde los zopilotes me lleven a volar por pedacitos —apenas escucho la voz cansada de mi tío. Pero ya falta poco; que espere un rato, ya vamos a llegar, un rato más, lo vamos a curar, va a sobrevivir.

—No llores, Manuel, no llores, ya falta poco, mi corazón me duele al escucharte llorar —le susurro a sus oídos, con sus ojos cerrados, la respiración cortante, ahora "el Pedrano" lo lleva en sus hombros.

Con una sola camisa de rayas desabotonada, pantalón de manta blanca, un cinturón sin color, mi tío aún deja caer algunas lágrimas que desaparecen en el aire quemante. Pedro también tiene ganas de llorar, ¿pero por qué lloramos?

6. Muchachos.

—Ya sólo un momento, tío, la carretera está cerca, sigue respirando —le anuncio en sus oídos para fortalecerlo, hemos caminado mucho tiempo, ya no habla, se ha quedado dormido después de tanto cansancio, de llorar, de lamentarse, eso espero. El camino nos secó, ¡que no se duerma! Lo muevo, le levanto la cabeza y nada. ¡No es posible! Sus manos cuelgan en la espalda de Pedro, su cabeza apunta al suelo.

—¡Pedro, espera!

Lo bajamos, tratamos de sentarlo, ya no responde.

—¿Qué vamos a hacer, Pedro? Dime, ¿no está muerto, verdad? Se ha dormido por el cansancio, no responde, míralo, haz que hable.

—*Ch'ul tot, ch'ul me'*[7] . . . —Pedro, hincado, murmura algunas frases mirando el cielo.

Lo hemos dejado con todo el dolor de nuestro corazón, antecito de llegar a la carretera de Altar, Sonora, medio cubrimos de tierra a mi tío Manuel para que no se lo comieran los zopilotes. Ahí lo dejamos descansando para siempre: pobre de él, ya no podíamos regresarlo hasta su casa ¿cómo y con qué? Su cuerpo se descomponía cada minuto que pasaba, dos días lo tuvimos cargando: un día vivo y al otro, se lo dejamos al *Kits'an bak*, la muerte. Todavía le noté en sus labios, en sus mejillas, el deseo de vivir, ya no le pudimos llorar más, el tiempo se adelantaba, el sol ya iba de bajada a nuestras espaldas cargando la tarde; por sorpresa una camioneta venía, ¡vaya, por fin, esta vez no era la policía!, nos subió sin mucha dificultad.

En el transcurso del viaje el sueño hizo que la vida se olvidara de nosotros, incluso el hambre no pudo hacer nada para despertarnos sino hasta que llegamos, no supe cuántos días ni horas nos tardamos, ni por dónde. El señor, chaparro y moreno, nos dice que trabajaremos con él. Pedro y yo comenzaremos mañana de peones, antes de que el sol se levante a caminar y quién sabe qué otra cosa más, mientras tanto ayudamos a los albañiles. Nos pagará mucho, creo que con dólares y supongo que está bien, no andamos ni un centavo en la bolsa, nada.

—Bueno, ya saben, mañana tempranito ustedes estarán trabajando —dice.

—Disculpe, patrón, ¿dónde vamos a dormir y comer? Traemos mucha hambre, tiene varios días que no hemos probado una tortilla —le imploro.

Con toda seriedad y sequedad, propone: —Eso lo veremos mañana —nos retira de su casa.

Los carros no nos dejan caminar libremente en las calles, de verdad que es

---

7. Padre sagrado, madre sagrada.

"Ta o'olol takin osil" / "En medio del desierto" / "In the Middle of the Desert"
by José Carlos de la Cruz

otro mundo, lleno de ruido, las personas huelen diferente a las de Jlumaltik. Miro alrededor y veo mucha gente caminando, todo se ve distinto, aunque con mucho miedo. Las casas tan grandes y el cielo medio azul, hace mucho calor. Pedro va conmigo. Desde que murió mi tío ya no se entiende lo que dice, constantemente le llora a su recuerdo, más que yo.

—Pedro, ya no aguanto mi estómago, mira, allá hay un basurero, vamos a buscar algo de comer.

—No, Mateo, en nuestra casa siempre hay pozol.

—¡Ten, prueba esto! Aunque huela a mierda, lo que sea es bueno para engañar al hambre; no importa, mañana comeremos bien, hoy traguemos esto. Mañana seremos otros, ya no sigas llorando, ya estamos aquí, en Nueva York.

—Esto no es lo que nos habían dicho, Mateo, ¿dónde dice que lo es? Hemos pasado cerca del mar. ¿En dónde estamos? ¿Quiénes somos?

—No lo sé, Pedro, mientras tanto come un poquito, si quieres siéntate un rato pero no te duermas ¿qué te pasa? ¡Levántate, Pedro!

In the Middle of the Desert

My eyes sting. My soul suffers with me under the scorching sun, and doesn't fight back. The blood smells of death, the stink chokes my breath, and I dry up. The ground is a burning comal,[8] and with each step I feel I'm melting onto it. The hands of the air play with the dust, my body turns into ash.

Skeletons of bushes seem to burn in the fiery light fallen from heaven. Back in my town there are trees, green pastures, fresh air, good and fresh. And here the sun leaves embers, only embers. Still, here I must walk, in front of me burnt branches of invisible wood are cracking, and my mind goes dark, I watch the blue blanket of the sky, blue like the sea. Vultures in circular movements, a ritual in perfect harmony, descend slowly, nobody talks; the silence becomes our prayer from this place, in the middle of the desert, warning us of evil. Land without blood!

Exhaustion is the accomplice of defeat, so we have to keep walking in spite of everything. Pedro and my uncle go past me, we follow in the steps of our dream for the future.

"What are you doing there, *cabrones*? Don't fall behind!" says a voice, strong and clear, forcing its way into my ears like the steps of a spider.

It's Mario, the one guiding us across the desert, always going forward boldly, but this time stopping his feet to wait for us, his voice showing no tiredness: just thirty-five years of toughness and strength; mustache and beard mixed together give a sign of maturity.

"You all keep going, I don't want to walk anymore," I tell him, and without giving me an answer he decides to lengthen his stride.

This trip has swallowed up my longing to see New York, I can't forget the count: sixty days from Jlumaltik[9] to cross this desert, and we haven't done it; we left January 2, a new year; and today is the second of March: sixty days. Memories fill me with sadness, as I think of my parents, memories weigh on me and sap the strength in my feet. I'm fed up with walking, running, hiding from the police! Fear, thirst, my body without a drop of water, my hands and feet shaking, bones burning in the air . . . my steps get shorter. I don't want to cry! What would the others say? They'll think I'm a little boy, scared of walking in strange lands: with no footprints to follow except Mario's, among the veins of the earth absorbed by the sun, through the imperfect nights, the roots of the trees come out to search for life, air to breathe.

8. Flat metal surface for cooking.

9. See note 11 on page 140.

"But where are we going? Will we die far away from Jlumaltik?"

"No, we'll find the will, we'll get through. Hurry!" answers my uncle, a man consumed by the work of the field, tired of bearing his poverty.

"That Mario wants to leave us in this hell-faced place, I have a feeling. He's not waiting for us anymore. Look at him, walking like my grandfather when he was young, without caring what happens behind him."

"Enough! We're not fighting here, we're going to get there. Jtatatik[10] is with us, and that coyote is taking us where we asked." My uncle's words take hold in my mind.

The silence again, I keep walking. My lips ask for water, my thoughts become dust and go down my throat; in the distance, the empty hills, the reddening horizon. What my teacher in school said was right: "The desert is a hell." No water, rivers, nothing, not so much in the night, but the day burns the blood, and it boils till it's dry.

My companions' steps leave no tracks. They walk on alone and lost in the world.

"I'm dying of hunger and thirst, and I need to sleep," says Pedro Arias, from Chenalhó, "el Pedrano" we call him; with his falling face, trembling cheeks, eyes like blurry clouds, hair losing its color, the image of a man thought to be a good Tatatik of twenty-five years. Three days ago we found him half-dead on the trail; his brothers left him there in the hills because he was slowing down their pace, and we helped put faith back in his heart, and he's come with us, his soul torn apart. Together we must withstand this fire that increases with each step of the sun.

"Lots of men have made this trip," says Mario without turning his head or slowing his pace, as he now comes near me, "and lots more haven't made it," he goes on, "whether from wearing out or giving up, eaten up by the heat, the earth, and the scavenging animals."

Finally we sit down under some branches, looking for shade where we can rest and wait for it to get a little darker. A dry leaf falls on my head and I remember my community, Chicumtantic, and then Jlumaltik, Chamula.[11] If it weren't for the failure of the potato, bean, and corn crops, I wouldn't be

---

10. Honorific name; the *J* of "Jtatatik" indicates first-person possessive, used when speaking to someone.

11. Chicumtantic is a community in the greater municipality of Chamula. Jlumaltik (with capital *J*) is Tsotsil for Chamula, but *jlumaltik* (with lowercase *j*) roughly means "our community" or "our land."

stuck in this misery here. The crop enhancements and fertilizers the govern-
ment sent us didn't work. It seemed the spirit of the fertile earth was robbed
by the gods. My uncle convinced me to leave the mountain.

My parents stayed, waiting for money, the good that I promised them.
Carajo, if they knew how I am now! "Don't worry, I'll go far away to earn
money, this place isn't any good, there's no good work, my studies don't get
me work in the city, don't think about them . . . what for, better I go away,
to see what I can do," I told my father, all ready with my backpack that I'm
not carrying anymore. With the ribbon from her braids my mother dried the
tears that follow me bitterly in my memories.

"Come on, get up, we've gotta keep moving, the night is coming, we'll
walk more," says Mario, his blood-colored eyes shining.

Sitting on a rock, I saw him smoking a cigarette that smelled like burnt
herbs, puffs of stifling smoke coming from his mouth, his nose; but most of
it he swallowed. In his small backpack, almost empty, he keeps rolls of paper
that reflect the light of the sun. Now we're in a line behind him and his white
T-shirt, blue jeans, leather shoes. It makes him mad that we talk in *bats'i
kop*,[12] he doesn't understand us.

After walking for a while among the bushes, Mario suddenly stops and
takes a knife out of his little bag; that edge could cut all day, and with one
chop he cuts off the branch of a spiny plant, and out of it comes a little bit
of water. We drink it anxiously, it's bitter. Thirst and hunger leave me for a
while; we finished the tostadas on the way. They were moldy, we didn't care.

"With this water you'll get the strength, in two or three days we'll be with
our 'gringo friends' earning dollars! That'll be a new thing." Mario's words
revive us.

We each paid Mario ten thousand pesos to help us pass. We'd heard in
Jobel that we could find him, and from there he's brought us this far. Some-
times he talks to himself, humming a song I don't know.

"What are you saying, Mario? That we're close to the highway?"

Okay, I'm coming.

The truck that was moving along in the fresh air curved slowly, leaving
behind the trees, the rocks, and the animals that hid behind them. We left the
desert after three hours, we see fields, farmland.

We had barely stepped out of the truck when immediately we heard the
squealing tires of pickups slamming to a stop, almost smashing us. I tell you,
we had no way to pull back, fear had tied up our feet.

12. Tsotsil.

"Oh my god, we got 'em . . ." said the tall *güero*,[13] stiff, with an evil face as he came out of the right-hand side of the car.

"Tell him to let us pass, Mateo, talk to him, you understand Spanish better, say something," exclaimed Pedro in *bats'i kop*, surprised.

I wanted the earth to open so I could throw myself into its deepest pit, after all that walking, hunger, exhaustion . . .

I was more convinced that the Jtatatik had forgotten us. Ch'ul San Juan was not going to help us. In vain I had prayed to him with soft drinks, *pox*, and a mountain of candles and incense before I left my parents' house. On the other hand, Mario has gone, who knows where. Only the güero would know, they talked and he went, I kept trying to find him, but I couldn't. He left us crowded together on the side of the highway like rats just born and taken from their nests, and just as ugly.

"Don't do this, let us pass, please, don't be cruel," I begged, kneeling at the feet of the evil *güero*, like I used to pray to Jtotik[14] San Juan, almost crying. My words fell away; my uncle was behind me, he bent down and picked up a rock.

"Okay, if the *tsajal tson*[15] is going to see who we are, I'm done with crying. Do you think I want to stay here like this? Help me, Mateo," he said to me.

I jumped to my feet and told him, "No, *tío*,[16] don't do it, killing him wouldn't help anything."

"But he came alone, we'll beat him, you said you wanted to kill him."

"Better we talk with him. Maybe he'll let us pass since he's alone."

"Ch'ul San Juan, heaven help us, look well at our situation, how much money we've spent, wasted," said my uncle to the heavens with his dry voice, swallowing his fury. Against his will he let the stone fall.

"Get inside, *cabrones*, if you don't want me to screw you!" said the gringo, pistol in hand, forcing us onto the truck. His kicks hurt a lot, but along with the sweat of our rage we withstood the pain. My feet trembled. Inside the truck I sensed a calming smell, rich and fresh.

We arrived at this old, abandoned house in Nogales, as they call it; again they pushed us inside with hits and kicks as if we were dogs. How lucky we are! The others watch us, exchanging looks, a few words, and then they shut up. The pain from the blows changes to sadness in this horrible house. We

13. Blond.
14. Our father.
15. Red beard.
16. Uncle.

breathe a sickening odor, nobody ever cleans here. Through the little holes in the roof threads of light visit us in the darkness, illuminate rays of hope; the house is big and full of abandoned dreams. We stay lying on the ground and sleep—and dream. My father finishes receiving the Staff of the Passion in the village; he is praying to the saints, thanking the Lord for allowing him to continue to live and to serve under his feet, side by side with his people. Kneeling in front of a thousand flowers, with the intoxicating smell of incense, he talks with the lord of heaven.

"Go back to your land, leave now, *pinche* Indians!" yells the one in charge, with words full of fire and fury. We've stayed fifteen days in this pigsty. And this fat guy, dark-skinned and short, along with others of different sizes, forces us to leave with kicks, again treating us like stray dogs.

The destination now is Mexico, where everyone can then go to their homes. Hordes of starved-to-death people leave the cave, where the food isn't food. Our dreams also stay closed up in that horrible house of spiders and rats.

Out there, far away, we hear the howl of a coyote as we wander after midnight under the clear light of a smiling moon; the fresh wind of the coming dawn passes its fingers through my hair, feeling, breathing. After some hours, the tenderness of the morning strengthens my steps, while still the dust chokes my breath.

After Nogales, we separated from our *paisanos*[17] from Chamula. They went to Mexico City, and the three of us decided to make another attempt to cross the border. We haven't left our dreams behind; on the contrary, they're still here, going after another story, we still have the hope to get there, beyond the border of Sonora, which is what this place we're passing through is called.

"My children who are there in the north sent me some money and we can pass, we'll risk it, in the hands of Ch'ul San Juan we'll get there. The others may have left, but we'll cross, whatever it takes."

My uncle's desire also pushes us, he has quite a young heart, he's really convinced us, through the merit of San Juan; I couldn't, I didn't want to be the same person anymore, stuck inside my body, weighed down by suffering, without consciousness. Now I'm thinner, with no more meat than the skin on my bones. Seventeen years of having swallowed the illusions of my parents.

"This time we'll do it. You're young. On the other hand, I'm kind of old, but I still want to cross. We're going," he affirms with the same confidence my uncle always has.

---

17. Countrymen.

"You're right, Don Manuel, we're going," adds "el Pedrano," which is a miracle because he never talks. Something inside me starts to say that we'll also have to fight, go through it again, and anyway my family doesn't know where I am, how I am. What must they be thinking of me?

And so we take up the road again, fearful yet attentive to the squeals of the cars, ready for the furious flames of the hills, of the earth, of the sun that is never late coming out, of course.

Ten in the morning, my head burning from the intense sun, high in the sky some vultures lower their flight. The desert land, peopled with lost souls, begins to wake up as we go along.

My companions question me with their eyes, I don't answer. I just think about what we've walked, I don't know where we're going, don't know where it is or how to find it; earlier my companions were telling me that I hadn't forgotten the route Mario used to bring us the last time, but the fact is, I don't know how he did it and now we're lost, with no footprints appearing, or anything else to show us a path to follow. I don't know what to do, my mind melted by the boiling plain, among these bare bushes.

"We should go this way to see where it gets us," proposes my uncle. And there we go. That doesn't solve everything, of course! My heart beats quickly, a buzzing sound in my ears, my blood going cold, my tongue stiff, and I can't move it to form any words; my soul submerges into my bones.

"Are you guys sure this is the way?" I finally manage to force out. Not even a breeze answers me, so we keep going without a fixed route, toward where the hours take us.

"Wait, look what's here!" desperate yells break the silence, I turn my head. It's Pedro, his face pale, like some ghost has stolen his soul, he wants to speak again but can't, he stutters, senseless words escaping his lips, he shows us that behind some rough little rocks are the remains of some T-shirts on the ground. Going back a little ways into the hills, out of curiosity, we see faded old shoes without laces. Something hits my body, the stench attacks our breath, I feel a collapsing in my head, and we look farther in spite of it all. Wait, what is that? What's behind those bushes? Now my heart is paralyzed, my skin crawls, and my face cringes. Bones, a human skeleton, and another, worms coming out of one of the skulls, still holding a bit of flesh and hair. Mounds of green flies, bigger than wasps, come startled out of the mouth and stomach and pass over us. A bit farther on we see flying away a shadow that was eating the remaining flesh; from one of the shoes emerges a rattlesnake, passing close to my uncle, dragging itself in curves. Pedro and I stand still, wordless, beside my uncle.

"Ta o'olol takin osil" / "En medio del desierto" / "In the Middle of the Desert"
by José Carlos de la Cruz

"Go! Run!" We hear Manuel's shouts from far away, very far.

Too terrified to know what time it was when we ran away from there, my heart is still racing beyond measure, memories tormenting me, every moment the blazing images crushing my mind: worms, flies, rattlesnake, vultures, hairs. The stink follows us, its steps sounding like boots of rubber.

"Wait for me, I can't go on anymore!" I hear the weak and sickly voice of my uncle. I stop and go back to where he waits.

I find him sitting on a rock, moaning in pain, on his forehead appear the last drops of water his body had hidden, soaked in sadness, regret, his face very pale, wilting. He lets go some tears. My mind flashes to when we used to carry wood together.

"What happened to you?" asks Pedro, also scared by the moaning.

"I don't know, my feet gave out, I can't breathe, I want to rest. I can't go on foot anymore. Aay!"

"Don't worry, we'll carry you, we'll get there, nothing will stop us," I say, full of doubt—he looks bad.

Walking through the afternoon with him on my back, on my right shoulder my uncle keeps ranting, his words disjointed. Near my ears his long breaths come out, and he cries, sobs miserably. Dry man, bones covered in clothes, I shift him on my back. I tell him to hang on, it won't be long now, the highway is in sight. From far off we can see some cars passing, finally we arrive at the low hills.

"*Keremetik*,[18] leave me here!"

"Don't talk, just breathe," I tell him, and I keep walking, staggering.

My head is heavy with the image of the skeletons.

"Keep breathing, you're not breathing," I beg him again. He can't die, he can't; Ch'ul San Juan can't forget his son in this land without a master, without a soul.

"Leave me here, here where the vultures will fly away with me in pieces." I can barely hear my uncle's tired voice. But now we're almost there, just a little bit left, we're gonna get there, a little longer, we'll get him better, he'll survive.

"Don't cry, Manuel, don't cry, there's not much left, it hurts my heart to hear you cry," I whisper in his ears, with his eyes closed, his breaths sharp, now "el Pedrano" is carrying him on his shoulders.

With only a striped shirt missing some buttons, white muslin pants, a colorless belt, my uncle still lets fall some tears that disappear into the burning air. Pedro also feels like crying, but cry for what?

"Hold on a minute, *tío*, the highway is close, keep breathing," I say into his ears to give him strength. We've walked a long time, and now he doesn't talk. He's gone quiet from so much exhaustion, crying, regretting, is what I hope. This trip has left us dry. Don't sleep! I move him, I lift his head, and nothing. It can't be! His hands are hanging down Pedro's back, his head pointed at the ground.

"Pedro, wait!"

We lower him, try to sit him up, but he doesn't respond.

"What do we do, Pedro? Tell me. He's not dead, right? He's asleep from exhaustion, look at him, make him talk."

"*Ch'ul tot, ch'ul me'*,"[19] Pedro, kneeling, murmurs some words, looking at the sky.

We've left him behind, with all the pain of our heart, right before we made it to the Altar, Sonora, highway. We half-buried my uncle Manuel so the vultures wouldn't eat him. We left him to rest there forever; poor man, now

18. Boys.

19. Holy father, holy mother.

never to return to his house. How and with what? His body was decomposing with each passing minute. Two days we carried him, one day alive and the other, we left him to Kits'an bak, death. I still saw in his lips, in his cheeks, the will to live, and we couldn't cry for him anymore, time was moving on, the sun was going down at our backs, carrying the afternoon; by surprise a truck came along. Finally! And this time it wasn't the police! We got on it without much difficulty.

In the course of the trip, sleep let life forget us, not even hunger could do anything to wake us until we arrived. I don't know how many days or hours went by, nor how we got there.

The man in charge, who is short and dark, tells us we'll work for him. Pedro and I will begin tomorrow as laborers, before the sun rises, to go and do who knows what; in the meantime, we'll help the construction workers. He'll pay us well, in dollars I think, and I guess that's good, as we don't have even a centavo in our pockets, nothing.

"Okay, as you know, early tomorrow morning you'll start working," he says.

"Excuse me, *patrón*,[20] where will we sleep and eat? We're so hungry, it's been days since we've had a tortilla," I beg him.

Serious and gruff, he only says: "We'll see about that tomorrow," and kicks us out of his house.

The cars don't allow us to walk freely in the streets, really this is another world, full of noise, the people smell different from those in Jlumaltik. I look around and see lots of people walking, everything seems different, but full of fear. The houses so big and the sky half-blue, so much heat. Pedro goes with me. Since my uncle died, I don't understand what he says, he constantly cries over his memory, more than I do.

"Pedro, my stomach can't stand it. Look, there's a trash can. Let's see if we can find something to eat."

"No, Mateo, in our house there's always *pozol*."

"Here, try this! It smells like shit, but it'll be good to cheat our hunger; it doesn't matter, tomorrow we'll eat well, today let's swallow this. Tomorrow we'll be other people, don't keep crying, we're here now, in Nueva York."

"That's not what they told us, Mateo. Where does he say it is? We went by the sea. Where are we? Who are we?"

"I don't know, Pedro, but for now eat a little bit. Sit down awhile if you want but don't fall asleep. What are you doing? Get up, Pedro!"

20. Boss.

Ma'yuk bin ora la jna'

Alberto Gómez Pérez

Ajnumal beel yakalika. Te k'unil sikil ik' yu'un ajk'abale k'ax swejlube yijk'al elawik sok sbak'etalik te winiketike. Ajnumal xp'itp'un yo'tanik yakal st'un-belik talel ta beel te xojobil spoko te Kojtome. Ta Jujubael te yijk'al sitike ya sk'ejlu ta spatxujkik; te te'ak'etik tek'ajtik ta jujuxujk te xoyajtik sok tanlum-tik kareterae, k'ajonik ta nojk'etalil ya snik sbaik ta yuma'il ajk'abal. Ya snop sbaik, yilojikix sbaik ta jtejklum la ya'iyik, ta snaik, banti wen stse'tsun ya xmajliyotik yu'un yijnamik, sok yu'un ak'a yilika te ay stse'elil yo'tanike ya x-abotik swe'ik ach' pajyel chenek'. Axan te snamalil k'inal banti ayike ya x-abotik jajk' o'tanil, ya yijkita sbaik. Pablo Wech, jtujl komil winik, junwan metro sok ojlil snajtil, pak'alix lujbel ta yelawa.

Muk'ul j-ak'ix ta leka, te Jpablo Weche yakalix sna'nubel skuxel yo'tana: yo'tanukxanix k'an snajkan sba ta xujk karetera yu'un ya xko jtebuka te sk'uxul ya' stunojix sba ta skaj beele, ta snopel bin yu'un te chopol *pensar* yakal ta t'uninel, ta uts'inel yu'une; axan teynix yakal ta beel baela, yu'un machuk xjil ta spat te Jwel Kojtom, te sjoy ta beele. Ta patil, ma'yuk sna'ojibal yu'unika, la staik ja'me wits' lejchupat ayix ta sitik ae, k'ajonax ta jun nojk'etalil la yilik ta namal, mel o'tantik sba, ch'aben. Tey ta sk'unil xojobil te u, te jujuteb xch'ailel k'ajk' yakal ta lok'el bael ta sjatabul pajk'e, xjoyoyet muel ta ik' sok ya xch'ay ta yijk'al ajk'abal. Te winiketike chapalix yu'unik te ya smajanik te nae, muik bael te ta wits' witse; nopolix ayika te ta awilale, leknax la sk'eluyik ta xojobil poko te nae: jit'bil ta ste'el bat, jatiklabil ta ojlil; te sti'ile stojliyej bael te wits Ijk'al lum sbiile. Te Jwel Kojtome la yak' bael sk'ajk' ta swa'el te banti jit'bil ta jalal te nae, chuktiklabil ta pat xwax, tey jok'ol jun chojak', jun mamal xanil pixjolol, sok te ta yan xujke tey latsal najtil te'etika. Te chilchiletike k'ayojinik ta patxujk, ta yutil ja'maletik; te kukayetike xliplunikxanix ta tijlel ta sjoyle-jal k'inal. Te winiketike ochik bael ta yijk'al k'inal te amak'e, la sk'ojk'oyik te ti'nae sok, k'alal bin ora la sjam sbae, chiknaj lok'el jtujl mamal. Te poko yich'oj ta sk'ab te Jwel Kojtome la sjajtaltes te ts'a'antikix yelaw te mamale, te sakal yisim sok sakal sjole ya yal te k'ajon k'axemix ta chaneb xcha'winik yabilale. Machuk jich aymeto, jujp'en ta ilel; skots'ikal sok in sbotikal sit, muk'iknax stsa' sk'ab, ja' jich te tulanil winik yilele; jxut'nax uts'inbil ta ilel yu'un te yalal jabiletikex. Te sk'u' spak'e lut'umtikix. Maba la sna'ik mach'a jejchukil, la skuyik ta ja' pajal sok te mach'a k'ajyem ta skanantayel yixim ta lejchupate, yu'un ma xyak' ta we'el ta chanbalametik o yu'un maba ya xbajt ta elk'anela.

—¿Binti ka leik, winiketik? —ta k'unil k'op la sjok'o, k'ajonax ya sti' yak' o k'ajon maba sk'an ya xlok' tal te mamal k'opetik ta ye te ma'yukix bayel sbakele.

—Ma'yuk tatik, jajchonyotik tal ta Campanario, ay binti xk'otuk kabeyotik jilel te j-a'tejpatane; yo'tik ini ya jsujtonyotikix bael ta Petalcingo, ja'nax te k'ax ajk'abalix, ja' yu'un tal kilyotik teme ya xju' ka wabonyotik ta majanel junuk ajk'abal te anae, yu'un ya xjilonyotik ta wayel —la sjak' te Jpabloe, sok jteb cheb o'tanil.

J-ajk' maba k'opoj te mamale; k'ajonax la sup' sba ta sk'ubulil yuma'il k'inal yu'un jich ya ya'ibe sk'opa te spensare, te xch'ulele; k'alal la xcha' t'ojan sit ta Jpabloe, jul ta sjol te ayix cheb semana talel, la yil alok' jtujl winik tey ta slejchupate, jichnix ja'chuk yilel sok te Jpabloe, skuchoj bael jun bulto ixim ta ajnumal beel; k'an snut sbael, axan p'ijnax la snop sok la sk'ej ta yo'tan te yato staix ta yan welta ae: "¿Ja'lajbal ja'in winik te mach'a la yelk'anbon kixim ae?", la sjok'obe sba. "Teme ja'e, to'na' teme jiche", xchi la xcha' jal. K'alal yakal smuken nopbela meto, k'ax ta jujch'ibeyel ta k'unil ik' te sakal stsotsil sjole, k'ajonax tey stsoboj sba ta sjol te sts'u'bil jabiletike. Sok teya me ine, ta yijk'al yuma'il k'inal, la sk'ejlu te Jwel Kojtom sok Jpablo Weche, la st'ojan jilel jmelxan te sbotikal sit ta stojol te Jpablo Weche, najtnax la yich' ik'; la smuts'ila sit; la sjak' snuk' yu'un wen jamal ya xlok' sk'opa. Patil, la yal: "Xju' ya xjilex ta amak', jipnax ja' jochol ku'una", jich la yal k'alal yakal xch'utubta-bel te awilale. Te Jpablo sok te Jwele lek la ya'iyik te binti japbotike, machuk yo'tanuk ta yutil na la sk'anik jilel, maba teyuka te ta sikil lum yu'un amak'e.

Te awilale, melel, maba k'ax chopol ta ilela, ta sk'ajk'al poko la yilik te tik' ya x-och bayelxan ch'ich'bak'et ae. Patil, te mamale la yik' ochel ta yutil na te winiketike. Ja'tik ini ochik, la yilik te pasbil wolwolte'etik ya xtuun ta nakta-jibale; te xojobil kantil jok'ol ta oy sok te k'ajk' tsunbil ta lume, la yak'ik ta ilel te ch'ujmetik jemel ta xujk lejchupate, te iximetik latsal ta yan xujk, te wabal slak'oj sba ta sts'ejl pajk' sok te cheb oxeb chojak'etik jok'ajtik ta slawuxil oye-tike. Te mamale la sjapbe jun tsima kape te yula'e, jich te k'alal yakal yuch'be-lik ae, la yich'betal jpajk' pojp sok jpajk' k'aal tsots yu'un ya smuk sbaik k'alal ya xwayik te ta amak'e.

K'alal lok' te mamale la smak ti'na sok mabayix jaymejl chiknaj; ta juera, tey ta amak'e, wen lamal k'inala, jich bin ut'il ma'yuk mach'a ay ta yutil na mi ja'uk ta spat xujke; te kinkee teynix tijlema, axan te k'ajk' tsunbil ta lume tup'ix stukela. Teyameto, te Jwel sok Jpabloe och sbajlan sbaik; maba mero koltayotik yu'un te wajam tsotse, ja'nax mukbot ta sjol yakan k'alal ta yelawik. Te Jpablo Weche oranax och swayel; k'ax tulan yakal ya'ibela te yalal lujbele sok yakalix ta makbeyel sit yu'una te wayele. Te slujbele manax ja'uk ta skaj te ipal beele, ta skaj te muel koel ta chopol beetike, ja'me ta skaj euk te k'un yo'tan xch'ulele: maba tojuk te ya xkujch yu'un namal beele.

———

Kuxu lajelto jbalanbel jbayotika, jich te Jpabloe oranax och swayel, k'ax lujbena; och jok'etel sni' sok ja'meto maba la yak'on wayel. La jnikula ta snejkel yu'un ak'a ch'abuk, axan jts'inax ya xkejchaj sok ora ya xcha' lijk; machuk la jmuts' ta lek te jsite sok maba la jk'an sts'ejl-chikintayel te yok'el sni'e, maba ju' ku'un wayel . . . Stukel wen sna'oja teme ya xjilotik ta kux o'tan ta bee maba swentauk bayel ya xwayotik, ja' ini sna'oja . . . axan tame ch'aywan ta yo'tan, jichon euk maba jul ta ko'tan, ja'nax jna'oj te ko'tan ya jkux ko'tan ae.

———

Yakal sna'nubel te Jwele, nijil ta mexa ta yaanil t'imbil yaxal lona, banti xch'apch'un sk'op te ants winiketike; ja'nax tey ora meto, ta spisil skuxlejal, te maba tal swayel te Jwele. Sok tey balal ajila, jachal; awil la ya'i bitik achiknaj ta yik'al te ijk'al k'inale; te chilchiletik muk'ul j-ajk' ya xk'ayojinik, patil ya xch'abik yu'un ya xcha' lijkik xchajk'ol. Yakalix stajbel yojlil ajk'abala, te Jwele xch'inetxanix lijkel yutil xchikin. Maba ju' snakel ta sjol te xch'uunel me'iltatiletik, te k'alal jich ya spas me ine, yu'un yakal ta na'el teme ta swa'ele sok yakal ta labanel teme sk'exan chikin te ya x-ok'e. Axan te Jwele stsawetxanix lijkel xch'ixal, kome tojnax lijkel ok' sk'exan sok swa'el chikin; jk'axel maba la sna' bin yu'un te jich k'ot ta pasele. Jasal tey ora me ine ajn k'axel te swayele, mabayix la sk'an smukel sba ta spak'al te wayele; jilnax ta sk'ejluyel te jolna sok ma'yuk bin la sta ta ilela.

———

Maba jaymejl la jna' bin yu'un te maba tal jwayele. La jmuts' te jsite, axan maba tal te jwayele, ja' la yabon slab ko'tan; patil jul ta kjol te k'alal bin ora jich ya spas ine yu'un nopol xtal jun wokolil . . . Awil mabayix la jk'an stenel jba, och jle ta kjol te bin la jpasyotik ta bee: te Jpabloe wen lujbenixa; jna'oj te la yalbone: "Ke Wel, jkux ko'tantik jts'inuk, ma xju'ix jbeel, k'uxikix kok", la yalbon ta tulanil k'op. "Ma jna' bin yu'un maba ja'uk la stikun tal te kerem jchukawaletik te j-a'tejpatane, ja'ik ora ya xbeenik, maba jichuk bin ut'il jo'on mamalonixi sok lajemonix". Jich meto la yal, axan teynix yakal ta beela sok jujubael ya stek'an sba ta swejluyel sba ta sk'a'al pixjol. Jo'one oranax la jk'an beenel tal, yakalto jnabel ya xjulon ta jnaa, smuk'ulinej ko'tan ya xjulon ta skanantayel sok ayinel sok te kijname, axan te jo'one ma'yuk bin la jna' . . . Ja' yu'un maba la kjak'be ta ora, ta patilix la kalbe: "Lumto bael ya jkux ko'tan-tike, ma x-amel awo'tan; ilawil k'ax ajk'abalix, ja' yu'un ma xju' ya xtek'ajotik; sok ayxan bin yan ya kalbat, ma x-awal te k'ax mamalatixe kome jk'axunt-abeyejat cheb oxeb u te waklajuneb yox winik awabilale; jich te jo'one mato k'ax mamal ya ka'i jba, yato xju' ku'un smuibinel beetik ta yut ja'mal sok yato jsujton tal sok jun bulto ixim", la jak'be sok maba la jk'elube sit.

––––––––

Te bin ak'ax ine ya xt'uninbot xch'ulel ta spisil ora, ta bayuk xbajt ya xbeen ta xchijnam sok ya sk'ejlu ta sts'ejl te jujuxojt' sbeel Jpabloe. Te binti swokole ja' te ma xpas ya yijkita sna'nuyele; xway ta staniw wabal ta sna sok ya xtal ta sit ta ora te yelaw Jpabloe: komil winik, alko ts'a'antikix jujuteb yelaw: "La jk'oponat, axan maba la awich'on ta muk'; ay bitik k'an jtsak jileljbaa, ja'nax te mamal yajwal lejchupate la sjochinon, la yik'on bael ta tulan". Patil wen xp'itp'un yo'tan ya sna' k'inal.

Yo'tik ini teytonix nakal ta sts'ejl te yijname, ya xch'ay koel ta lum te ya'malel tamale lajelto swebel sok mel o'tane, ya yuch' j-ujm ch'aal kape, ja' te ya swoch'obtes yijnam ta Xmarta ta lumil samet sok ya sjuch' ta molinoe. Ya ya'ibe te sk'op winiketik nakajtik ta sjojylejal mexae, ta yajlanil te t'imbil lona yich'oj yip ta jch'ix ajb ta yojlile. Ta snamalil ch'ulchan xmuts'inaj sit ek'etik, xk'ax wesetel sikilal k'unil ik', jich bin ut'il ta ajk'abal tey ta be bin ora jilik ta wayel ta slechupat te mamale.

––––––––

K'alal boonyotik te ta Campanarioe, la kil te xchebet yo'tan te Jpabloe; la kalbe te maba lek xchebet ko'tantik teme ay bin ya jpastike, kome jich ya yal te xch'uunel me'iltatiletike, melel k'alal yakalotik ta beele tame ay bin woko-lil ya jnup'intik. Ja' ini melel stukel, ja' yu'un ja' lek te maba ya xlok'otike; axan k'alal la snop ta leke, la yal: "Lekwan ya xboon, bin stuul te bayel ya jpensartae, teme maba ae, te ants winiketike xba yalik te maba jpas ta lek te ka'tele, te li'nax yakalon tsa'tsunele". Axan binti k'an jna' te jo'one, ma'yuk mach'a sna' teme ay bin ya xk'ot ta pasele.

Ta xchebalwan ora stibiltayel k'inala te la yijkitayik jilel te jteklume, ajnumal beel bajtik ta spasel te binti yich'ojbeyik sk'oplale; te xojobil k'ajkale yakalix ta koel sk'uxula, te ja'malmutetike ya yak'ik ta a'iyel sk'ayojik ta yajk'olal te nopajtik te' ak'etike; te winiketike k'ajonax ja' yakal st'unbelik bael te sbeel oraetike, swentame te'ayikixa te ta Campanario k'alal ya x-och te ajk'abale, yu'un yato xju' yu'unik sujtel talel ta Petalcingoa, teme la yabeyik j-a'tejpatan te binti yich'beyejik baele. Ja' yu'un, la ya'iyik xot'be ta yutil kapetal sok k'al-tiketik; la sbeentayik snojk'etal te' ak'etik pastiklabil ta xojobil k'ajk'al; k'ax wilajanel xenenetik ta sit yelawik; ta jujubael ya xlok'ik ta karetera sok ja' tey ora wen ajnumal ya xbeenika, jich ta patil ya x-ochik ta banti nopol bik'tal beetik yu'un jich ya sk'axuntabeyik sbeela te k'ajk'ale.

K'alal k'ax chaneb ora, ochik bael ta xoral yu'un te jtejklum banti p'ichaj p'ichajtiktonax naetik ae, pastiklabil spajk'ul ta te' sok te sjole pasbil ta ak. Bin ora k'otik ta sna te Jponcho Ernantese, ta sti'il wits' plasa, la yabeyik te jun banti yakal ta ik'el ta Petalcingo ta swenta yilel sti'sts'akanil te xchebal jtejklume. Patil la yabe sba sk'abik sok sujtik talel.

Te yijk'al k'inale och snojesix k'inal, jujuteb ya spet bajlumilal ta kolem yijk'al k'ab. Te winiketike jujubaelnax ya sk'opon sbaik: la yalik sk'oplal bin ut'il xmu xko stojol te kapee, k'alal teme wen lek ya sitine ya xko stojol, teme mabae ya xmu; ja'tik k'opetik ini te bitik ya xchiknaj ta xchijnamike sok maba ya sk'uj bael sbaika, k'ajonax yakal smajlibel ya xjulik ta jtejklum yu'un jich ya slajinik ta jalela te bitik ya sk'an ya yalike. Ja'me ini te bitik ya spasike: te yayinelik ta yamak'ul te kawiltoe, ya xmiub bael bitik ya xcholik sk'oplala, ta swenta te ts'unbil ixim chenek'e, bin ut'il ya yelk'an jkaxlan te bitik ya sts'unike. Jasal te xchebal jabil slijkel ta a'tel ta chukawalil te Jpabloe, ja'tonax sbabeyal sok ja' slajibalix weltaa te lok' bael ta yan jtejklum sok te Kojtome. Xchebal sna'ojbeyik ta lek sbelal, kome yak'el ay sbeentayejikixa, ja'nax te jun yo'tanik ya xk'axik ae; tey ya xk'axika te bin ora ya xbajtik k'alal ta *Salto de Agua* ta smanel xapon, ats'am ae . . . Yo'tik ini, te Jpablo Weche, ta sk'ubulel xch'ulel, teynix yakal ta kolela te sjajk'al yo'tane, te chopol *pensar*.

Tey sjochinej baela te chopol pensarile k'alal k'ot ta lejchupate, la yak' ta yo'tan, jasal och ta wayel; yan stukel te mamal Kojtome, ja'nax jil smuk'ul o'tanin te yakuk xtal swayele. La sjawan sba, la sts'ean sba sok la spajkan sba ta sleel swayel; mero tey ora meto, k'alal yakal smajlibel ya xyajl ta sk'unil k'ab wayel, yu'un jichuk ya xch'aba te slujbele, ay binti k'un sok jchajpxanix chiknaj tal ta yutil te lejchupate, jich ja'chuk te bin ut'il ay mach'a ya xyajl ta wabale. Ja' tey abajt yo'tana, k'an sts'ejlchikinta xchajk'ol te binti toj lijkel och ta wijlel yo'tan yu'une; axan ma'yukix bin la ya'i, ja'to ta patil, la ya'i xchajk'ol ta pana, ta stojil te wits Ijk'al lume. Te Kojtome la skuy ta jkojt jxi'el chanbajlam; jich muem yo'tana, maba stejk'anej sba, la sjach muel sjol sok la yil ta spatxujk, bin ut'il mach'ayuk ch'ich' bak'et te ya skananta sbae, k'an stij smojlol yu'un jich skolta sbaika teme ja' jtujl j-u'ts'inwaneje; axan te k'alal ochix ta k'uxubela te snuk'e, la yil ta sk'unil xojobal u te nopij talel jun ijk'al wolol tokale.

Te Jwele xi'eltik la sk'elu te chopol nojk'etal jijts tal ta sts'ejle; stsawetxanix lijkel xch'ixal, wen alxanix sok sik la ya'i te sjole, la yil xp'ijtawetxanix a jits talel, muk'ub te bak'etalil maba nabil sbae. Te xi'ele la yak'sba ta xch'ulel, la

xchuk sba ta xchial sok jujubael tulan ap'ebot stajn; sokto xi'el, la sna' yilel te
bak'et maba nabil sbae, jkojtmati j-onkonak, k'ax muk', k'ax ma'yuk banti
jich ta ilel, in sbotikal sit, ma'yuk bin ora jich yiloja. Te yo'tane teytonix yakal
p'itp'unel ta stajna, k'an snik bael swa'el k'ab ta stojol Jpablo, k'an snitbe sk'u'
o k'an sk'ojila ta yakan sk'ab yu'un ak'a sna' k'inala; axan maba ju' yu'un spa-
sel. La st'ojan bael sit me ta chanbajlame: ijk'xanix snujkulel sok uch'-uch'tik
yilel, wolwoltikxanix xchinul; la yil te la xchijman sni' ta banti maba mukbil
yok te Jpabloe, ta mero sts'ejl stajn yok; jchajpxanix la sje'ula sok smakula te
yee, k'ajonax yakal sk'oponbel lum, la smuts'ila te sbotikal site sok oranax
wijl jukeb welta ta jujun swa'el te okile. Jts'ijn ta leka chiknaj spojchawetel
jkojt mut, jich bin ut'il yakal sk'anbel ya xkojl ta sk'ab lajel. Te Jwele sikub la
ya'i skojtlejal sbak'etal; kome ta mero sts'ejl, maba la sna' yilel ta lek, la ya'i a
chiknaj pojchawetel te mute, k'ajonax esmaj ta mero yok te sjoye. Jich nojelto
ta xi'el, ja'nax ju' yu'un sk'ejluyel sjojyobal spat xujk, axan maba ju' yu'un
yilel jkojtuk chanbajlam te ya spas pochinajele; ja'nax la yil te j-onkonak la
sutp'inix sba sok ta skaj te k'ajyem ta yijk'al k'inale, bajt lujt'inajel ta ora ta
banti jajch talele. K'alal yakal ta k'axela meine, teynix tulan yakal ta wijlel
yo'tana te Jwele; mabayix la smuts' sit sok jich ajilixi, jachal, k'alal sakub
k'inal. Te bin ora k'an yal te yorailix ya xcha' tsak sbeelike, maba chikanix
ya sna' k'inal te Jpabloe, tojolnax te jwersa k'an xot'be swayele, jich stukelix
sujt talel ta jtejklum. Ta ojlilwanix k'ajk'ala te sujt bael xchajk'ol ta banti ay
ae, axan joyinbilix ta jmeltsa'anwanej sok yan chantujl jchukawaletik, spisi-
lik, xkats'et sk'uxul yo'tanik ta snuk'ik, la yak' sk'abik ta skuchel tal, jok'ol ta
alabak', te sbak'etal Jpablo Weche.

————

La jkuy ta lek aya. Bayel welta la jnikula ta snejkel; kome la kil te maba ya
snik sbae, la jk'elu ta lek. Awil la jojt'an jba sok la jtsakbe te sk'exan k'abe
yu'un jich aka'ia teme yato x-a'tej te xchiale, axan ma'yukix bin la ka'i; maba
xp'itp'unixa te yo'tane. La jxi', bajt jk'ojk'obe sti' sna te mamale yu'un akil
teme ya sk'an skoltayon ae; jts'ijn ta lek la jk'ojk'o sok maba la sje'bon. La
jkuchyotik talel ta jtejklum, la kich'yotik bael ta sna, tey ta muk'ul barrio, ta
sts'ejl te mukenale. Tey ak'ota te mamal Jteofilo Sitmise, jtujl j-ujul wen nabil
sba ta ants winiketik, la sjachbe sok spikbe te stajn sk'exan oke, ja' jich la kily-
otik te wen joyajtik ta yaxubele sok xchi la yal: "Bin k'an kutik, mabayix li'ay
te xch'ulele". Patil ma'yukix bin la jna'a, ja'nax yato jna' te ajk'abal bin ora la
kil ak'ot te j-onkonake, jts'ijn ta lek ayin teya; ta patil xchajk'ol la ka'i la ya'i
pojchawetel jkot mut ta yojlil ajk'abal, ja'me la ka'i, jich bin ut'il sk'an ya x-ajn;
awil la kjach muel kjol, axan ja'nax la kil te j-onkonak yakalix ta sujtel bael ae;

bayelix welta kjojk'obeye jba bantiwan alok'tal te mute kome jna'oj te ma'yuk la kich'yotik bael jkojtuke. Ta swenta te mamale ma'yukix bin la jnabe stojol.

————

Te yijnam ta Xchusa sok te jo'tujl snich'nab, oxtujl kerem sok cha'tujl ach'ix, k'ax bayel ok'ik, k'ajonax ya sk'an ya yak'ik ta ilel te smuk'ul smel o'tanike o yu'un ya yabeyik ya'i xchamen chikin anima te k'ux ya ya'iyik te sma' ayinele . . . Axan stukel ayix ta skaxail, sok te sk'u' spak' la stuun ta skuxlejale, sok jch'ix smachit ta sna, k'ajon ya xbajtix ta a'tel ta swajam k'al animaetik sok ta sts'unel teya, ta sk'inalel te lajele, te stse'elil yo'tan te jujubaelnax la sta ta spisil skuxlejale.

Nunca supe nada

En este cuento, dos hombres, Manuel Kojtom y Pablo Wech,
viajan por el bosque denso de las montañas de Chiapas.

Avanzaban de prisa. El suave y frío soplo del aire nocturno les rozaba el rostro moreno, el cuerpo entero. Con la respiración agitada, caminaban siguiendo la luz de la lámpara de Manuel Kojtom. De vez en vez sus negros ojos miraban a su entorno: los árboles a los lados de la carretera serpenteada y polvorienta, parecían sombras moviéndose en el mutismo del anochecer. Se pensaban, se imaginaban ya en el pueblo, en su hogar, donde sus esposas les recibirían sonrientes y en señal de alegría les servirían frijoles recién cocidos. Sin embargo, la distancia aún era motivo de nostalgia, de resignación. Pablo Wech, hombre de poca estatura, tal vez un metro y medio, tenía pegado el cansancio en el rostro.

Desde hacía mucho rato Pablo Wech sentía ganas de un descanso: deseaba sentarse a la orilla de la carretera y aflojar las piernas entumidas por el viaje; meditar respecto al mal presentimiento que le acosaba, le torturaba; no obstante, continuaba la marcha para no quedarse atrás de Manuel Kojtom, su compañero de camino. Más tarde, como por mera casualidad, hallaron esa pequeña choza que ahora tenían enfrente. A lo lejos era como una sombra, de aspecto triste, silencioso. Bajo la tenue claridad de la luna, el humo apenas visible de una fogata escapaba por las rendijas de la pared, subía como espiral en el aire y desaparecía en la oscura boca de la noche. Los hombres dispuestos a pedir alojamiento subieron por la colina; y ya más cerca del lugar, contemplaron la choza más detenidamente con la luz de la lámpara: estaba construida con troncos de corcho partidos a la mitad, cuya puerta daba al cerro Ijk'al lum.[1] Manuel Kojtom iluminó el rincón derecho del corredor cercado con carrizos, atados con mecate; ahí colgaba un morral, un sombrero viejo de guano y al otro extremo había un montón de palos largos. Los grillos cantaban en rededor, entre los montes; las luciérnagas parpadeaban en la intemperie. Los hombres penetraron el oscuro pasillo del corredor, tocaron la puerta de tabla y, al abrirse, apareció un viejo. El foco que Manuel Kojtom traía en la mano derecha iluminó del anciano el rostro lleno de arrugas, su barba y cabello encanecido daba la impresión de que debía tener más de ochenta años. A pesar de ello, se veía gordo: el rostro fruncido, ojos saltones, el brazo fuerte, le daban una dura apariencia; el peso del tiempo parecía

---

1. Nombre que significa "tierra negra".

haberle afectado en lo muy mínimo. Traía camisa y pantalón remendados. No tuvieron idea de quién podría ser, creyeron que tal vez era uno de aquéllos que acostumbraba cuidar su maíz en la troje, para evitar que los animales se lo comieran o que los ladrones se lo fueran a robar.

—¿Qué buscan, señores? —preguntó con voz lenta, como mordiéndose la lengua o como si sus palabras viejas se resistieran a salir de su boca con varios dientes perdidos.

—Nada, *tatik*,[2] regresamos de El Campanario, fuimos a dejarle un encargo a la autoridad; ahora ya vamos a Petalcingo, sólo que ya es muy noche, por eso venimos a ver si nos puedes prestar tu casa una noche, para quedarnos a dormir —respondió Pablo, con cierta incertidumbre.

El anciano no habló por un momento; parecía haberse sumergido en el abismo del sosiego para escuchar la voz de su conciencia, de su alma. Fijando la vista en la persona de Pablo, recordó que dos semanas antes vio a un hombre con las mismas características salir de la misma troje, con pasos apresurados, llevándose en la espalda un pergamino repleto de maíz; trató de seguirle, pero reaccionó con prudencia y se guardó en la memoria la idea de que volvería a encontrarlo. "¿Será éste el hombre que robó mi maíz? Si fue él, entonces es un tonto". Mientras duraba aquel secreto pensamiento, un aire suave sopló su cabello blanco, como si el polvo de los años se le hubiera amontonado en la cabeza. Y ahí, en el nocturno silencio, alternó la mirada entre Manuel Kojtom y Pablo Wech; detuvo una vez más sus ojos saltones en los de este último, respiró hondo, parpadeó, carraspeó para aclarar la voz. Enseguida dijo: "Pueden quedarse en el corredor, es el único lugar vacío que tengo", y señaló con la mano. Pablo y Manuel aceptaron el ofrecimiento, aunque hubieran preferido reposar adentro y no sobre la tierra fría del pasillo.

El espacio no se veía tan mal, con la lámpara observaron que el corredor daba cabida a varias personas. Luego, el anciano invitó a los hombres a pasar dentro de la choza. Entraron, contemplaron los troncos esculpidos que servían de asiento; la luz del candil colgado en un horcón y la fogata hecha en el suelo alumbraban las calabazas amontonadas en la esquina del jacal, las mazorcas de maíz en otra esquina, la cama de carrizo pegado a la pared de madera y unas redes colgando de los clavos en los horcones. El viejo ofreció un guacal de café a sus visitantes y mientras éstos bebían les trajo un petate junto con una chamarra vieja y delgada para que se cubrieran al dormirse.

---

2. "Padre" o "abuelo"; se le dice principalmente a los ancianos como una demostración de respeto.

Al salir ellos, el anciano cerró la puerta y no apareció más; afuera, en el corredor, había una profunda calma, como si nadie estuviera dentro de la casa ni a sus alrededores; el candil siguió encendido, mas el fuego hecho sobre la tierra se había extinguido. Ahí, Manuel y Pablo se dispusieron a tenderse; la cobija les protegía poco del frío, no les cubría más que de las rodillas hasta el rostro. Pablo Wech durmió pronto; le atormentaba el peso de la fatiga y la modorra le cerraba los párpados; su agobio no se debía sólo a la larga caminata, por subir y bajar senderos escabrosos, sino también por su espíritu débil: no era natural que resistiera tan largos recorridos.

———

Apenas nos habíamos acostado y a Pablo le entró muy rápido el sueño, estaba cansado; se puso a roncar fuerte y eso no me dejó dormir. Lo movía de los hombros para que se calmara, pero apenas se callaba un rato y luego seguía, por más que cerré bien los ojos y quise no escuchar sus ronquidos, no pude dormir . . . Él sabía que cuando uno se queda a descansar en el camino no debe dormirse mucho, eso lo sabía . . . pero tal vez se le olvidó, yo tampoco me acordé de eso, sólo sé que quería descansar.

———

Manuel recuerda, inclinado a la mesa bajo la carpa de lona verde en donde se oyen voces confusas de hombres y mujeres, que esa fue una de las pocas veces, a lo largo de su vida, que no logró dormir. Y ahí permanecía acostado, despierto oía entonces cómo de la negrura de la noche surgían ronroneos provocados por el viento, por los grillos que cantaban largo rato y luego sosegaban para volver a empezar. Daba medianoche, Manuel escuchó un ruido que parecía producirse en el fondo de sus propios oídos. No pudo evitar traer a su memoria la creencia de que, cuando eso ocurre, a uno le pueden estar extrañando si es del lado derecho y burlándose si es del izquierdo; sin embargo, a Manuel se le erizó la piel porque fue simultáneamente de ambos lados; no tuvo siquiera una pizca de idea acerca de por qué le sucedía aquello. Desde ese instante se le escapó el deseo de dormir, de encobijar su cansancio con el abrigo del sueño; quedó observando el techo de zacate sin lograr distinguir nada.

———

Nunca supe por qué no podía yo dormir. Cerraba los ojos, pero no conciliaba el sueño, eso me dio coraje; después llegó a mi mente que cuando eso sucede es que un peligro se aproxima . . . Entonces ya no quise insistir, me puse a recordar en lo que hacíamos durante el camino: Pablo sí estaba muy cansado, recuerdo que me había dicho con voz fuerte: "Manuel, descansemos un ratito, ya no puedo caminar, me duelen los pies. No sé por qué el agente no mandó a los policías más jóvenes, ellos caminan rapidito, y no yo que estoy viejo y acabado", dijo, pero seguía caminando y se detenía de vez en cuando para ventilarse con su viejo sombrero. Yo quería avanzar más rápido, todavía pensaba llegar a casa, tenía esa esperanza de poder llegar y cuidar de mi mujer, de estar con ella, pero yo nunca supe nada . . . Por eso no quise responderle pronto. Ya después le dije: "Vamos a descansar allá adelante, no te preocupes; mira que ya es muy noche, por eso no debemos detenernos, y otra cosa, no digas que ya eres muy viejo porque te llevo por unos meses de los 56 años que tienes; y pues yo no me siento tan viejo, aún puedo subir las veredas de la montaña y regresar con un pergamino lleno de maíz", respondí sin mirarlo.

Aquel recuerdo le acosa el alma a todas horas, en todas partes, camina en las redes de su memoria y observa cada uno de sus pasos a lado de Pablo. Le resulta para su desgracia, inevitable acordarse de él; duerme en su cama de caña brava, en su casa de tierra y le asalta la figura de Pablo: hombre bajo, con algunas arrugas rondando en su semblante: "Te hablé, pero no me hiciste caso; intenté agarrar algo para detenerme; pero el viejo del jacal me arrastró, llevándome con fuerza". Luego despierta con la respiración agitada.

Ahora sigue sentado al lado de su mujer, tira al piso de tierra la hoja de tamal que acaba de comer con tristeza, bebe un sorbo de café amargo, de aquello que su esposa Marta tosta en el comal de barro y muele en el molino. Escucha las voces de los hombres sentados alrededor de la mesa, bajo las lonas apuntaladas en el centro con un palo de bambú. En el cielo infinito las estrellas parpadean, el aire sopla suave y frío, como aquella noche en el camino que durmieron en el jacal del anciano.

Al encaminarnos hacia El Campanario, vi que Pablo estaba muy indeciso; yo le dije que no es bueno pensar dos veces para hacer una cosa, pues eso dice la creencia, porque en el transcurso del viaje puede suceder una desgracia. Eso es seguro, por eso mejor es no salir, pero después de que lo pensó mucho, dijo: "Mejor me voy, para qué lo pienso bastante, si no la gente va a pensar que no cumplo con mis deberes, que sólo estoy aquí de flojo". Pero qué iba yo a saber, uno nunca sabe lo que va a pasar.

A eso de las dos de la tarde abandonaron el pueblo a pasos ligeros, avanzaron en cumplimiento del encargo; los rayos del sol empezaban a ser menos fuertes, los pájaros dejaban escuchar su algarabía sobre los árboles cercanos; los hombres iban como siguiendo el ritmo de las horas, debían estar antes de oscurecer en la comunidad de El Campanario para que pudieran volver a tiempo a Petalcingo, después de entregarle a la autoridad el recado que le llevaban. Para ello, cortaron camino internándose en cafetales y milpas; atravesaban sombras de árboles proyectados por el sol; los zancudos volaban rozando los rostros; a ratos salían a la carretera y avanzaban con más prisa, para luego internarse en la vereda más próxima y así ganarle la marcha al tiempo.

Cuatro pesadas horas después arribaron a las calles de la comunidad apenas salpicada de casas, hechas de madera y techo de zacate. Al llegar a la de Alfonso Hernández, frente a la pequeña plaza, le entregaron el documento donde se le invitaba a presentarse en Petalcingo para tratar un asunto relacionado con las mojoneras de ambos pueblos. Luego se despidieron estrechándose la mano.

La oscuridad comenzaba a llenar el espacio, poco a poco abrazaba a la tierra con sus enormes brazos negros. Los hombres sólo de vez en vez intercambiaban palabras: hablaban de cómo el precio del café subía y bajaba, de que cuando se daba buena cosecha el precio bajaba y cuando no, se elevaba; pláticas de ese tipo rondaban en sus pensamientos y no se prolongaban sobre el tema, como si esperaran llegar al pueblo para gastar todos los términos posibles en conversaciones. Esto era la rutina: la estancia en el corredor de la agencia rural se prolongaba en pláticas y comentarios acerca de los cultivos de maíz y frijol, de cómo los ladinos robaban las cosechas . . . De dos largos años que Pablo llevaba trabajando de policía, era la primera y última vez que salía a un paraje con Kojtom. Ambos conocían bien el sendero, pues en períodos anteriores lo habían caminado, sólo que con más calma; por ahí pasaban cuando iban hasta Salto de Agua a comprar jabón, sal . . . Ahora, en lo profundo del alma de Pablo Wech seguía creciendo una inquietud, una mala impresión.

Arrastró aquel mal presentimiento hasta llegar al jacal, lo mantuvo en su corazón, hasta antes de dormir; en cambio, Manuel Kojtom sólo se quedó con el ansia de cerrar los párpados. Se acomodaba boca arriba, de lado o boca abajo, buscando el sueño; justo en ese lapso de tiempo, mientras esperaba caer en las caricias tibias de la somnolencia para aliviar su cansancio, se produjo un extraño y corto ruido dentro de la casa, como si alguien hubiese caído de la cama. Eso llamó su atención; deseó volver a escuchar aquel rumor que, de manera brusca, le había provocado un acelerado palpitar del corazón; mas nada volvió a oír, sino hasta más tarde, fuera de la choza, en dirección al cerro Ijk'al lum. A Kojtom le pareció oír a un animal asustado, jadeante; sin ponerse de pie, irguió atemorizado la cabeza y miró a su alrededor y como toda persona precavida, quiso despertar a su compañero para defenderse en caso de que se tratara de un enemigo, pero cuando comenzaba a cansarle el cuello, vio entre la poca luz de la luna acercarse una nube negra.

Manuel miró con terror cómo aquella sombra misteriosa y deforme se acercó saltando, se le erizó la piel, sintió pesada y fría la cabeza, vio que a cada salto el cuerpo extraño crecía de tamaño. El miedo imperó en su alma, le enredó las venas y le apretaba el pecho cada vez más fuerte; aún tembloroso, vio que aquel cuerpo enigmático era de un viejo sapo, enorme, descomunal, de ojos saltones, como nunca antes había visto. El corazón seguía golpeándole el pecho, quiso mover la mano derecha hacia Pablo, tirarle de la camisa o moverlo con el codo para despertarlo, pero no pudo. Fijó sus ojos en el animal: negra piel como corroída, espantosas protuberancias; vio que inclinó las fauces cerca de los pies descubiertos de Pablo, a muy corta distancia del talón; las abría y cerraba de un modo extraño, como si hablara con la tierra, parpadeó sus ojos saltones y enseguida dio siete brincos de un lado al otro del pie. Al poco rato se escucharon aleteos de un pollo, como si intentara escaparse de la muerte. Manuel sintió helarse su cuerpo entero, pues junto a él, sin que pudiera distinguirlo, se oían los aleteos, como si surgieran justo en los pies de su compañero; presa de terror, apenas pudo mirar a su alrededor, no obstante, no logró ver a ningún animal semejante capaz de producir aquel murmullo; sólo el sapo que ya había dado la vuelta y acostumbrado a la noche, iba saltando con rapidez por donde había venido. Mientras transcurría ese tiempo, Manuel le seguía latiendo con fuerza el corazón; ya no pegó los párpados y así permaneció, despierto, hasta el amanecer. Cuando quiso anunciar la hora de reanudar la marcha . . . , no vio señal alguna de que Pablo despertara, intentó en vano interrumpirle el sueño, volvió solo al pueblo. A eso del mediodía regresó al lugar pero acompañado por el agente municipal y cuatro policías más; todos con un dolor anudado en la garganta, ayudaron a traer cargando, colgado de una hamaca, el cuerpo de Pablo Wech.

Yo creí que él estaba bien, lo moví del hombro varias veces; como vi que no se movía, lo miré bien. Entonces me agaché y lo tomé de su mano izquierda para asegurarme si sus venas todavía palpitaban, pero ya no sentí nada, su corazón no latía. Me asusté, fui a tocar la puerta de la casa del viejo para ver si me quería ayudar; toqué un buen rato y no me abrió. Lo trajimos cargando al pueblo, lo llevamos a su casa en el barrio grande, cerca del panteón. Ahí llegó don Teófilo Sit Mis, un curandero muy conocido por la gente, le levantó y tocó la planta del pie izquierdo, así vimos que tenía unas ruedas moradas. "Ni modos, ya no está aquí su ch'ulel", dijo. Después yo no supe nada, de esa noche sólo recuerdo cuando miré que llegó el sapo, ahí estuvo buen rato; ya después oí que aleteaba un pollo en medio de la noche, como si quisiera escaparse, entonces levanté la cabeza, pero no más miré el sapo que ya regresaba. Me he preguntado muchas veces de dónde habrá salido el pollo porque recuerdo que no habíamos llevado ninguno. Del viejo ya nunca supe nada.

––––––

Su esposa Jesusa y sus cinco hijos, tres hombres y dos mujeres, lloraron bastante, como si trataran de mostrar el tamaño de su pesar o que el difunto oyera con sus oídos muertos que lamentaban su ausencia . . . Pero él estaba ya en su ataúd, con las ropas que había usado en vida, con su machete dentro de la funda como si fuera a trabajar en el acahual de los muertos y sembrar ahí, en el terreno de la muerte, la felicidad que muy pocas veces encontró en todos sus años.

"Ma'yuk bin ora la jna'" / "Nunca supe nada" / "I Never Knew Anything"
by José Carlos de la Cruz

I Never Knew Anything

In this story, two men, Manuel Kojtom and Pablo Wech, travel through dense forest in the Chiapas mountains.

They were going along quickly. The soft, cold pull of night air brushed their brown faces, their whole bodies. Breathing heavily, they followed the light of Manuel Kojtom's lamp. From time to time their black eyes turned to look at their surroundings, the trees along the serpentine, dusty road. They seemed like shadows moving in the silence of the oncoming night. The men were thinking, imagining themselves already in the town, in their homes, where their wives would receive them with smiles, and as a sign of their happiness would serve them some freshly cooked beans. Still, the distance remaining was cause for nostalgia, for resignation. Pablo Wech, a man of small stature, maybe a meter and a half, wore his weariness on his face.

For quite a while, Pablo Wech had been wanting to take a rest: he wanted to sit on the edge of the road and relax his legs, numb from the trip, and meditate on the evil presentiment that was troubling, torturing him; however, he kept marching along so he wouldn't fall behind Kojtom, his traveling companion. Later, as if by mere chance, they came upon a little shack. From a distance it was like a sad and silent shadow. Under the faint light of the moon, smoke was barely visible escaping through the slits in the wall, spiraling up through the air and disappearing into the dark mouth of the night. Thinking to ask for lodging, the men climbed the hill; and closer to the place, they contemplated the shack more carefully with the light from their lamp: it was built from cork trunks split down the middle, its door facing the hill Ijk'al lum.[3] Manuel Kojtom shined his light on the right corner of the passageway enclosed by a reed fence tied with rope. There hung a bag and an old balsa hat, and at the other end was a big pile of firewood. Crickets sang around them in the hills; fireflies flickered under the starlight. The men went into the dark passageway, knocked on the wooden door, and when it opened, an old man appeared. The light in Manuel Kojtom's right hand illuminated an old face full of wrinkles, its gray beard and hair giving the impression that he must be over eighty. In spite of this, he looked fat: the furrowed face, protruding eyes, the strong arm, gave him a look of toughness; time's weight seemed to have had minimal effect. He wore a patched shirt and pants. They had no idea who he could be, maybe one of those men used to caring for his corn in the granary, keeping animals from eating it and thieves from stealing it.

"What are you looking for, *señores*?" he asked in a slow voice, as if chewing on his tongue, or as if the words resisted leaving his mouth, which was missing several teeth.

"Nothing, *tatik*[4], we're returning from El Campanario. We went there to do a job; now we're going to Petalcingo, only it's very late, so we came to see if you could let us use your house for one night, to sleep here," answered Pablo with some uncertainty.

The old man didn't speak for a moment; he seemed to have immersed himself in an abyss of stillness to hear the voice of his conscience, of his soul. Staring at Pablo, he remembered that two weeks before he'd seen a man with the same features leaving the granary with hurried steps, bearing on his back a sack full of maize. He had tried to follow him, but then reacted with caution and kept in his memory the idea that he would encounter him again. "Could this be the man who stole my corn? If it is, he's a fool." While he was having this secret thought, a light breeze blew over his white hair, as if the dust of the years had piled atop his head. And there, in the silence of the night, he alternated his gaze between Manuel Kojtom and Pablo Wech; he rested

3. Name meaning "black land."
4. "Father" or "grandfather"; used mainly with older men as a sign of respect.

his bulging eyes once more on those of the latter, breathed deeply, blinked, cleared his throat to speak. Right away he said, "You can sleep in the passageway here, it's the only empty place I have," and signaled with his hand. Pablo and Manuel accepted the offer, although they would have preferred to sleep inside and not on the cold earth.

The space didn't look so bad, with the lamp they saw that the corridor had room for several people. Later, the old man invited them to come into the shack. They entered, looked at the carved trunks that would serve as seats; the light from a candle hanging from a wooden post and a fire on the ground showed the squashes piled in one corner, ears of corn in another, the bed of reeds stuck to the wall, and some nets hanging from nails in the posts. The man offered a gourd of coffee to his visitors, and as they drank he brought them a mat and a thin, old coat to cover themselves while they slept.

When they left, the old man closed the door and did not appear again; outside, in the corridor, there was a deep calm, as if no one was inside the house or around it; the candle kept burning, but the fire on the ground had been extinguished. There, Manuel and Pablo prepared to lie down; the blanket gave little protection from the cold, not covering more than from the knees to the face. Pablo Wech soon slept; the weight of his fatigue tormented him and weariness closed his eyelids; his anxiety was not due just to the long travels, climbing and descending steep trails, but also from his weak spirit: it was not natural to bear such long journeys.

———

As soon as we lay down, Pablo fell asleep, he was tired; he began snoring loudly, and that kept me from sleeping. I nudged his shoulders to calm him, but after a little time of quiet he'd continue, so no matter how tight I closed my eyes and tried not to hear his snores, I couldn't sleep . . . He knew that when someone stops to rest on the road, they shouldn't sleep long, he knew that . . . but maybe he forgot; I didn't remember that either, I only knew I wanted to rest.

———

Manuel remembers, leaning on the table under the green canvas tent where a confusion of male and female voices are heard, that it was one of the few times in his long life when he wasn't able to sleep. And he stayed lying there awake, hearing what sounded from the blackness of the night like purring brought on by the wind, by the crickets who sang a long time, then calmed down, only to begin again. Around midnight, Manuel heard a noise that seemed to well up from his own ears. He couldn't avoid bringing to mind the belief that when this happened, it meant someone was missing you if it was in the right ear, or laughing at you if it was in the left; however, Manuel got goose bumps now because it came simultaneously from both sides; he had no idea why that would happen. From that instant he lost the desire to sleep, to blanket his weariness in the coat of dreams; he kept observing the thatched roof without being able to distinguish anything.

————

I never knew why I couldn't sleep. I closed my eyes, but sleep never came, and that made me angry; soon it came into my mind that when this happens it means a danger is approaching . . . Then I didn't want to keep trying, so I started to recall what we had done during the walk: Pablo really was tired, I remember he had told me in a loud voice: "Manuel, let's rest awhile, I can't walk anymore, my legs hurt. I don't know why the agent didn't send some younger policemen, they walk fast, and I don't because I'm old and worn out," he said, but he kept walking, only stopping long enough to fan himself with his old hat. I wanted to go more quickly, I was still thinking about getting home, hoping that I'd be taking care of my wife, be there with her, but I didn't know anything . . . So I didn't answer him right away. After a while I told him: "We'll rest a little farther on, don't worry; look at how late it is, for that reason we shouldn't stop, and also, don't talk about how old you are because I'm a few months younger than your fifty-six years, and I don't feel that old, I can still climb the slopes of the mountains and come back with a sack full of maize," I answered without looking at him.

————

That recollection haunts his soul at all hours, all places, walks in the web of his memory and revisits every one of his steps next to Pablo. To his dismay, he cannot help remembering; he sleeps in his bed of coarse reeds, in his house of earth, and the figure of Pablo assaults him: a short man, with some wrinkles around his face: "I told you, but you didn't listen to me; I tried to hold on to something to stop myself; but the old man from the shack dragged me away, carrying me with force." Then he wakes up, his breath shaking.

Now as he sits at the side of his woman, with sorrow he throws the leaf from the tamale he has just eaten onto the dirt floor, takes a sip of bitter coffee, which his wife Marta roasts on the clay *comal* and grinds in the *molino*.[5] He listens to the voices of the men sitting around the table under the canvas supported in the center by bamboo poles. In the infinite sky the stars twinkle, the air blows soft and cold, like that night on the path when they slept by the old man's shack.

———

During the walk to El Campanario, I saw that Pablo was very indecisive; I told him it's not good to think twice about doing one thing, as the saying goes, because in the course of the trip misfortune can happen. That is certain, so it's better not to leave, but after a lot of thought, he said: "I'd better go, because as I see it, if I don't, people will think I don't pay my debts, that I'm just a loafer." But what did I know, one never knows what will happen.

Around two in the afternoon they left the village behind with light steps, moving on to fulfill the assignment; the sun's rays began to weaken, the birds allowed their rejoicing to be heard in the nearby trees; the men went along with the rhythm of the hours, hoping to reach the community of El Campanario before dark in order to be able to return on time to Petalcingo, after giving the authorities the message they were carrying. To do that, they took shortcuts through the coffee trees and cornfields; they crossed the forest's shadows that the sun projected; mosquitoes flew around their faces; at times they went onto the highway and advanced more quickly, so that later they got on the closest path and thereby gained time.

Four heavy hours later they arrived at the streets of the community scattered with just a few houses, made of wood with thatched roofs. When they reached the one belonging to Alfonso Hernández, in front of the little plaza, they delivered the document inviting him to come to Petalcingo and help settle an issue regarding the boundaries of the two villages. Then they shook hands firmly and said good-bye.

Darkness began to fill the space, little by little embracing the earth with its enormous black arms. The men exchanged words only now and then: they talked of how the price of coffee rose and fell, about when there was a good harvest it fell, and when there wasn't, it went up; discussions of this type went around in their thoughts and they didn't spend a lot of time on any theme, as if they were expecting to use up all possible conversation topics on their way. This was the routine: their time in the hallway of the rural agency was lengthened by discussions and commentaries on the cultivation of corn and beans, on how the ladinos stole the harvests . . . In the two long years that Pablo had been working for the police, it was the first and last time he went to a community with Kojtom. Both knew the trail well, as in earlier times they

5. Mill.

had walked it, but with more calm; they had gone that way when they went to Salto de Agua to buy soap, salt . . . Now, in the depth of Pablo Wech's soul, there continued to grow an anxiety, a sense of misgiving.

Dragging that foreboding along until they arrived at the shack, it stayed in his heart, until he went to sleep; on the other hand, Manuel Kojtom's only anxiety was over shutting his eyelids. He tried lying face-up, on his side, and face-down, seeking sleep; during this lapse of time, while he was waiting to fall into the tender caress of slumber and relieve his exhaustion, a short, strange noise came from inside the house, as if someone had fallen out of their bed. This got his attention; he wanted to hear again that commotion that had gotten his heart pounding; but he didn't hear anything else until later, outside the hut, in the direction of the hill Ijk'al lum. To Kojtom it sounded like a scared, panting animal; without getting to his feet, he raised his head, terrified, and looked around, and, like any prudent person, he sought to wake his companion in case an enemy came, but when his neck began to tire, he saw in the faint moonlight that a black cloud approached.

Manuel watched in horror as that mysterious and deformed shadow came leaping up. His skin shuddering, his head heavy and cold, he saw that with each jump the strange form increased in size. Fear took over his soul, tangled his veins, squeezed his chest; still shaking, he saw that the shadowy shape was of a monstrous old toad, gigantic, with bulging eyes like he had never seen. His heart kept pounding in his chest. He wanted to move his right hand toward Pablo, tug on his shirt or shake his elbow to rouse him, but he couldn't. He fixed his eyes on the animal: skin black as if corroded, hideous growths; he saw that its jaws were moving toward Pablo's exposed feet, a tiny distance from the heel; its jaws opened and closed in a strange manner, as if it were talking with the earth, its jutting eyes blinked and right away it made seven jumps from one side of the foot to the other. In a little while he heard the beating wings of a chicken, as if it were trying to escape death. Manuel felt his whole body freeze, while next to him, without quite knowing what it was, he heard the wing beats, as though they were emanating from the feet of his companion. Seized with terror, barely aware of his surroundings, he still couldn't see any animal that could be capable of producing that murmuring; only the toad, which had turned around and, accustomed to the night, gone jumping back to where it came from. During this time, Manuel's heart kept racing; he couldn't close his eyes, and there he stayed, awake, until dawn. When he wanted to announce that it was time to resume the march . . . , he saw no sign that Pablo was awake. After trying in vain to interrupt his sleep, he went back to the village alone. Around noon he returned, but accompanied by the municipal agent and four more policemen. With pain knotted in all of their throats, they carried back, hanging from a hammock, the body of Pablo Wech.

———

I thought he was okay, I pushed his shoulder several times. When I saw that he wasn't moving, I looked carefully at him. Then I bent down and took his left hand to make sure he still had a pulse, but I felt nothing, his heart wasn't beating. It scared me, I went to knock on the door of the old man's house to see if he wanted to help; I knocked a long time and he didn't answer. We brought Pablo to the village, carried him to his house in the main neighborhood near the graveyard. There we met Don Teófilo Sit Mis, a *curandero*[6] well known by the people, who lifted Pablo's left leg and touched the bottom of his foot. We saw that he had some round bruises. "Nothing to do now, his *ch'ulel* is no longer here," he said. After that I didn't know anything, from that night, I only remember when I saw that toad arrive; it was there a good while; later I heard a chicken flapping in the middle of the night, like it was trying to escape, then I raised my head, but I only saw the toad, which was retreating then. I've asked myself many times where the chicken could have come from because I knew we hadn't carried any. Of the old man I never knew anything.

———

His wife Jesusa and their five children, three men and two women, cried a lot, as if trying to show the size of their sorrow or so that the departed would hear with his dead ears that they were mourning his absence . . . But he was already in his coffin, with the clothes he had used in his life, with his machete in its sheath, as if he were going to work in the tall grass and sow there, in the land of the dead, the happiness he had rarely encountered in all his years.

6. Traditional healer.

꧁

Glossary

This glossary provides definitions or explanations for the Mayan language words or phrases the authors opted not to translate into their Spanish versions, as well as for some Spanish terms not translated to English. It should be noted that some Tsotsil and Tseltal terms can be difficult to translate. For example, though *ch'ulel* is often translated as *alma* and "soul," its meaning for Mayan language speakers encompasses more. In Robert M. Laughlin's *The Great Tzotzil Dictionary of San Lorenzo Zinacantán* (1973), the entry for *ch'ulel* states: "soul of everything naturally created, and of manufactured objects that have been used and so receive soul of owner, dream" (139). The definitions provided here should be taken as useful but not exact. Alphabetization is by Mayan term first, then by Spanish term if no Mayan term is provided.

Mayan (Tsotsil or Tseltal)	Spanish	English
bats'i k'op, bats'il k'op	*tsotsil, tseltal (lengua);* "*la verdadera lengua*"	Tsotsil, Tseltal (language); literally, "the real/true language"
bolom	*jaguar*	jaguar
chauk	*rayo*	lightning bolt
ch'ayk'in	*días festivos en el calendario tsotsil actual*	festival days on the modern Tsotsil calendar
ch'ixtot	*pajarito*	little bird (specifically, rufous-collared robin)
chojak'	*red de henequén*	bag made from agave fibers
ch'ul	*sagrado*	holy/sacred
ch'ulel	*alma/espíritu*	soul/spirit
ch'ul tot, ch'ul me'	*padre sagrado, madre sagrada*	holy father, holy mother
ch'uy k'aal	*autoridad religiosa*	religious authority
—	*comal*	flat metal surface for cooking
—	*curandero*	traditional healer, seer
—	*curtidos de nance*	pickled nance fruit, which is a tropical yellow berry
—	*güero*	blond
—	*huipil*	traditional blouse worn by indigenous women
jlumaltik	*nuestra comunidad;* "*nuestra tierra/patria*"	our village/land (literally, "our land/country"; the United States is *jlumaltik* for its residents)

Mayan (Tsotsil or Tseltal)	Spanish	English
Jobel	San Cristóbal de las Casas, *una ciudad en Chiapas*; *"zacate"*	San Cristóbal de las Casas, a city in Chiapas (literally, "grass." San Cristóbal was a valley of grass.)
jtotik	*nuestro padre*	our father
keremetik	*muchachos*	boys
k'in	*festival*	festival
kuxlejal	*vida*	life
mats'	*pozol*	cold drink made from tortilla dough and water. For a "meal on the go," Tsotsils carry a ball of tortilla dough that they mix with water when they're hungry. Over the course of a day or two, especially in hot weather, the dough may become sour, in which case the drink becomes *paj mats'*, or "sour *mats'*."
—	*molino*	mill
—	*nagual/nahual*	nagual, a spirit guardian in animal form
ojovetik	*guardianes ancestrales de las montañas*	ancestral guardians of the mountains
oventik	*fruta nativa de Chiapas*	fruit native to Chiapas
Oxyoket, Tsonte'vits, Jmatsab	*nombres de montañas en Chiapas*	names of mountains in Chiapas
—	*paisano*	countryman
pojp	*petate*	mat made of woven straw
pox	*aguardiente*	homemade cane liquor

Mayan (Tsotsil or Tseltal)	Spanish	English
pukuj	*demonio*	demon
Tatatik	*nombre honorífico*	honorific name
tsajal tson	*barba roja*	red beard
tsobojeletik	*organizadores del carnaval*	organizers of the carnival
tsuk'	*cabellos de maíz*	corn silk
ts'unobalte', kilon, tilín	*tipos de plantas usados en altares religiosos*	types of plants used on religious altars
wakax pojp	*torito de petate*	bull costume made of the same material as *petate* mats
Xmal	María	Mary
yantsileletik	*hombres vestidos de mujeres tseltales*	men dressed as Tseltal women
Yoxo'	*agua cristilina de la región tsotsil*	crystal clear water from the Tsotsil region

※

Contributors

María Concepción Bautista Vázquez was born in the Tsotsil-speaking city of Huixtán. Her first artistic endeavors were in drawing and painting, which she started at a very young age. She began writing poetry in Tsotsil, teaching herself the letters based on their sounds. She continues both forms of creative expression. Later, she attended programs at CELALI to perfect her creative activities.

Her awareness of the lives, culture, and cosmovision of the Maya communities inspired her to collaborate with organizations in defense of the rights of women and children, as well as in educational intervention with marginalized indigenous women and children of San Cristóbal de las Casas, Chiapas.

Bautista presents different aspects of the indigenous world in her poetic expressions to help promote her people in a different way.

Bautista has degrees in pedagogy and visual arts. Her completed programs include Gestalt Treatment (2001) and Intercultural Education (2003) at the National Pedagogical University. Her artwork has been exhibited in various locations in Chiapas and elsewhere in Mexico, and she has published writings in several national anthologies and magazines. She is coauthor of the book *Ocho voces* (Eight voices; 2004). She received grants from the Fondo Nacional para la Cultura y las Artes (FONCA, National Fund for Culture and Art) for its 2007–2008 and 2010–11 distributions.

María Concepción Bautista Vázquez es originaria de un pueblo Tsotsil llamado Huixtán. Sus primeras actividades artísticas fueron en dibujo y pintura, que empezó a muy temprana edad, iniciando así misma en las letras basadas a partir de su sonido. Continúa las dos formas de expresión creativa. Más adelante, cursó diplomados en el CELALI para perfeccionar su actividad creativa.

Su entendimiento de la vivencia, cultura y cosmovisión de las comunidades mayas la inspiró a enfocar su labor junto a otras organizaciones en la defensa de los derechos del niño y la mujer, así como en la intervención educativa con mujeres e infancia indígena en contextos de marginación en San Cristóbal de las Casas, Chiapas.

Bautista presenta diferentes aspectos del mundo indígena en sus expresiones poéticas, para ayudar a promover su gente de otra manera.

Bautista es licenciada en pedagogía y arte plástica. Ha cursado diplomados, entre los que destacan: Entrenamiento Gestalt (2001) y Educación Intercultural (2003), en la Universidad Pedagógica Nacional. Ha realizado exposiciones pictóricas en diversos lugares del estado de Chiapas y de México. Tiene publicada sus obras en diversas antologías y revistas del país. Es coautora del libro

Ocho voces (2004). Fue Becaria del Fondo Nacional para la Cultura y las Artes (FONCA), emisión 2007–2008 y emisión 2010–11.

———

Ruperta Bautista Vázquez is a Tsotsil Maya writer from San Cristóbal de las Casas, with parents from the Tsotsil community of Huixtán. In the years of her childhood, few indigenous people lived in the city, and Bautista says that most of those who did were forced to erase all trace of their culture so they could avoid mistreatment from the *kaxlantik*, the mestizos—but not Bautista's mother. She decided to stay firm in her Tsotsil identity and make sure her children learned Maya culture and history. "When I first knew of the *Popol Wuj*, it was in her voice," Bautista says.

At her school, Bautista was the only indigenous student. She faced both verbal and physical abuse from other children, and no support from teachers. She wrote her first poem for an assignment in sixth grade, but her teacher gave her a bad grade, saying it was so good that she must have copied it from some book. During these years, Bautista began writing in Tsotsil, figuring it out for herself based on her understanding, as a way of alleviating the suffering she felt growing up Tsotsil in that semiurban environment in those times. Her writing still addresses the Maya people's suffering—marginalization, discrimination, forgetting—but goes on to celebrate the longing that keeps alive the spirit of the song, the wisdom in the ancestors' witness, the rejoicing at the sight of a growing cornfield, and the eternal message of life in nature.

Bautista holds degrees in creative writing from Sociedad General de Escritores de México (SOGEM; General Society of Writers from Mexico), Chiapas chapter, and in indigenous rights and culture from Centro de Investigaciones y Estudios Superiores en Antropología Social (CIESAS; Center for the Investigation and Study of Social Anthropology)–Southeast. She is currently an anthropologist with the Autonomous University of Chiapas.

Bautista writes poetry, plays, and stories. Her collection here was originally published by CELALI in 2003 as *Ch'iel k'opojelal* (*Vivencias*). Other publications include *Xojobal Jalob te'* (*Telar luminario*), published by CONACULTA in Mexico City, 2013, and *Realtà non necessaria*, published by the Universidad of Siena Department of Philology and Literary Criticism in Italy, 2009. Her play *Indigenous Children: We Are Not to Blame* was included in the book *Women of Chiapas: Making History in Times of Struggle and Hope*, published by Routledge in New York, 2003.

Ruperta Bautista Vázquez es una escritora maya-tsotsil de San Cristóbal de las Casas, Chiapas, sus padres del pueblo tsotsil de Huixtán. En los años de su niñez, pocas indígenas vivían en la ciudad, y Bautista dice que la mayoría eran obligados a borrar todo rasgo de su cultura para evitar sufrir los maltratos de parte de los *kaxlantik*, los mestizos—pero la madre de Bautista no. Ella decidió mantenerse firme a su identidad tsotsil y asegurar que sus hijos aprendieran la cultura e historia maya. "La primera vez que supe del *Popol Wuj* fue en voz de ella," dice Bautista.

En su escuela Bautista fue la única estudiante indígena. Sufrió abuso verbal y físico de otros niños, y sin apoyo de los maestros. Escribió su primer poema para una tarea en sexto grado, pero su maestro le puso mala calificación, diciendo que era tan bueno que ella lo debió haber copiado de algún libro. Durante estos años, Bautista empezó a escribir en tsotsil, con sus propios conocimientos basándose en su entender. Estos primeros escritos eran una estrategia de aliviar el sufrimiento que vivía creciendo tsotsil en el contexto semiurbano en esos tiempos. Su escritura aún aborda el sufrimiento de la gente maya—marginación, discriminación, olvido—pero sigue su fluir para celebrar el anhelo que aún vela el espíritu del canto, el testimonio del conocimiento ancestral, el regocijo al ver el brote del maizal, y el eterno mensaje de la vida en la naturaleza.

Bautista es diplomada en Creación Literaria por la Sociedad General de Escritores de México (SOGEM), capítulo Chiapas; diplomada en Derechos y Cultura Indígenas por el Centro de Investigaciones y Estudios Superiores en Antropología Social (CIESAS)–Sureste; actualmente es antropóloga con la Universidad Autónoma de Chiapas.

Bautista escribe poesía, obras de teatro y cuentos. Su colección aquí fue publicada originalmente por CELALI en 2003 con el título *Ch'iel k'opojelal* (*Vivencias*). Otras publicaciones incluyen *Xojobal Jalob te'* (*Telar luminario*), publicado por CONACULTA en México, D.F., 2013, y *Realtà non necessaria*, publicado por la Universidad de Siena, Departamento de Filología y Crítica de la Literatura, Italia, 2009. Su obra de teatro *Indigenous Children: We Are Not to Blame* (*Niños indígenas: No es culpabilidad*) fue incluida en el libro *Women of Chiapas: Making History in Times of Struggle and Hope* (Mujeres de Chiapas: Haciendo historia en tiempos de lucha y esperanza), publicado por Routledge en Nueva York, 2003.

Manuel Bolom Pale was born in 1979 in the Tsotsil municipality of Huixtán. From 1999 to 2003 he studied social psychology at the Universidad Maya in Tuxtla Gutiérrez. In 2004, he obtained the "Y el bolom dice . . ." ("And the jaguar says . . ."; *bolom* is Tsotsil for jaguar) prize for narrative. In 2005, he won the "Pueblos y palabras" (Peoples and Words) indigenous essay prize; in 2008, he won the "Pat o'tan" indigenous poetry prize. All of these competitions were organized by CELALI, through which Bolom also completed courses and seminars on literary creation.

Bolom is the coauthor of two books: *Xpulpun sbek'tal jch'ulme'tik* (*La luna ardiente*; The fiery moon) and *Mol, pukujil ka' xchi'uk saben* (*El anciano, el caballo salvaje y la comadreja*; The old man, the wild horse, and the weasel). He is the author of the book *K'anel: Funciones y representaciones sociales en Huix-tán, Chiapas* (K'anel: Social functions and representations in Huixtán, Chiapas). He is coauthor of *Desarrollo sustentable, interculturalidad y vinculación comunitaria* (Sustainable development, interculturality, and community connections).

Bolom's first experience in writing was with essays, but he began cultivating the words for poetry, using tools CELALI provided. He hopes his writing might help awaken the spirit of his people. He believes the indigenous have been viewed as a silent people, and he wants his poetry to help show the voices hidden in the silence.

Manuel Bolom Pale nació en 1979 en el municipio tsotsil de Huixtán. De 1999 a 2003 estudió psicología social en la Universidad Maya en Tuxtla Gutiérrez. En 2004 obtuvo el "Y el bolom dice . . ." premio de narrativa. En 2005 ganó el "Pueblos y palabras" premio de ensayo indígena; en 2008 ganó el "Pat o'tan" premio de poesía indígena. Todos estos concursos fueron promovidos por el Centro Estatal de Lenguas, Arte y Literatura Indígenas (CELALI), con que Bolom también cursó diplomados y seminarios de creación literaria.

Bolom es coautor de dos libros: *Xpulpun sbek'tal jch'ulme'tik* (*La luna ardiente*) y *Mol, pukujil ka' xchi'uk saben* (*El anciano, el caballo salvaje y la comadreja*). Es autor del libro *K'anel: Funciones y representaciones sociales en Huixtán, Chiapas*. Es coautor de *Desarrollo sustentable, interculturalidad y vinculación comunitaria*.

Su primera experiencia en escritura fue con ensayos, pero empezó a cultivar las palabras para poesía usando las herramientas provenidas por el CELALI. Bolom espera que su escritura pueda despertar el espíritu de su pueblo. Cree que los indígenas han sido vistos como personas calladas, y quiere que su poesía muestre las voces escondidas en el silencio.

––––––––

Juan Julián Cruz Cruz, born in Petalcingo, Chiapas, in 1987, grew up bilingual in Tseltal and Spanish. Racism was strong at the time, he says, and that led his parents to speak Spanish more—*castellanización* (Hispanicization) was considered a vehicle for the development and progress of the nation. His schooling was completely in Spanish. He began learning to read and write Tseltal as a teenager, thanks to Marceal Méndez, a Tseltal writer from Petalcingo who hosted weekend classes at his house. Cruz continued improving through his own efforts, and he found that the best way for him to learn was by writing stories. At first he wanted to be a writer to make something of himself, but through practice and courses at CELALI he developed an appreciation for the discipline writing requires and the commitment necessary to write in a way that expresses the richness of his language and helps strengthen it.

Regarding "Carnival Disaster," Cruz says "ninety percent is real" (*noventa por ciento es real*). It happened when he was seventeen and "my temperament had no bounds" (*mi temperamento no tenía orillas*). For him and his friends, the carnival provided the climax for their energies. He says that nobody involved in the carnival incident knows he has written this story about it.

Cruz holds a degree in language and culture from Universidad Intercultural de Chiapas (UNICH). He completed a workshop in literary creation (2004) and a seminar on literary analysis and composition (2007) at CELALI, as well as a workshop on stylistics in indigenous poetry of Chiapas (2008–2009) at UNICH. He is the author of *Petul Ach' Poxtawanej / Pedro un nuevo curandero* (2005) and *Te Swokolil Jtul Mamal* (2008), published by CELALI; he has also written two stories about migration: "Na'tel Slok'ombail Reina / El espejismo de la reina" and "Sujtele / El regreso" (2009). Currently he is a cultural promoter with the Indigenous Culture Organization of Chiapas (Organización Cultural Indígena de Chiapas, OCICH; LEJ KLUMAL) in Petalcingo.

Juan Julián Cruz Cruz, nacido en Petalcingo, Chiapas, en 1987, creció bilingüe en tseltal y español. El racismo era fuerte es ese tiempo, dice Cruz, y por eso sus padres hablaban más en español—castellanización se veía el vehículo para el desarrollo y progreso de la nación. En las escuelas enseñaban netamente en español. Cruz empezó a aprender leer y escribir tseltal cuando era adolescente, gracias a Marceal Méndez, escritor tseltal de Petalcingo quien alojaba clases en su casa cada fin de semana. Cruz continuaba mejorando por su iniciativa propia, y encontró que la mejor forma de aprender era escribiendo cuentos. Primeramente escribió para ser alguien en la vida, pero con práctica y los cursos de CELALI desarrolló un aprecio para la disciplina requerida y el compromiso necesario para expresar la riqueza de la lengua y ayudar fortalecerla.

Sobre "Carnaval de desgracia", Cruz dice que "noventa por ciento es real." Pasó cuando tenía 17 años y "mi temperamento no tenía orillas." Para él y sus amigos, el carnaval proveyó el climax de sus energías. Dice que ninguno de sus amigos del carnaval saben que ha escrito este cuento.

Cruz estudió la licenciatura en Lengua y Cultura en la Universidad Intercultural de Chiapas. Ha cursado un diplomado de Creación Literaria (2004), un seminario de Análisis y Composición Literaria (2007) en el CELALI y un diplomado sobre Estilística en la Poesía Indígena de Chiapas (2008–2009) en UNICH. Es autor de *Petul Ach' Poxtawanej / Pedro un nuevo curandero* (2005) y *Te Swokolil Jtul Mamal* (2008), publicados por el CELALI; también ha escrito dos relatos sobre migración: "Na'tel Slok'ombail Reina / El espejismo de la reina" y "Sujtele / El regreso" (2009). Actualmente es promotor cultural de la Organización Cultural Indígena de Chiapas (OCICH; LEJ KLUMAL) de Petalcingo.

Angelina Díaz Ruiz is the only author in this book who learned to write in an indigenous language in her primary school. She was born in the Tsotsil community of Las Ollas in the municipality of San Juan Chamula, Chiapas. She attended a school where Spanish was the language of instruction, but Tsotsil was a subject.

She has a degree in social anthropology from the Autonomous University of Chiapas, Campus III. She is coauthor of the anthology of poems *Sbel Sjol yo'ntom ik'* (Memory of the wind), 2006. She completed programs in literary creation (2004) and literary composition and analysis (2007) with CELALI.

Díaz grew up among forests and mountains. She liked to wander and eat outside, and says she was always planting trees. Nature and the environment became her inspiration to write, to express what she felt in the mountains.

Angelina Díaz Ruiz es la única autora de este libro que aprendió escribir en una lengua indígena en su escuela de la niñez. Nació en la comunidad tsotsil de Las Ollas del municipio de San Juan Chamula, Chiapas. Asistió una escuela en que la lengua de instrucción era español pero tsotsil era un sujeto.

Es licenciada en Antropología Social de la Universidad Autónoma de Chiapas, Campus III. Es coautora de la antología de poemas *Sbel Sjol yo'ntom ik'* (*Memoria del viento*), 2006. En 2004 cursó el diplomado en Creación Literaria y en 2007 el seminario de Análisis y Composición Literaria en el CELALI.

Díaz creció entre los bosques y las montañas. Le gustaba pasear afuera y comer afuera, y dice que siempre plantaba árboles. La naturaleza y el medioambiente se hicieron su inspiración para escribir, para expresar lo que sentía en las montañas.

———

Alberto Gómez Pérez was born in 1982 and is a Tseltal storyteller from Petalcingo, Tila, Chiapas. As a boy he spoke Tseltal, his mother tongue. He began to read Spanish in third grade with the poem "El tejoncito maya" (The little Maya badger) by Rosario Castellanos. In fourth grade he read the poem "Yo soy un hombre sincero" (I am a sincere man) by José Martí; he liked this poem and thought that he, too, could write poetry. He continued reading in Spanish, but also, on his own, began to read the Tseltal translation of the Bible that his father was always reading.

In Technical Secondary School Number 89, Gómez continued his writing. During this time, he kept a notebook that he filled with short texts that he considered poems. It wasn't until 2004 that he began to dedicate more time to literature. In about March of that year, Juan Julián Cruz Cruz came to Alberto's house to tell him that Marceal Méndez was going to open a literary workshop for students of COBACH. Gómez was not a student at that time, but he discussed with the teacher the possibility of participating in this workshop, and he was accepted. At first he brought his poems to the workshop, but at one point Méndez introduced a story competition called "Y el bolom dice . . ." ("And the jaguar says . . ."; *bolom* is the Mayan name for jaguar). The three students who were still attending the workshop participated. Gómez received two prizes in this competition. Now he focuses generally on narrative.

"I Never Knew Anything" is purely fiction, but it incorporates elements of the oral tradition: Gómez heard a story from his father about traveling in the mountains.

Gómez has completed workshops, programs, and seminars on literary creation at CELALI. He received a grant from the Fondo Nacional para la Cultura y las Artes (FONCA; National Fund for Culture and Art) for 2011–12. Currently, he is writing a series of stories about political and social conflicts in Petalcingo.

Alberto Gómez Pérez nació en 1982. Es narrador tseltal de Petalcingo, Tila, Chiapas. Desde niño habla en tseltal, su lengua materna. Aprendió a leer en español hasta el tercer grado de primaria, con el poema "El tejoncito maya" de Rosario Castellanos. En cuarto grado leyó el poema "Yo soy un hombre sincero" de José Martí; ese poema le gustó y pensó que él también podría escribir poesía. Luego continuó con la lectura en español y, por sí mismo, comenzó a leer la Biblia traducida al tseltal que su padre leía constantamente.

En la Escuela Secundaria Técnica Número 89 continuó su escritura. En ese período mantuvo un cuaderno que llenó de textos cortos que él consideraba poemas, mas fue hasta 2004 cuando comenzó a dedicarle más tiempo a la literatura. Aproximadamente en marzo de ese año, Juan Julián Cruz Cruz llegó a casa de Alberto para avisarle que Marceal Méndez abriría un taller literario para estudiantes del COBACH; como en ese entonces Gómez no estudiaba, platicó con el maestro para ver si le daba posibilidad de participar, y fue aceptado. En un principio estuvo llevando sus poemas al taller; pero en cierta ocasión, Marceal llevó una convocatoria del concurso de narrativa "Y el bolom dice . . .". Los tres alumnos que quedaban del taller participaron. Gómez obtuvo dos premios en este concurso. Ahora le dedica más tiempo a la narrativa.

"Nunca supe nada" es pura ficción, pero incorpora elementos de la tradición oral: Gómez oyó de su padre una historia sobre viajes en las montañas.

Gómez ha cursado talleres, diplomados y seminarios de creación literaria en el CELALI. Fue becario del Fondo Nacional para la Cultura y las Artes (FONCA) en la disciplina de Letras en Lenguas Indígenas, generación 2011–12. Actualmente escribe una serie de cuentos sobre conflictos políticos y sociales en Petalcingo.

Inés Hernández-Ávila (Nimipu/Nez Perce, enrolled on the Colville Reservation, Washington, and Tejana) is a Professor of Native American Studies at the University of California, Davis, with a Ph.D. in English from the University of Houston. She is one of the six founders of the Native American and Indigenous Studies Association (NAISA). She is currently Co-Director of the three-year

UC Davis Social Justice Initiative funded by the Mellon Foundation. She is a scholar, poet, and visual artist. One of her major research and teaching areas is contemporary indigenous literature of Mexico. She regularly teaches a UC Davis Summer Abroad course in San Cristobal de las Casas on "Chiapas: Indigenous Literary and Social Movements."

Inés Hernández-Ávila (del pueblo Nimipu/Nez Perce, registrada en la reservación Colville, en el estado de Washington, y Tejana) es profesora de Estudios Indígenas en la Universidad de California, Davis. Tiene un doctorado en inglés (literatura) de la Universidad de Houston. Es una de los seis fundadores de la Asociación de Estudios Indígenas [Native American and Indigenous Studies Association] (NAISA). Actualmente es Co-Director del trienal Initiativa sobre Justicia Social en la Universidad de California, Davis—la initiativa es apoyada por la Fundación Mellon. Ella es investigadora, poeta, y artista visual. Uno de sus areas mayores de investigación y enseñanza es la literatura indígena contemporánea de México. Enseña con regularidad un curso de la Universidad de California, Davis, de verano en el extranjero en San Cristobal de las Casas sobre el tema "Chiapas: Movimientos Indígenas Literarios y Sociales."

————

Nicolás Huet Bautista studied anthropology at the Autonomous University of Chiapas (Universidad Autónoma de Chiapas; UNACH), where he became interested in linguistics and how its connection with history and culture helps shape and show a people's values. At the university he was part of the Bertolt Brecht Literature Workshop, a club for writing and discussion of literature. This group of fifteen to twenty members helped Huet appreciate the power of creative words.

Huet wanted to promote his culture's values, bolster Tsotsil language and writing, and locate his people's consciousness. At the time no classes existed for learning to read and write Tsotsil, so he learned through books and talking to others who were studying the language.

Huet now works to encourage other indigenous writers to show the world there are cultures beyond what they may know. Although he wants to promote Tsotsil, he acknowledges that the literature, and the values it presents, must pass to other languages in order to reach other people, and so he thinks translations like the ones here are a vital part of the movement.

Nicolás Huet Bautista estudió antropología en la Universidad Autónoma de Chiapas (UNACH), donde conocía lingüística y como su conexión con la historia y la cultura ayuda formar y mostrar los valores de un pueblo. En la universidad era socio del Taller de Literatura Bertholt Brecht, un club para discusión y escritura de la literatura. Este grupo de 15–20 personas ayudó Huet a apreciar el poder de palabras creativas.

Huet quiso promover los valores de su cultura, fortalecer el lenguaje y la escritura, ubicar el conocimiento de su pueblo. En ese tiempo no existieron clases para aprender leer y escribir tsotsil, así que aprendió por libros y consultas con otros que estudiaban la lengua.

Huet trabaja ahora para animar otros escritores para mostrar al mundo que hay otras culturas más allá de lo que pensaron. Aunque quiere promover la lengua tsotsil, reconoce que la literatura, y los valores que presenta, deben pasar a otras lenguas para lograr esas personas, y por eso piensa que traducciones como las de aquí son una parte vital del movimiento.

———

Adriana López was born in 1982 in the Tseltal community of Chalam del Carmen in the municipality of Ocosingo. She became interested in writing poetry in secondary school after studying the poems of Sor Juana Inés de la Cruz. Her formal education as a child was all in Spanish. She began learning to read and write Tseltal in 2002 and developed her interest in poetry through courses and seminars on literary creation at CELALI. She hopes her poetry can help show the wisdom of her people and strengthen the Tseltal language so that more children will learn to read and write in it. Her poems in this collection address *o'tan*, the heart, which means not just the human organ but also the heart as the essence of her community and her people.

López is an anthropologist at the Intercultural University of Chiapas and author of the poetry collection *Jalbil K'opetik / Palabras tejidas* (Woven words) and coauthor of *Xpulpun sbek'tal jch'ulme'tik / La luna ardiente* (The fiery moon) and *Naetik / Hilos* (Threads), the latter of which is part of the collection La Ceibita from the periodical *Tierra Adentro*. She received a Jóvenes Creadores (Young Creators) grant from the Fondo Nacional para la Cultura y las Artes (FONCA; National Fund for Culture and Art) for 2009–10.

Adriana López nació en la comunidad tselta de Chalam del Carmen en el municipio de Ocosingo. Desde la secundaria le nació el interés por la escritura y la poesía después de estudiar los poemas de Sor Juana Inés de la Cruz. Cuando era niña, su educación fue totalmente en español. Empezó a leer y escribir en Tseltal en 2002 y desarrolló más su interés en los concursos y seminarios de creación literaria en el CELALI. Quiere que sus poemas puedan mostrar la sabia de su pueblo y que se fortalezca su lengua para que más niños aprendan a leer y escribir en tseltal. Sus obras abordan *o'tan*, el tema del corazón, que significa no solamente el órgano humano sino también el corazón como la esencia de su comunidad y su pueblo.

López es antropóloga que trabaja en la Universidad Intercultural de Chiapas y autora de la colección de poesía *Jalbil K'opetik / Palabras tejidas* y coautora de *Xpulpun sbek'tal jch'ulme'tik / La luna ardiente* y *Naetik / Hilos*; este último forma parte de la colección La Ceibita de la revista *Tierra Adentro*. Obtuvo la beca de Jóvenes Creadores del Fondo Nacional para la Cultura y los Artes (FONCA) en el período 2009–10.

––––––––

Andrés López Díaz was born in the Tsotsil community of Ch'ilinjobeltik in the municipality of Chamula on December 1, 1977. He holds a degree in social anthropology and a master's in cultural studies from UNACH. From 1999 to 2001, he was an instructor and indigenous community trainer for CONAFE; from 2004 to 2007 he served as a cultural promoter for CELALI; from 2007 to 2010 he helped run workshops for the Bilingual Preschool Project of Educational Innovation of the French National Institute for Demographic Studies (Institut national d'études démographiques; INED). Currently, he teaches Tsotsil classes at UNICH. He is coauthor of the book of poems *Jowil Yaxinal / Delirio de sombra*, 2004, and coauthor of the poetry anthology *Sbel sjol yo'nton ik' / Memoria del viento*, 2006.

In 2000, as a prize for his poetry, López won a trip to Mexico City, where he was able to work with indigenous writers from other parts of Mexico, and he credits this experience with helping him understand what his writing could help accomplish.

López's long poem "Ojov" in this collection refers to the ancestral deity recognized in all ancient Maya cultures, generally written as "ajaw" in Tsotsil and Tseltal, a word that is most often translated as *señor*, or "lord." He hopes to help restore the awareness of this spiritual force among today's young Maya, whose religious views may be limited to European-style Christianity.

López finds his poetry readings often get a better reception among Ladino audiences in places like San Cristóbal than among his own Chamula people, whose literary traditions are based more on oral folk stories and ritual prayers, so he is now working on creating words to go with music in hopes of better reaching his own community.

Andrés López Díaz nació el 1 de diciembre de 1977 en la comunidad tsotsil Ch'ilinjobeltik en el municipio de Chamula. Es licenciado en Antropología Social de UNACH y con maestría en Estudios Culturales, Campus VI, Humanidades, Tuxtla Gutiérrez. De 1999 a 2001, fue instructor y capacitador comunitario indígena del Consejo Nacional de Fomento Educativo (CONAFE); de 2004 a 2007, promotor cultural del CELALI; de 2007 a 2010, tallerista y responsable del Proyecto Preescolar Bilingüe de Innovación Educativa (INED), A.C., S.C.L.C. Actualmente, es docente de la asignatura Lengua Originaria Tsotsil en la Universidad Intercultural de Chiapas (UNICH). Es coautor del poemario *Jowil Yaxinal / Delirio de sombra*, 2004, y coautor de la antología de poemas *Sbel sjol yo'nton ik' / Memoria del viento*, 2006.

En 2000, como premio para su poesía, López ganó un viaje a la Ciudad de México, donde pudo trabajar con escritores indígenas de otras partes de México.

Atribuye a esta experiencia su mejor entendimiento de lo que su escritura puede realizar.

Su poema largo "Ojov" en esta colección refiere a la deidad ancestral que fue reconocida por toda la región maya en tiempos ancianos, generalmente escrito *ajaw* en tsotsil y tseltal, y traducido al español como *señor*. López espera restaurar el conocimiento de esta fuerza espiritual entre los mayas jóvenes de hoy, cuyas ideas religiosas pueden ser limitadas al cristianismo de estilo europeo.

López encuentra que en general sus recitales de poesía son mejor recibidos por las personas afuera de la comunidad indígena, en lugares como San Cristóbal, que entre su propia gente de Chamula, cuyas tradiciones literarias incluyen cuentos orales populares y rezos rituales. Por eso él actualmente trabaja para crear palabras que acompañarían música, para alcanzar mejor su propia comunidad.

Marceal Méndez is a Tseltal writer and scholar from Petalcingo with a master's degree in social sciences and humanities from the Universidad de Ciencias y Artes de Chiapas. He has helped compile several collections of tales from oral literature.

Marceal Méndez es escritor y erudito tseltal de Petalcingo con maestría en ciencias y humanidades de la Universidad de Ciencias y Artes de Chiapas. Ha ayudado a compilar varias colecciones de cuentos folklóricos de la literatura oral.

Miguel Ruiz Gómez, born in 1985, speaks of the barrier created by his formal education in Spanish, as his family and community all spoke Tsotsil. As a teenager, he continued his education in San Cristóbal, where Spanish was necessary for everything, but he became interested in writing in his native language after he read some Tsotsil stories.

He eagerly began reading all the Tsotsil texts he could find, but he was disappointed to find that they were all folktales or prayers transcribed from oral literature. He began putting his own ideas on paper, and in the process started teaching himself to write his native language. His first creative efforts were in poetry, but he began to think narrative would be more effective for expressing tone, imagery, timing, and voice.

Although at one point in his life Ruiz says he was "very close" (*muy cerca*) to becoming a migrant, "In the Middle of the Desert" is based not on his own experiences but on those of uncles, cousins, and friends who undertook the journey north to look for work and survived. Hearing their stories, he felt an urgent need to create a record of this new but substantial aspect of his community's life.

Ruiz holds a degree in Spanish American language and literature from the

Autonomous University of Chiapas and a master's degree in contemporary Spanish American literature at the Austral University of Chile. He is coauthor of the books *Xpulpun sbek'tal jch'ulme'tik / La luna ardiente* (The fiery moon), 2009, and *Compilación de cuentos en lenguas indígenas* (Compilation of stories in indigenous languages), 2009.

He is also the author of the novel *Los hijos errantes* ("the wayward children"), 2014, and is currently writing his second novel, about drug trafficking in the indigenous world of Chiapas.

Miguel Ruiz Gómez, nacido en 1985, habla de la barrera de su educación formal en español, cuando toda su familia y comunidad hablaron tsotsil. Como adolescente, continuó su educación en San Cristobal de Las Casas, donde el español fue necesario para todas cosas, pero se interesaba en escribir en su idioma nativo después de leer unos cuentos en tsotsil.

Empezó afanosamente a leer todos los textos tsotsiles que pudo encontrar, pero fue decepcionado pues generalmente eran recopilaciones de historias o rezos y narraciones orales transcritas. Inició escribiendo sus propias ideas al papel, y en el proceso enseñándose a sí mismo a escribir en tsotsil. Sus primeras obras creativas fueron poemas, pero empezó a pensar que la narrativa sería más efectiva para expresar tonos, imágenes, tiempos y voces.

Aunque en alguna parte de su vida Ruiz dice que estuvo "muy cerca" de ser un migrante, "En medio del desierto" no está basado en sus propias experiencias sino en las de sus tíos, primos y amigos que sí hicieron el viaje al "norte" para buscar trabajo, quienes sí lo vivieron. Escuchando sus historias, Ruiz sentía una gran necesidad de registrar este aspecto nuevo pero sustancial de la vida de su gente.

Ruiz es licenciado en Lengua y Literatura Hispanoamericana por la Universidad Autónoma de Chiapas y tiene una maestría en Literatura Hispanoamericana Contemporánea en la Universidad Austral de Chile. Es coautor de los libros *Xpulpun sbek'tal jch'ulme'tik / Luna ardiente*, 2009, y *Compilación de cuentos en lenguas indígenas*, 2009. También ha publicado traducciones en el libro *Sjalel Kibeltik / Tejiendo nuestras raíces*, 2010.

También es autor de la novela *Los hijos errantes* (2014), y actualmente está escribiendo su segunda novela sobre el narcotráfico en el mundo indígena de Chiapas.

————

Sean S. Sell has a B.A. in English and a J.D. from the College of William and Mary, and an M.A. in English from San Diego State University. He completed the teaching credential program at the University of California–San Diego and taught high school English and history in San Diego for ten years. He is currently a PhD student in comparative literature at the University of California, Davis.

Sell's master's thesis compared literature by indigenous writers in Chiapas with Chicano literature from the United States. Studying in San Diego, California, he found many books of traditional Chiapas folklore but little original work by contemporary writers, though articles often addressed the flourishing literary scene in Chiapas as part of the greater cultural development there. Thus, after completing his M.A., Sell went to Chiapas to learn more about this contemporary literature and to work on translating it to English. He met with Enrique Pérez López and Nicolas Huet Bautista of CELALI, and they agreed to allow him to seek U.S. publication for his English translations. The U.S. publication of this collection by Oklahoma University Press is a result of their agreement.

Sean S. Sell es licenciado en inglés y derecho del College of William and Mary y tiene maestría en inglés de San Diego State University. Completó el programa de educación para maestros en la University of California, San Diego, y enseño inglés e historia en escuelas secundarias en San Diego por diez años. Actualmente es estudiante en programa doctoral de Literatura Comparada en la University of California, Davis.

El tesis de Sell comparó literatura de escritores indígenas de Chiapas con literatura chicana de los Estados Unidos. Como estudiante en San Diego, California, encontró muchos libros de folklore tradicional de Chiapas pero poco trabajo original de escritores contemporáneos, aunque artículos académicos frecuentemente abordaron la escena floreciente de literatura en Chiapas como parte del gran desarrollo cultural allá. Por eso, después de terminar su maestría, Sell fue a Chiapas para aprender más sobre esta literatura contemporánea y trabajar traduciéndola al inglés. Se reunió con Enrique Pérez López y Nicolás Huet Bautista de CELALI, y ellos permitieron que Sell pudiera solicitar publicación en los Estados Unidos para sus traducciones al inglés. La publicación de esta versión por Oklahoma University Press es un resultado de ese acuerdo.

Printed in the USA
CPSIA information can be obtained
at www.ICGtesting.com
LVHW090455161223
766608LV00004B/422